ALSO BY JENNIFER GILMORE

Something Red
Golden Country

THE MOTHERS

A Novel

Jennifer Gilmore

WITHDRAWN

SCRIBNER

New York London Toronto Sydney New Delhi

Scribner
A Division of Simon & Schuster, Inc.
1230 Avenue of the Americas
New York, NY 10020

First Scribner hardcover edition April 2013

SCRIBNER and design are registered trademarks of The Gale Group, Inc.,
used under license by Simon & Schuster, Inc., the publisher of this work.

For information about special discounts for bulk purchases, please contact
Simon & Schuster Special Sales at 1-866-506-1949 or
business@simonandschuster.com.

The Simon & Schuster Speakers Bureau can bring authors to your live event.
For more information or to book an event contact the Simon & Schuster
Speakers Bureau at 1-866-248-3049 or visit our website at
www.simonspeakers.com.

Manufactured in the United States of America

1 3 5 7 9 10 8 6 4 2

ISBN: 978-1-4516-9725-4
ISBN: 978-1-4516-9788-9 (ebook)

For Pedro

Part 1

GETTING THERE

1
—

November 2009

We were headed for the Verrazano Bridge, caught in traffic. It was several weeks before Thanksgiving, which I remember because there was a massive billboard hanging from a crumbling brick building off the highway in Sunset Park. It depicted an enormous cartoon turkey standing, feathers unfurled, on a dining room table, a family of six seated around it.

Though we were well into fall, the heat and gas from the cars rose up in waves; looking out it could have been a summer day, except for the trees lining the blocks off the highway, their branches reaching up, sky slipping through brittle claws. Ramon's hands were tight on the steering wheel. And Harriet, sweet Harriet, sat behind me, panting in my ear.

"Honey." I reached back to calm her. "Settle down, darling."

We were dropping her off at her favorite place on earth: my parents' house in Northern Virginia where she ate scraps of grass-fed venison and beef tenderloin, fetched tennis balls on the lawn, and where at night my father carried her, curled in his arms, up and down the stairs.

We were leaving Harriet and heading down south, to North Carolina, for a training session at a national adoption agency.

Ramon's hands went white, then relaxed, the color returning to them, as if pigment were being poured into the casing of his skin.

"We're not in a hurry." I craned my neck to see ahead.

"No," he said.

"We can just get there whenever."

"That's not really true. I mean, we need to be in Raleigh by six."

"We've got plenty of time," I said.

Ramon looked at me and laughed. "We don't actually. And since when did you become so easygoing?"

"I am willing it so," I told him, but inside? I did the math like I always did the math, though I am not a math person: It's 7:30 A.M. If we get to Virginia by noon, and stay fifteen minutes, we'll be fine. Other math: If I have a baby right this minute, I will be seventy-six when the child is my age now. But I am not pregnant, so I have to add on nine months and change the equation: if I get pregnant right this minute. But of course, I'm not getting pregnant. Which is why we're taking this trip in the first place.

Four hours and fifteen minutes after leaving Brooklyn, we pulled up in front of my parents' house, once my home, but now my home is a fourth-floor walk-up in Brooklyn. Not for the first time, I realized that the sweep of their corner yard and the way the hill at the front led around back to a rose stone patio with wrought iron tables and cushioned chairs, a barbecue flanking the house ringed by azaleas and hydrangea bushes and, marking the end of the property, a large woodpile to feed the fireplace in winter, were all too enviable. I saw myself as a child running in the sprinkler out back, a rainbow arcing in the mist. I saw Lucy trying to catch hold of me and I shielded my eyes from the memory.

When had I stopped disparaging my parents' way of life and had instead begun to covet it?

Ramon parked on the street, leaving enough room for my mother to zoom out of the garage, as she often did, without hitting our car. Madame Harriet took the quickest of pisses before she bounded up the lawn to the front door and sat, tail wagging, waiting for my mother to let her in. In and out of this door, summer nights thick with lightning bugs. Winter, trailing in snow from the treads of our Moon Boots. The soft white light of the kitchen.

"Hello!" The door swung open. Harriet reared up on her back legs, squealing and snorting. And there she was:

The Mother.

"Hey, Mom." I entered the hallway.

"Hi, honey."

"Joanne!" Ramon embraced her.

"You two want some lunch before you get back on the road?" my mother asked.

"Quickly," I said.

"Thank you so much for taking Harriet." Ramon handed over the leash.

"Are you kidding? We love watching her. She's our granddog!"

I breathed in sharply at this, as we didn't have a grandkid to offer up, but a dog. Lucy, three years younger, was off teaching in South America. Or she was surfing there and building huts? Or scuba diving? Whatever she was doing, there didn't seem to be a deep commitment to family on her part. She'd lived away for over five years now, and I hadn't seen her in nearly three.

Lucy and I had had no falling-out to speak of, no argument that had divided us, and yet we rarely communicated now; we had not spoken in ages when we caught each other on the phone last week.

"Jesse?" I had heard birds squawking in the background; had there also been the sound of the ocean?

"Lucy!" I cried on hearing her voice. "How are you? Where are you?"

"Panama?" she said. "With a friend."

A parrot screamed in Spanish, *¿Dónde está la carne de res?*

Last time we'd spoken, my sister had been in Costa Rica. Now, in Panama, she was doing some sort of community outreach with an animal refuge and making jewelry with disabled young mothers. All this she'd told me with a sigh of exhaustion, as if she'd acquired seventeen companies or traveled to the moon; and she was also helping this friend open a café specializing in Greek food. And she was surfing, too, which was why she had originally landed in Costa Rica. She had become a surfer, my sister, Lucy.

As she spoke I made a note to never send my hypothetical child to college in California.

My sister and I knew so little about each other now. The last time we'd talked I told her I was about to embark on my final fertility treatment. I hadn't followed up to tell her it was unsuccessful, and she hadn't called to find out. She was off, out there, somewhere; it was hard to fix an actual image of her that held still, that wasn't in motion.

My mother, however, was here before me, before a backdrop I knew well, but she too had become unrecognizable. My whole life, she'd worked, traveling for months at a time. It was our housekeeper, Claudine, who raised us by day. She kept her entire wallet stuffed in her brassiere and wore an Afro wig of fake, gleaming black hair that she would take off when she was in the house, revealing that her head was bald in parts, the remaining hair straightened, greased with pomade, and pinned back.

"Just one minute, let me make you a sandwich for the road," my mother said, as if she had been feeding me lunch and milk and cookies every day of my life.

"And coffee," I called after her, enabling her fantasy—and mine—that she had always been here just to serve me.

What is a mother? I have asked myself this often. As Ramon and I hauled back into the car, waving good-bye to my mother and Harriet, who didn't give a lick that we were leaving, I thought about my own mother's arrivals, her unpacking, Lucy and I anticipating our gifts. We sat cross-legged on her bed watching her remove her travel kits and her perfectly folded garments as we waited for our packages to emerge from the depths of her suitcase, which smelled of saffron, or cleaning solution, or used bookstores. She would then turn to face us. That was back when my mother let herself go out into the sun without the sunscreen that could protect her from a nuclear explosion, and her face was several shades darker, her nose and cheekbones sprinkled with the freckles I have inherited. Why, I wondered then, was the developing world, where I knew my mother went, always in the sun?

The gifts were regional and various: small woven baskets, iron figurines, wooden napkin holders carved into elephants and giraffes, a cloth envelope containing three clay beads. One particular time, she handed me a small package folded in a wrinkled, waxy brown paper bag and wrapped in one of her long peasant skirts. Inside were several copper bracelets.

"They're pretty," I'd told my mother. But in truth I didn't like them. What I really wanted was a dangling metal heart suspended on a golden chain, tilted on its side, like my Andy Gibb–loving babysitter wore. I didn't want what was for purchase in a marketplace in Africa.

Now I wonder how she could have left us for so long, what that was like for her.

"Bye," I yelled, watching my mother and Harriet in the front yard, her waving as we pulled away.

Ramon and I met in Italy when I was traveling there alone. I'd been working on my dissertation—a small portion was on gender and generational politics in contemporary Italy—which enabled me to receive grant money for the visit. I hadn't known when I planned the trip how anxious I'd be when traveling alone, securing hostels, acquiring proper currency. On night trains, fearing Gypsies, I wore my passport taped to my heart.

I have often imagined that I would never have met Ramon had I had companionship in those tired, dusty afternoons. In Rome, I slept in a hostel run by nuns. Ramon was visiting his mother in Terracina, not two hours from Rome, where he'd come to stay with friends, and he too was unaccompanied when we met in Santa Maria in Trastevere.

My mother's sadistic touristic rigor had put me off cathedrals altogether—villages across France must bear the heavy marks of my dragging footsteps as I was pulled in to investigate each town's church—but on this trip they offered relief from the heat, and I remember walking out of the sun and into the familiar musty darkness.

Why do synagogues contain light, churches darkness? I wondered at this, looking up at the dusky ceilings, the dark walls embossed in gold, the carved decorations. I crept into the chamber behind the altar, where their relic was stored: Saint Apollonia's skull encased in glass on a bed of red velvet.

There was a slot to insert a coin and when I dropped a lira in, the skull lit up and in the trembling church light I could see its grooves, the wavy lines separating the different parts of the cranium. The light did not last long and when it switched off I turned to see Ramon waiting behind me.

"Want to watch again?" He held a coin between his thumb and forefinger.

And then there it was, illuminated. Like a heartbeat, I thought.

I had not been thinking of a child's then. Once all the math I did was mere subtraction: I had been ill—I'd had cancer—but I had survived my illness. Perhaps I was thinking only of the surprising durability of my own heart.

That first night, Ramon spoke with the nuns at the convent where I had secured my little cot in the row of women, the bed's sheets pulled up tight like a scared child's, like the girls in the Madeline books, as I retrieved my bag from the convent. As I walked away, I knew the sisters were thinking that the stories they'd heard about American women—especially the Jewish ones—had been true. That night in Rome was the first time since I'd had my surgeries that I'd let someone touch me. The moonlight streamed in through the window, and when I lifted my shirt, tentatively, the line that bisected me, that jagged cut, was illuminated in the eerie gray light.

Ramon had paused. "Looks like you lost that catfight," he'd said before moving on.

After two days of pizza and pasta and coffee and ice cream and fried artichokes and street cafés and piazzas filled up with pigeons, and the exchange of stories about our separate lives in New York

City, where Ramon now lived, we sat eating at a place in Campo de' Fiori. The restaurant boasted a choice of no less than 3,456 types of mozzarella and as far as I could tell not one of them was not the most delicious, creamy, delectable morsel I'd ever tasted. I was on not my first, second, or third "taste" when Ramon asked me if I'd like to meet his mother.

Beneath my deep uncomplicated love of the mozzarella, I liked Ramon. But I did not know if this was a lasting relationship. So, no, I was not dying, just then, to meet his mother. And yet I was intrigued. When Lucy and I traveled with my parents, they sought out a farmer to cook a typical meal for us, or a restaurant with four chairs in the mountains one couldn't find in a guidebook (or without one, it turns out), a special ceremony only locals—which somehow seemed to include us?—could attend. The goal: a true experience that legitimized the privilege of our tourism, rendering it authentic and therefore qualifying us as atypical Americans. When traveling, never turn down the opportunity to visit the home of an indigenous person, I thought, and so I told Ramon that I would love to meet his mother.

I thought of all the indigenous objects my mother had brought from her travels: a mask from Kenya that had been danced in a renewal ceremony and so had once come alive; a voodoo doll from Haiti with rusted pins in its back; a Moroccan woven basket. As we drove from the highway onto the dirt road that took us to Ramon's home in an agricultural section outside of the *commune*, I wondered what I could bring back, proof that I had traveled there.

Ramon explained that his mother, Paola, had grown up in Terracina, which is a town in the region of Lazio. "But she's just come back to live permanently only recently," he said.

Ramon had described his experience of living all over the world due to his Spanish father's work for BP. He told me about living in

West Africa and Argentina, about Holland and Colombia, about how his mother held him so close, afraid of what lay beyond the confines of their company-provided homes.

"Where's your father?" I asked as we made our way down the pitted road.

"He's still in Jakarta," he said. "Now they're temporarily separated."

"Jakarta!" Did I even have an image to attach to this place? Had my mother ever brought me a gift—a hand-painted puppet made of paper, batik cloth—from there? I saw a city with the tallest building in the world. I saw women covered head to toe. "Temporarily?" I asked.

"Yes. It's just temporary." Ramon looked straight ahead.

I glanced at him, but he did not turn to catch my eye, and so I sat back, my bare feet on the dusty dashboard of his navy blue VW Golf (the car of a Nazi, my grandmother would have said, just as she told my father when he bought his used Volkswagen from a hippie in Arlington). The road was bumpy, and edged by high stone walls and swaying cane, so that we could see only straight ahead, an endless path of loose dirt and gray stones.

"Anyway, my mother's family is from here," Ramon continued. "Their old stone house is actually on our lot, but now there is the new house," he said. "Long story, but my mother told everyone in the village I was an architect. In order to keep up the ruse, she and my father asked me to design the house, like an architect would."

The car thumped along, and Ramon kept his eye on the road. I loved his profile. Like a man on a nickel.

"Seriously?"

He turned toward me. He stopped the car and took his hand off the gearshift. "Yes," he said, placing it on my knee. "She thought

11

a graphic artist meant painting billboards, like the ones in Rome, which made her think that I would have to stand on a ladder to paint them, which of course meant that I could fall, and not only that I could fall, but that I most certainly *would* fall, and so, better to be an architect, leave New York, and come back to Terracina and build up the village."

"Wow," I said.

"Yes." Ramon removed his hand from my knee and began again to drive. "And so it was built and so the house makes no sense."

"You mean to tell me you actually drew up the plans and then someone just built the house?" A little ways up a truck was making its way toward us rather speedily, alarming, as there was only room for one car on this road.

"The point is, this is not what you would call an American family situation." This seemed to be an insult of some kind and I thought of the earlier girlfriends Ramon had told me he'd brought home to Paola: a Swiss ballerina, a Mexican painter, and most recently, a photographer from Brazil who had visited Java with Ramon. They had taken a trip into the jungle and had hiked down into a special cave and Ramon had opened an umbrella in front of his face to keep the bats away.

I looked at Ramon. What did he see when he looked at me, aside from my Americanness?

What he didn't seem to notice or care about was the pickup truck barreling toward us. "Also," he said, "you need to get rid of everything before you come in the house. Cigarettes, condoms, any kind of alcohol."

I pointed at the truck. "Alcohol? And all my firearms?"

Ramon put the car in reverse and began backing up at an uncomfortably rapid pace.

"Ramon!" I grabbed what I thought was the armrest on the

door but turned out to be the manual window crank. It promptly fell off in my hand. "Shit." I felt my anxiety rise.

Ramon had backed into a little patch of flattened cane and we watched the truck scream by, its wheels rattling as they spit dust and stones at us.

"Close the window!" He reached over me.

"Here." I handed the plastic contraption over to Ramon.

He leaned over me again, sticking it back on with a focused push. "It has fallen off for years," he said. "You really have to be careful not to pull it at all, just push it, gently."

"Have you thought of fixing it?" I asked, afraid now to touch the handle.

"Why? If you handle it gently, properly, there's no problem," he said. "Anyway, listen, here's where you need to dump any cigarettes, condoms, anything of this nature."

"Yes, but I don't have any of those things."

"You sure?" Ramon pulled out onto the road. "Do you have any lingerie? Because my mother will go through your bags. She will search everything," Ramon said.

"First of all, had I backpacked through Europe alone, with lingerie, and met some Italian-Spanish guy who lives in New York who I'd been sleeping with for three nights, don't you think he might have seen it by now? The lingerie, I mean."

He smiled.

"And second of all? That's ridiculous," I said. "You're how old, thirty-five?"

He nodded again. "Well, thirty-three."

I was twenty-nine then.

He couldn't be serious, I thought as he slowed down to a stop in front of a large metal door, sea blue, a color I have only seen painted on toy boats and the twirled domes of the churches on

Greek islands. Pink and pinker bougainvillea and twisted bright green vines climbed up the sides and over the doors.

Ramon took a key out of the clean ashtray. He went to the door and pushed it open: a flash of light and then the tips of citrus trees with their green waxy leaves, branches heavy with lemons and oranges. Then he returned to the car and drove us slowly inside, gravel crunching beneath our tires.

There was the house, the house that Ramon had planned, with a red clay roof and wooden shutters, opened wide (the windows, I soon realized, were sealed shut), and a marble staircase leading up to a small terrace overlooking the driveway. Mountains rose up, hazy, in the distance.

There at the top of those stairs stood a stout woman, her black hair swept up, her tanned arms folded across her chest. She was screaming in Italian, a language I could barely make out even when it was not being shot off like artillery fire. And then there was wild pointing, at the car, or at me, perhaps both, as I pushed my way out, as if I were defying gravity, and then, before I could greet her with an Italian *Buongiorno!* I'd been practicing—inwardly—in the car, there was more screaming. Ramon opened his arms wide, his head tilted as he walked up the steps to her and took her in his arms.

"Mama!" he said.

Her voice was muffled now, but still, she made wild gestures with her hands, even as she hugged her son. I could see a sliver of her mouth curve into a smile:

The Mother.

2

—

I had always thought about what a mother is in relation to what she is not. I knew, had I the choice, for instance, that I would not choose to be my mother. My mother was stretched thin. My mother was nervous. She grew up in the fifties. For her, working was a political act. Being a mother was both the equal and opposite of a political act. As an adult I believe in my mother's politics, and I understand as a chronicler of history—women's history in particular—that making a choice was necessary. But as a kid, I did not care about postwar American society and the myth of the feminine mystique; I just wanted my mother to take me to soccer practice.

Claudine used to call me home to read to me at 4:30 P.M., when other kids were still eating cereal together in front of televisions or kicking the can along tar-pocked streets.

It was always winter, and twilight, and I remember leaving my friends' houses and crossing the darkening street for home. Lucy would be waiting there, and Claudine would read us the story of the magic pot, a folktale about a poor farmer who found a magic pot that would multiply to the hundreds whatever anyone placed inside it. My mother heard the story on one of her trips to Kenya and later found a book that illuminated the tale with batik-like illustrations. The pot kept giving and giving but soon the king heard about it, and, being king, wanted it for himself. Fighting ensued, which eventually led to the unjust death of many villagers, and the pot grew dusty, its magnificent talent wasted, the villagers still unfed but with the knowledge now of the luxury they were missing. Lucy would be curled in Claudine's lap, and I, propped on my elbows, imagined our mother doing what she described in her postcards like testing the water supply or showing women how to make milk from U.S. government–provided nutritional powders, a property almost as astonishing as the magic pot's.

Once my mother asked me what I would put in the magic pot. Candy of course, I told her, but what I'd meant was her love. And now? I have wished on every eyelash, each ladybug touching down on a bare freckled shoulder, for all the grade-A fertilized embryos a girl could hope for. Or no: actual babies are what I want. A magic pot full of babies, one for every childless mother, two for me so they can have each other, the way Lucy and I once did. A magic pot filled with a chance to fix the past. Because that is also what a mother does. She fixes the past from the future. If you cannot be a mother, how do you fix the way in which you were mothered?

Ramon and I were back on 95, heading south toward the adoption agency. Every state has different adoption laws and practices, and it turns out New York is one of the most difficult places to adopt in. National adoption agencies, with offices in the baby-making hubs of our country, were what many of the people we'd spoken to had chosen, and so here we were, going to the closest office, that magical place that held our future. We were to arrive at six o'clock for an initial meeting—a mixer! the informational packet had said—

that would begin our weekend of adoption training. Should I bring sneakers? I'd asked Ramon while packing. This training, will it involve a track? A long jump?

To his credit, he'd laughed. Wouldn't it be nice if it was really just a grueling boot camp? he'd said.

"I wonder what this is going to be like." Ramon looked away, out his window at the red brick buildings off the highway, nearing Richmond.

"Me too," I said. "I'm excited though. Are you?"

"I am. Relieved, too."

By "relieved," Ramon meant that we had finally jumped off the in vitro fertilization journey—and by "journey," I mean path through the fairy-tale forest to hell—and had moved on to a newer gamble, the gamble now not being *whether* we get a kid, but *when* we would get a kid, and what that child's genetic makeup would bring. Why gamble on science, Ramon and I reasoned with each other, when our luck has always been suspect?

Ramon had wanted out of the science before we'd even begun, believing my body, which had undergone surgeries and chemo, had withstood enough. Ramon's mother, who had perhaps taken three Tylenols in her entire life, was against any shred of medication, and Ramon had inherited her resistance. He bludgeoned his hangovers with an occasional Advil and his bouts of depression with drinking. He had never told his mother about my illness—when we went to the lake or the sea with her, I wore a one-piece suit to hide my scars.

Had we unlimited finances, there is no telling what we would have done, but Ramon and I had come to terms with not being genetically linked to our child. And sometimes, we agreed, too much choice gives you, well, too much choice. I remember thinking of the march on Washington senior year of college, how I'd held that round blue sign high: TAKE YOUR LAWS OFF OUR BODIES!

I thought I'd never be able to use a surrogate for this reason. We are not, I used to scream at the boys in sociology class, incubators!

Looking at Ramon in profile as he drove, I could register my own sadness that we would never see his dark face and long nose replicated. Other parts of him that I have blamed on Spanish and Italian temperament, I reasoned, I would be glad to never encounter in my children.

And there was also the cancer. I would be happy not to pass that along to anyone.

Relief. I wasn't sure I could use that word. I was relieved to be done with my body as Western: a place where the fertility cowboys, spurs of their boots dragging in the sand, tied their horses to my body's rotting post. They kicked open its rusty-hinged doors, guns blazing, dead bodies and cracked eggs left behind them in clouds of red dust. And either you won the shoot-out and ran off with your own kid swaddled in your arms or you got shot down in some horrible haunted ghost town, ended up with nothing but a moonshine hangover.

When all the science we could muster had failed, we thought we'd adopt internationally. Ramon was international, after all. We went to a very fancy adoption agency—Smith Chasen, on the Upper East Side—for an introduction to international adoption. It was as if we were applying to prep school. The chairs lined up perfectly, the metal of each arm touching the next just so, and pristine forms on clipboards were fanned out on tables, which made us feel we needed to be special, chosen even, for entry into this arrangement. And so we sat, straight as pins, poles up our hopeful, anal-retained asses, as we waited for the social workers to illuminate us about what countries we might plunder for a baby.

This was 2009. The whole world was on the verge of financial collapse, and in regards to international adoption, I had the sense that, like going to college in the eighties, I had missed a quintessential moment. While I still banged around Washington, DC, shaking my fists, it was hardly the age of protest. The Freedom Riders, beaten, had already come home. Civil disobedience was long over. It seemed we had missed the opportunity to adopt a child abroad by a hair as well. Ten and twenty years previously, due to the one-child policy, Chinese girls were easy to come by. There were so many Chinese girls in New York City schools that our friend's child, Zoe—the third Zoe we knew—thought anyone Asian at her school had been adopted. Now I knew that the removal of all those Chinese girls had clearly taken a toll on the country: China was now a rich country of young men. It would be quite difficult to get a Chinese child, we were told, under the age of five.

A five-year-old. I had gotten Harriet at eight weeks old; she'd been teenier than a loaf of bread, and just as soft and delicious. I'd adopted her in part to recover from illness, to take care of instead of only being cared for, a final escape from the invasiveness of having been opened and basted closed.

Harriet. I was in graduate school then, with more time than I would ever have again in my life, and so I did obsessive obedience training with her—sitting, staying, handing over the paw, a game where I shot her and she played dead—all to prepare her for future visits to sick children in cancer wards, places she would never go because I could never go back.

Commands aside, it had been important to me to raise a puppy as my companion, and I felt similarly about a child. I could let go of the genetic link quite easily, and with it release a child from inheriting my mighty nose, my proclivity toward migraines, my rash rush to anger, but I could not let go of the prospect of mothering an infant.

Given my family, a heady combination of Eastern European Jews, I was inclined to choose a child from Russia. When the criteria for adopting a Russian child went up on the screen at that first meeting at Smith Chasen, we found we made the cut—bravo!—but what the country was offering was hard to bear. Children in orphanages, the environments unclear, and I thought of a child perhaps untouched from infanthood. The long wait for a Russian child flashed on the screen, along with a chart of how orphanages tried to adopt those children out first locally, in the town or village, and then state-wide, and then nationally. So by the time the possibility of that child arrived here, she was often three or four, and, I could not help but wonder, passed over *why*?

I could not have known at that introductory session that two weeks later, Russia would put a ban on U.S. adoptions as a result of an American woman who placed her adopted Russian child alone on a one-way plane to Moscow with a note that said: *This child is mentally unstable. He is violent and has severe psychopathic issues.* The child was dropped by a hired driver at the Russian Education Ministry in Moscow.

I thought about the woman who sent that child back to Russia as we drove south, where babies—babies available for adoption—came from. Because of religion, I thought, remembering the fanatics in front of the abortion clinics we defended in college, who held *Life* magazine's blown-up pictures of fetuses in uteri, the same photos my mother had shown me when trying to explain how babies were made.

Ramon had spent several years in Argentina and Venezuela, and so a South American child made sense to us. He was a native Spanish speaker, and Guatemala seemed a viable option until we were told that night at Smith Chasen that Guatemala had also recently closed to Americans. The Hague Convention, which prevented organizations from paying women to have children, as well as the trafficking of babies over international borders, had been signed into U.S. law. Of course I didn't want to take someone's baby, someone who was being forced into placing their child up for adoption. I didn't want to buy a child. And yet, I couldn't help but think of getting here before those laws had started to affect intercountry adoption, in the golden age, when you lined up and paid your fees and got your fingerprints taken and your HIV tests, and then you got in a queue and when it was your turn, you left that country with an infant. And then that infant became your baby. And that baby grew into your child.

We had been cut off from Asian countries, where one was not to have ever had a mental illness—no antidepressants, not a single therapy session, not a one. But for me it was not reasons of mental health that precluded Asia; it was cancer. No. Cancer. Never. None. We were ineligible to become parents of children from an entire portion of the world.

Now Ramon and I passed through Richmond, its factories billowing black smoke, the large buildings almost New England looking in their stoic red-brickness, and I remembered a couple who sat next to us on that row of chairs at Smith Chasen, two men in beautifully tailored suits, crisp shirts with the faintest blue stripes, pastel ties. One was dark—Latino, I think—and the other looked as if he'd spent his first twenty summers on the bow of a boat in topsiders and Bermuda shorts, one knee bent as he looked out to sea, his blond hair feathering in the wind. The darker one raised his hand as we watched slides of orphanages flip by.

"I know that some countries don't allow gay couples to adopt." He cleared his throat. "What are the criteria for Russia?"

I want to say the social worker looked uncomfortable, that she shifted her papers and cleared her throat, but she did neither of those things. "I'm sorry no one told you this before tonight," she said. "But we don't take on homosexual couples for international adoption. Most countries will not consider it." She smiled; her one concession seemed to be that she did so without showing her teeth.

The couple looked at each other, stunned. Then, as if on cue, they stood up and tried to leave the row with dignity, but they had to step over Ramon and me, who had not had time to stand and make room for them to pass. We tried to, believe me, but it was badly timed, and so we blocked them rather than cleared a path. When they finally exited our row, knocking several chairs imperfect, I began to cry. I sat down and put my head in my hands as I heard more rustling, the sounds of more same-sex couples exiting the room.

After they left, a single woman, also banned from parenthood, filed out, and then it was Ramon's and my turn. No cancer, we were told. No matter how long it's been in remission. Not for Asian countries. There was a ringing in my ears so loud, but I could not answer it. Ramon went to stand, but I jerked him back into his seat. I would not leave the room.

Perhaps, we thought, someone with experience could explain this process to us. A colleague gave me the name of an acquaintance—their kids were in school together—a lawyer facilitating adoptions who had adopted two Russian children, simultaneously, five years previously.

The lawyer was kind enough to meet me for coffee uptown. It was just after she'd had a hair appointment and as she approached my table, I could see her hair was rather purple, like an elderly person's, and, because it was combed back and sprayed high, away from her face, it revealed two slits at each ear, where her skin had been pulled too tightly and then resewn.

"This is how you get the best ones," she said, meaning the children, after we'd said hello and ordered. "You send flowers to the people helping you." She blew into her tea. "You just do it. They say it's a queue but it's not really a queue. Send flowers, and you can get better ones than the ones you're supposed to get."

I had no idea what this woman was talking about. It felt similar to the beginnings of my peregrinations through the underworld of infertility treatments—needles filled with Follistim and Menopur, hot stone massages, progesterone, acupuncture, wheatgrass shots, estrogen patches, potassium IVs. Once I did not know the meaning of some of those words. Here, I began to write everything down in my adoption notebook, a red leather-bound book I'd had for years. I did not yet understand that what the lawyer meant was: try not to get the Russian kid who has never been touched, she will have bonding issues.

"Bonding issues can ruin your life," she told me. "If you're at all unsure about the condition of the child, that's where Felicia Hirschfeld comes in. She's famous for looking at videos and measuring the heads of Russian children—actually she measures heads from all the Stans: Kazakhstan, Uzbekistan—any Stan she'll do. She did it for Angelina Jolie, and," she said, "for a well-worth-it fee, she will also do it for you."

"Did Angelina Jolie adopt from a Stan?" I asked, after writing down the name of the woman who measured heads. In addition to securing my memory, writing these facts came with the bonus of removing myself entirely from what, I was finding, was a one-way conversation.

She waved me away. "No, she didn't, but it's Angelina and Felicia Hirschfeld is the best—The. Best.—so Angelina used her for her African child."

"Oh," I said. I would soon learn that most everyone adopting a child referred to Angelina Jolie often, and by her first name. "Ramon and I were thinking about Ethiopia as well." I looked up at the lawyer, the sides of her face tinted purple where the stylist had not wiped her skin clean of dye. We were thinking of Ethiopia because the criterion for Ethiopia was: you can get a child now. They can be six months old, and the orphanages were said to be clean, with loving caretakers, and they did not seem to care about cancer. I imagined getting a grant to learn about a feminist activist community movement in the Sudan while I waited for my baby to make her way to me. Perhaps my own mother, with all her access to the developing world, might be able to help in this situation as well. The Ethiopians, my mother once told me, are the most beautiful people on earth.

Was I allowed to care about beauty? I had no idea, but this lawyer looked at me, her chin quivering, pointed down. "You know . . ." Her index finger drew imaginary lines on the sticky table. "If you get an Ethiopian child, that child will be black."

I stopped writing and looked up. We were in one of the most diverse neighborhoods in one of the most diverse cities on earth. "Obviously," I said. "Of course we're aware."

"Well, I'm just saying that if you have a black baby you will have to pal around with black people."

I took a long sip of my coffee. "Okay." I went back to writing. *Pal around,* I wrote. *With black people.*

"I'm glad you see my point. Your people are Russian." She raised her chin.

I nodded. She was not wrong.

"It matters," she said. "Let me tell you about international adoption. It's not open. You do not want open. That's the way they do it now, domestically."

"Really?" I looked up from my note taking. "I thought research was showing open—where all of us know each other to some degree—was best for the child. I've got adult friends who didn't know their biological parents and I don't know that it was better for them. They have a lot of fantasies about where they might have come from, who their parents might have been. They have to decide as adults if they want to find these people, strangers really. It can turn their worlds upside down."

She smiled. Her face stretched, a drum, a lampshade. "I had a mother who would give me furniture and then take it back. Give me a beautiful dresser—inlaid, just gorgeous—and then take it back. A mirror. Take it back. I just couldn't bear that. Someone's mother coming back, I mean. Taking them back."

"Coming back for the child?" I asked.

She looked at me, incredulous. "For the child," she said. "Yes. I cried for weeks when my mother took the beautiful dresser. A stunning mid-century piece."

I had that same horrible feeling that I would leave many conversations about adopting with: paralyzing anxiety. They made me politically uncomfortable, or they made me fearful that I had made a fallacious choice, taken an incorrect path through the wrong forest, and, because of this, my magic pot would not only not be brimming with babies, it would not even be partially filled, not even with one infant. If every meeting, every conversation, each scrap of knowledge I accrued, told me something about adoption, here was my lesson from this meeting: When you are adopting a child, the rules of social conversation are not applicable. When you are adopting a child, you are allowed to say what you please about race. You will eventually have to write it down on a form for everyone to see, what race you want, what race you do not want. You will have to know this, but you will not have to explain your reasoning. You will not have to explain anything at all. You simply do not check the box you do not want. And, somehow, in this new country, because of the Hague laws and democracy and capitalism and America, and the fact that you will become the mother of this child, everything you say will be correct.

I couldn't imagine what it meant for a baby to be taken. Back.

As we were readying to part out on Seventh Avenue, a bright robin's-egg-blue day, I asked the lawyer why she'd waited so long to adopt.

"You know," she began, her fine hair separating in the wind, "my brother died when I was five. We were playing in the street up in Westchester, in our neighborhood." She paused. "He was hit by a car." Another pause. "I was five. I just didn't know if I could do it," she said. "Be a mother. And then before I knew it, it was too late. And then it was really too late."

That had been over six months ago. I was thirty-eight.

"Just yesterday," the lawyer said, "I went to pick up my children, and the teacher's aide, she called my children over and said that their grandmother was here."

"How awful," I told her, with emotion.

"Their grandmother!" She had nodded her head, and I could tell she was in that moment, turning the injustice of it over, of aging and biology, letting it roll around, a marble on her tongue, pinging against her teeth. And then she turned and began to walk uptown. She didn't wish me luck or tell me to be in touch if I had questions. She didn't even say good-bye.

In the end, Ramon and I decided on domestic adoption because we didn't meet the criteria of many countries due to my illness, but mostly it was because we desired an infant. I put out of my mind the notion that a mother could come back and take the child away and what that could feel like, because we were told that once there was a match with a birthmother, we could be in the delivery room, holding her hand. The birthmother, we were told, would be like family. This became the fairy-tale narrative we lived by, there from almost the beginning of our once-upon-a-time. I imagined, as we headed to this agency down south, away from New York and its difficult laws that few agencies were licensed in, that we would name our baby Grace, like a lot of the adopted girls I knew. Grace, as in "divine," as in "God's Grace," because of all we had to do to find her, the child that was ours from the ancient beginnings of time, but that we'd had to be tried and tested and trained to find.

The birthmothers, we told each other, are real. They have what we want: not the stitched pink stripe, the ticking black spot, not the hand-forced specimen swimming free in a sterile cup, but flesh and blood and bones, a thread sutured to life. I thought about Grace now, on this highway. Ramon and I were relieved when we decided on adoption, and we believed we would find comfort in going to Smith Chasen for that horrid meeting, and now we felt relieved that finally this process could make sense to us; there would be logic to this grace.

"This is going to be great," I said, as if we were on our way to Club Med. I looked out at the road. We had just left 95 and now were on the diminutive 85, which made us feel like we were headed somewhere undiscovered. "But also, I'm nervous." What had the sign said? Martina? I'd just seen a sign that said RALEIGH 100 MILES, I do remember that, as I remember thinking how close my parents were to Raleigh and how strange that seemed, as I consider my parents staunch northerners.

"I've been thinking about it," said Ramon, still the fingers gripping and ungripping the wheel. "I'm going to speak Spanish to the child, no matter what the ethnicity. I'm going to speak Spanish and Italian."

As he said this I felt a combination of psychotic rage and unbearable sadness. At first my violence-bordering anger was against all Europeans who, as we uneducated isolated Americans know, speak so many goddamn languages. It quickly, however, honed in on Ramon. "Really?" I asked.

"Of course! I'm Spanish and Italian. My mother spoke to me in Italian for my entire childhood, and that's important to me to pass on."

"But I don't speak either of those languages, Ramon." It was my great shame that, as many years as I'd been going to Terracina, I had never learned to speak Italian. The old farmers who lived next to his mother thought I was an idiot. Here comes the illiterate Jew who killed Jesus, they said to one another as we pulled in each summer. I don't know that they said this, as Ramon is the worst translator in the history of translators, but I'm quite sure it was something to that effect.

"Well, that's not my fault, Jesse." He looked straight ahead. "What will you do then? What will you pass on to the child?"

I didn't know if I would burst into tears or tear my husband's head off. What would I do? Take our African-American, Italian-and-Spanish-speaking baby to Hebrew school?

"What will I pass on to the child," I said, more to myself than Ramon.

I remembered Passover at my great-grandmother's house in Cleveland, all the cousins rushing to find the afikomen as if it held the key to something besides Nana Sadie's checkbook. Great-Uncle

Sid with his magic quarters, his colored silk scarves pulled out of the most unfathomable and, I now see, inappropriate places. There were long dinners and a photograph of Ronald Reagan my father had gotten for his grandmother-in-law, who, for some reason that no one could fathom, had cast her vote for him, the first and last Republican vote in our family.

"I blame Cleveland," my father had said, laughing, as he slid macaroon after macaroon off Sadie's delicate three-tiered dessert tray and dropped them down his gullet.

Three generations dipping our fingers into salted water, passing the bitter herbs and the charoset, three generations, piling the horseradish high on the gefilte fish, leaving the door ajar for Elijah, even if Sadie lived in an apartment building. It was three generations singing "Dayenu" as if our lives depended on it, my grandfather the attorney, bent and birdlike; his wife, three times larger than he, belting it out; even Great-Aunt Sylvia, who was deaf, sang, in her low sad voice. And Lucy asked the four questions. Wherever we were, always, Lucy was the youngest of us all.

Three generations. All at one table. I will be the one to break that.

"Yes," Ramon said. "You have to think about legacy."

My child would be heir to what? I closed my eyes as we drove, and I thought of Harriet, asleep at my mother's feet as she moved around the kitchen, before a new stove she had not used until three months ago. She'd had to go downstairs to the fuse box to figure out how to turn it on. I thought with regret how we had spayed Harriet, and so we would never have her puppies, and just the thought of never seeing her or her likeness again made me breathe heavily, tears collecting at the corners of my eyes. And beneath all that was this: where do I fit in here? Most women become pregnant and they carry their babies and then they breast-feed their infants, who need them to survive. Ramon and I were the same. We were two bodies. The baby would need us equally, and yet Ramon would have his seventeen languages and his countless rich cultural experiences to share. I didn't know what I could offer, and while I began to ponder all the perils of assimilated Judaism, really it was just this, only this: was I the mother?

Wasn't I supposed to be the mother?

3

Ellen Beskin was the first adopted person I met. We were eight years old and bored when she told me. We'd made an A-frame house out of giant Tinkertoys, and when we were done, we sat down, Indian-style, inside our transparent home. Neither Ellen nor I was a particularly girly girl. We both played soccer—Ellen had been the fortunate one who got Pelé's coveted number 10—but we did not wear tube socks pulled up to our scraped knees, nor did we trade baseball cards or walk around reciting hockey scores like a few of the tomboys we knew. And yet, as we were not built for tea parties, pinkies extended as we sipped from pretend china cups, and as my mother had put the kibosh on an Easy-Bake Oven, Ellen and I did not know what to do in the trappings of this Tinkertoy house, this bastion of domesticity, once we'd assembled it.

We were just sitting there, pulling at the stiff shag basement carpeting, when Ellen said, "Did you know I'm adopted?"

I shook my head. "Uh-uh."

"I am. Adopted. I didn't come from my mom's tummy. I came from a different mom's tummy."

"Huh." I couldn't look at her.

"My brother came from my mommy's tummy." Ellen gazed wistfully out of the pretend window. "So he's not adopted."

I nodded. And then I stood up. I decided I'd rather be roller-skating.

"Do you want to take this thing down?" I said as I began unscrewing the roof.

It was my mother who made a big deal about Ellen's being adopted by wanting to discuss it. My mother wanted to discuss a host of concerns, especially regarding disturbing topics, such as an assassination attempt on the president or the firing of a teacher for molesting a child at a local Catholic school.

"Yes, she *is* adopted," my mother said when I brought my conversation with Ellen up to her a few days later. She spoke with vigor and enthusiasm, as she had when film of the president being hoisted into an ambulance played on the six o'clock news. "Do you know what 'adoption' means?"

"Yes, Mom," I told her.

She raised her eyes and shook her head encouragingly.

"It means that she didn't come from her mom's stomach." As I stated this I realized I didn't understand what that meant at all. I imagined the book *Are You My Mother?,* that poor baby bird searching high and low, turning to all kinds of species and machines for comfort. But I had related to that bird too; my mother was away often. Claudine was the one reading to me. *Are you my mother?,* Lucy and I would both say together in the places I'd memorized. What, I wondered, did Ellen make of the question the book begged?

"That's right," my mother said. "How does that make you feel?"

"Fine?" It was a question that, going forward, I would be asked by her so many times I would begin to dread and despise it.

"What it means is that Mr. and Mrs. Beskin wanted Ellen so much they had to search for her," she said, and then she went on to explain to me the process of adoption. "Ellen might feel bad about it, because her brother wasn't adopted," she continued. "She shouldn't feel bad, mind you, but she might."

When Ellen's mother—the adoptive one—died two years later, from cancer, and I attended her funeral with my mother, I fixated on Ellen and her father and brother, seated in the hard pews, her blond head twitching beside the darker versions of her family. It was my first funeral and the ritual, the flung-open casket, the wreaths of flowers propped on metal stands, fascinated me. Our teachers were there; for the first time I'd gotten to see Mrs. Gross outside of her classroom. Teachers were all we knew then of celebrity, and spotting one now, as *one of us,* was nothing short of thrilling.

As the minister spoke—so many firsts in one special day!—I thought of how Ellen's being adopted was surely connected to the death of her make-believe mother. Precisely how, I was not certain. All the kids were saying that if your hand was bigger than your face you had cancer, and I could see many students in the pews that day, testing this out. I wondered if Ellen's mother's hand had been bigger than her face. But because Ellen was the first adopted person I knew, and the first person whose mother—if that was what she had in fact been—had died, then certainly there was something tethering these two moments together, even if it was only in the effect of Ellen's losing her mother twice.

Ellen was sent to a private school for junior high and high school, and I lost track of her. Before she left, she had grown very intense. She forged personal relationships with our favorite teachers. She seemed to have protracted and fraught romances instead of the timid schoolyard dances the rest of us were having. At the parties we threw in our parents' basements, while they swilled wine and ate fondue with their friends upstairs, we played Spin the Bottle and Two Minutes in Heaven, and sometimes smoked clove cigarettes on the covered garage tarmac, Ellen would often wander off into a dark corner, alone. I came upon her there as she was being comforted by one of the more fleshy, maternal figures of our bunch, and I was fascinated by Ellen's vulnerability and the other's willingness to soothe it, bodily, her arms around Ellen, a pudgy hand pushing back her white-blond hair.

Surely it was her mother's death that created this need for prolonged connection, for succor, due to this cleaving, a crucial sense of belonging cut. I thought of this flying along 85. As we'd crossed over into North Carolina from Virginia—when the rolling hills and barns and fences, horses swatting their stunning tails, cows asleep against the green of the thick grass—everything had come into focus. I could distinguish where the land met the sky, and I could discern the rise and fall of the earth as we made our way south. It occurred to me only then that I was off the fertility drugs and for the first time in a long while I was thinking clearly, seeing the world not blanketed in fuzzy contours, but in sharp definition. Everything was radiant.

Leaving the city can often make things brighter, the color of the moment, yes, but also the shades and nuances of home, too. The horses were placid and sweet as we drove by, and I'd wished that I had a carrot or some apple for them to eat from my palm. It was a silly wish, and I had given those up, as I had begun by then to think my wishes should be saved, that I'd used them too freely and quickly on lesser desires, like procuring a tenure-track position in New York City, no small feat, or on daily aspirations, like for the subway to just once get me where I needed to go on time. Such replaceable wishes. I wondered, as we passed the horses, if my wishes weren't all used up. Perhaps it was time for prayers.

My sister was a rider. She used to go with my father to a stable farther south in Virginia, and they would ride together. I remember watching her put on her hard hat, and that blue blazer with the golden buttons. I remember her soaping her saddle, a present from my grandparents, who had never so much as touched a horse. And I remember Lucy slipping a tall boot into the stirrups and sitting up straight and tall, and then the two of them moving, her body matching the rhythm of the elegant animal's pace. After, waiting for our father, we'd pick the buttercups and dandelions that grew in large patches by the wooden fence of the rings and place them under each other's chins. You like butter, we'd say, yellow reflected on the pale and delicate skin at our necks. And the deep yellow of dandelions. *Mama had a baby and its head popped off,* we'd sing, flicking the blooms from their tender stems.

Now, with my newfound coherence, my view of a shimmering world, I thought, Perhaps I will write a poem. "Ramon," I said, "I'm so hopeful I could write a poem right now."

He laughed. "A poem? About what?"

"About nature. Isn't that what poems are about? How now I can see the world again." I was smiling.

"Okay, shall we write it now?"

"I'm serious!" I said. "I'm feeling hopeful again."

"I'm glad." Ramon put his hand on my shoulder.

I tried to picture our child. How strange to have absolutely no idea what she will look like, or when he might arrive, and by what sort of delivery system. I remembered meeting Ramon, and then later that day, seeing him across the room at a café, moving toward me with two glasses of wine, and how I had a vision of him holding a child's thumbs and guiding that child across the room to me.

I'm not inclined to such fancy, but it was how I knew that I would choose Ramon. Since then I'd been looking so hard to catch sight of that child's face.

"Thanks for being glad." I sounded more sarcastic than I'd intended.

We were silent for a bit. I remembered us before any of this, on Capri, a last-minute trip we took to escape Ramon's mother for a few days. Our hotel had been carved into a cliff overlooking the sea, the famed Blue Grotto far below. Paradise, really, though our room—the only remaining one available—looked out onto the street; the sea and sky and cliffs were cropped out.

Before dinner we had walked down to the Grotto. It was twilight, when all the glass-bottom two-person boats were on their way out of the caves. Tourists (*Tourists!* I thought; I had with me an Italian!) made their way, beaming, shakily, out of the boats and onto the stone shore. We stood and watched, and then Ramon spoke to a few people in Italian, inquiring as to where was nice to eat, I think, and soon enough someone was taking us out onto their boat.

Come, Ramon had said, gesturing for me to step in. We ducked low in the boat and rode toward this tiny white light, the spectacular entrance to one of the sea caves, and the echo of the fishermen speaking to one another. Inside, Ramon gently pushed me to stand, and when I met his hand with resistance, he threw off his shirt and jumped in. He glowed—this is the thing about the Grotto: as dark as it is inside, it shoots what it holds in its waters through with silvery light. I watched Ramon, nacreous in the water. He looked luminous and also fearless. I was still scared of any of the ways my body could fail and shame me, and yet I jumped in after him, the fisherman clapping slowly behind us, and I felt the heavy water, watched my hands, as I lifted them, carry light.

When we went back to the room to change before dinner— a place the fisherman had recommended, not fancy, but authentic—we turned to each other in the dark of the room. The sun had gone down, and now the night sky appeared, illuminated with stars, like fish in the sea, I knew, even if I could not view it. I imagined Ramon, as I would often picture him now, indomitable in the water.

We stripped off our wet clothes and our bodies were clammy as we met each other.

"I have an idea," Ramon said.

We were standing. All of him was touching all of me.

"What." I placed my face at his neck. "Tell me." I looked up at him.

"Let's try to make a baby," he said.

What I remember most was giggling as he pulled me onto the bed.

"Oh my God!" On the highway, Ramon stopped short. We had come upon a row of five or six cars, the sun glaring off their shining hoods, a deflection of flaxen light. It took me a moment to see the true distraction, a bus that was turned slightly on its side, on the shoulder of the road. There was something painted on the surface of the bus that I couldn't make out, and several of the dark windows were smashed in; the remaining ones had white, spiderweb-like lines bursting across the glass. The front wheels still spun in the air, dismal pinwheels.

"Oh my God," I said again, covering my face with my hands.

Several people had gotten out of their cars and were on their phones, clearly calling for help.

"Jesus," Ramon said, driving along the opposite shoulder. I could feel our tires slowly turning beneath us, the sound of stray stones impressed in the tough, grooved rubber, and then the shift from the scrape of smooth, new asphalt to the soft rugged earth.

We saw someone inside the bus, propped sideways. Spread palms pushed against the glass of the doors, and then the hands, as if the fingers remembered the laws of reversals, began pulling at the door. And then this person, off-kilter, as if the world had turned upside down, stepped jerkily out of the bus. The shoulder-length hair, teased high, and the long legs, wrapped in tight denim, the high, slender hips, belonged to a man.

He wandered the road aimlessly, in circles, one leg crossing over the other, a foal learning to walk, as he looked up at the sky, his forehead smeared with blood.

The onlookers tried to still the man as we continued to drive on the shoulder.

"Do you think we should call anyone?" I asked.

Ramon shook his head. "Everyone is calling," he said, and, as if to prove his point, as we passed, I saw someone snap her phone closed and reach out for the man, touching his chest, an offering of comfort.

I turned around in my seat to watch the scene recede. The man just swayed and sat down in the road, and I watched several others start to leave the bus, one by one, startled and disoriented, and then soon they were merely toy soldiers, inky silhouettes against the darkening sky and black road, and then they were small dots on the horizon and then they were gone and again we were on our way.

4

—

We were headed into a new world. Also, we were rattled from the accident. And because Raleigh is a city of hotels, especially the little enclave of them on Arrow Drive where we drove in circles until we finally found ours, when we got back in the car to go to the adoption agency, to this mixer, we were already behind schedule.

"We're going to be late!" I turned frantically to Ramon. "Why are we the only people on earth without a GPS system?"

Ramon resisted, along with medical treatment, most of life's newest conveniences, which also included microwaves and light dimmers.

"It's no big deal," Ramon said. "Please, just check the directions again. What street is this?"

"I *am* checking, Ramon, I *am*. Oh wait." I rolled down the window. "Excuse me! Excuse me?" I screamed out into the evening air, vaguely toward the median strip, where two men in baggy jeans walked, hands shoved into pockets, their heads pitched down.

Ramon did not slow down. "Are you fucking kidding me?"

"What?"

"You're going to ask two homeless people how to get to the mixer?"

"Yes," I said, "I am. Because two homeless people—who are not homeless by the way, they're fine—know more about how to get to the mixer than we do." I started to cry.

"Please tell me you're not crying." Ramon looked straight ahead. "Honestly, Jesse, you have to pull yourself together."

"Thanks for the help." I crossed my arms.

"We are going to this thing and we need to be pulled together."

"Actually," I said, "what we need to be is on time."

Or we're not going to get a baby, I thought. I did not say it aloud, as I did not count aloud, or add up the years passing us by aloud, as if saying it out loud would make it so, but I did what I could not help, which was infuse absolutely everything with magical thinking. If we arrive on time for each event this weekend, we are that much closer to being parents. If we are late? Well, who knows what that means for our file. Perhaps lateness—along with being a bad baker, say, or cursing—would make becoming parents impossible.

"Perhaps you could look at the directions instead of crying and maybe we would get there sooner," Ramon said. Very loudly.

"I can't believe you're yelling at me," I sniffled. "We're going to a goddamn adoption party and you can't even be nice."

"Adoption party. Now that sounds like a whole lot of fun."

"I know," I laughed. I tried again. "So, what if an adoption party was like a Tupperware party, where people brought babies and women showed up and bought them, in sets of ten say, with color-coded snap tops." I pulled down the sun visor and checked for tear-smudged mascara. I wiped the corners of each eye with the tips of two fingers. "Color-coded," I said again.

Ramon sighed, turning the car around.

I looked at the directions and then at the road. I had no idea where we were.

Ramon stopped and tore the directions out of my hand. He shook his head. "It's right over there," he said. "It's been right there, the whole time."

"What do you mean by that?" I asked.

"That it was over there the whole time?" Ramon pulled into the lot. "Here?"

"Yes."

"Just what I said," Ramon said.

"Mmm-hmm," I said. But I knew it was some kind of metaphor. For what, and why it even mattered, who is to say?

The mixer. It was in a little mall-like stretch of buildings around the corner from a gas station and a Subway, about ten minutes from Arrow Drive, a trip we managed to stretch into thirty minutes. The mixer consisted of Ramon and me; five other couples; two twelve-year-old social workers, Crystal and Tiffany; and the branch director, Nickie.

Ramon and I were the last ones in, which I noted with anxiety as Nickie, tall and mahogany colored, stood up and handed us name tags, white stickers framed in blue, our names printed in childlike letters with a red marker. With a gesture, she invited us to sit at the table, which was really several tables, like we had in grade school, and nothing like the modern tables of Smith Chasen, pushed together. I could see the mini squares of light in between the fake wood where the corners of the tables met up.

"Hi. I'm Jesse, and this is Ramon." I pushed Ramon forward. "We're from New York."

He nodded his head. "Hi." He put on a smile.

I unpeeled my name tag and pasted it over my heart.

"I'm Tiffany," one of the blond social workers said. "I used to live in Manhattan!"

"Neat," I said. "We're in Brooklyn. Lots of babies in Brooklyn!" I laughed, too loudly.

It was impossible not to notice that the others, all of them, were same-sex couples.

Nickie stepped forward and reached out her hand. "We spoke on the phone. I registered you for this weekend."

"Yes." I shook her hand, which was dry and strong.

The lighting—bright, fluorescent, buzzing—was not the kind of lighting I associate with getting to know anyone in a civilized manner. I could see Ramon's pores, the size of dimes, and the little pubic-like hairs springing from Nickie's chin. And it illuminated all too clearly who was around the table: one set of lesbians and three sets of gay men. Ramon and I appeared to be the oldest by at least five years. At *least*.

Being the only heterosexual pair, while anthropologically fascinating, lighted the fear and panic-in-constant-waiting that we had come to the wrong place. Of all the agencies outside of New York, why, I wondered now, had we not chosen the one in Vermont, another popular agency with New Yorkers? Vermont would be beautiful right now, with the leaves, and the maple syrup, and the inns, and the straight couples, I thought, as I put aside that the Vermont agency's sessions were full through the year and that Ramon and I had been anxious to begin. And so here we were in a strip mall off a highway, in this place I now feared would not get babies for straight people in New York City, no matter how punctual they were.

Forget that there was no ambient music playing, not a single pig resting in a burnt or soggy blanket, nothing skewered—at least not chicken—at this mixer. And forget that everyone sat beneath the glare of the humming light, drinking Dr Pepper from cans. My heart flipped in my chest and I thought of the way this poor goldfish I'd won at a school fair slapped my cupped palms when I held him. I don't know why I would be so cruel as to take a fish out of water, though I do recall wanting to offer it comfort.

"Sorry we're late." I looked around the room, blinking. "We drove in from New York."

One of the men—Herman, his name tag said—rolled his eyes.

"I just meant it was far," I said. "And there was an accident."

"Oh, I heard!" another man, Gabe, said. "I heard Miley Cyrus's tour bus overturned."

"No way!" someone else responded.

Gabe nodded. "She wasn't in it though."

"Well, thank goodness for that," he said.

My head bobbed frantically at everything being said. Yes! It was Miley Cyrus! Yes! She wasn't there! Yes! Thank goodness she was okay. Yes! We were there!

The woman to my right, Anita, her fleece pullover flinty with animal hair, smiled back at me.

Ramon swallowed hard. He had not yet put on his name tag, I noted, as I wondered if, when we returned to the hotel, he would blame me for not signing up with that agency in Vermont.

"I'm Jesse," I again said, gesturing to my name tag and sliding into one of the two remaining chairs.

"Hi, Jesse!" the room said in unison.

I nodded my head around the room.

Ramon looked at the floor and sat down.

I unpeeled his name tag and slapped it on. "Ramon!" I pointed.

The room bubbled with laughter, and Ramon grabbed my hand

beneath the table, with an urgency that startled me. I wasn't sure if it was to stop me from speaking, to offer comfort, or to receive it.

Herman's partner, Alex, smiled at the side of his mouth. "Well hello, *Ramon*!" he said.

This happens all the time: Ramon, it should be noted, is a good-looking man.

Everyone laughed—again! What fun this was!—and said hello, and Ramon said hello back.

My heart flipped again, slippery in a hand. We are old and straight and we have tried a million other ways to have children, and we live in New York, where no one but Tiffany has ever been because, I would learn later, they think you can get shot there. And don't even bring up Brooklyn.

And then I had another one of my preternatural thoughts: if everyone here was gay and from the South—which in a way meant everyone here was the same—then maybe Ramon and I had a good chance. Maybe, if we did everything just as we were told, if we listened very well and did all the paperwork correctly, in the right order, and if we smiled properly, and didn't bicker in front of everyone, if we came on *time,* if we tried to always remember how once we had seen each other in a church and fallen in love, maybe we would get to be parents.

"Well," Nickie said, standing, leaning in on her spread fingers, her nails long and sculpted and red. "Shall we begin?"

Later that night, after finding our way back to Arrow Drive and the Crabtree Hotel that was not the Marriott Crabtree hotel but was right next to it, we turned on the news and lay back on the bed. Miley Cyrus was on, crying about her tour bus. Correction: crying about the *people* on the tour bus. She was grateful not to have been on it, but her band and the roadies had been, and two people had been killed. How old is this girl? I thought, doing my math. Could I be her mother? She is seventeen years old, the news tells me, and so yes, it appears that were I a different kind of woman, living in an alternate world, I could be her mother.

I pictured that man from her bus, unhinged in the middle of the road, the rolling hills green as moss against the black asphalt.

"Strange," I said to Ramon.

"What about this day, I would like to know, has not been strange." He took three pillows and propped himself up in bed.

I nodded slowly. I tried to be contrary, to find an argument *for* this day, but came up with nothing. "True," I said.

"The drive was strange, the place was strange, the people were strange, what is happening to us is goddamn bizarre."

"The people were nice, though. In the end. The couples, I mean."

"The mixer-that-was-not-a-mixer was not so bad in the end, yes. I see why they did it. We all got to meet each other before we do the training, whatever that is going to entail." Ramon punched at his pillows, readying, I could tell, for total obliteration. That's always the way he does it.

"Yeah, who knows what it will be tomorrow."

"I mean, training for what? The adoption ten-K?" Ramon turned onto his side, away from me, and then he said something I couldn't hear.

"What?"

"More like training for more heartbreak," he said, louder now.

I looked at my husband, taken aback, as I had been when he took my hand earlier that evening. My throat tightened, sewn shut. I tried to swallow.

"We need to stay positive." I put my hand on his shoulder.

"That's my line," Ramon said. "I will use it on you, tomorrow, when you're flipping out again."

I nodded at his back. "I know. I have been. I can't believe this is us. I just can't. How did this happen? Remember that first night in Rome, when you saw my scars and I told you I didn't think I could have children?"

Ramon's head nodded into the pillows.

"And then later when we were engaged? I told you again. You were like, who cares? We both said that. Who cares? Remember? But you know what? I don't think we believed it."

I remembered saying the words. *I can't.* But back then, what did we think we would not be able to overcome?

"Did you?" I asked him. "Did you believe it?"

"I don't remember," he said.

We were silent. "We need to stay positive." Ramon reached around to pat my hand and got my elbow instead.

I hit him on the shoulder. "You're right. We do. Let's try to get through this weekend and see." And just then I thought of that lawyer, her purple hair, the slit at her hairline, sewn tight. I hadn't known then the wait that prospective parents endure. I had always thought, in the very back of my head where my past is stored, where hope lies in wait, that we would just adopt if science didn't work for us. Making the decision to adopt would be the most difficult part, and I believed that the moment I let go of my self-absorbed need to give birth to my own biological child, a baby would miraculously reveal her face.

I did the math at the Crabtree Hotel the first night we arrived in Raleigh. It was roughly the same as yesterday and it would be the same tomorrow. But one day soon that number would radically shift.

"At least this isn't a gamble, though," I said.

Ramon was silent. He does this thing when we're in bed and he doesn't want to talk anymore, where he puts the pillow over his head and goes to sleep. But he hadn't done that just yet.

"We get a kid if we do this. Not like with the IVF, where we wait and spend all this money we don't have, and still it might not happen. This isn't like that." I thought of all the women in the waiting room at the hospital on the mornings I went uptown at daybreak for my appointments. Not one looked at another, as if we were competing for the few successes that day held. Statistics were statistics and there were not enough favorable outcomes for us all. If celebrities were there—and they always were, in their baseball caps and loose velveteen sweats and hoodies—we ignored them. Would they take everything due to their proximity to stardom? Would they get all the good luck, all the baby dust, all the magic, or had they too used up their wishes?

When they did call our names—first and last—we put our heads down and we went inside, and we took whatever we had coming, and then we went home or we went to work and we turned to chat rooms on the Internet. That's where we got the information we needed: drink wheatgrass, it improves egg quality; eat pineapple, it helps with implantation—acts that made us think we were affecting change. As we chatted anonymously, without bodies, about what our bodies weren't doing, it made us feel, however briefly, that the plans we'd made for our lives might transpire.

Still, I saw his expression when Ramon found out that I was not pregnant from our final course of IVF. I had gotten up for several mornings before he awoke and taken my own pregnancy tests, too impatient to wait for the doctor's official word, and I had not told him for days that, no matter how many times I checked it, no matter how I saved each strip, comparing it with the one the following day to see if perhaps it had darkened just the slightest bit, the answer was still the same. It was after the fifth day of silence—a disposition uncommon to me—that Ramon had woken to my steady weeping over the bathroom sink. I had not heard him outside the door, and I turned as he opened it, and we both knew in that moment that everything had run out.

"I can't think about this anymore right now." Ramon stretched out his arm and turned out the light, signaling that not only couldn't he think about it, but he wouldn't be talking about it either. "Can you just wake me when all of this is over?"

I lay in the hotel bed and thought of other hotels I'd been in with Ramon, that first night he had run his finger along the deep grooved scar. I enjoyed what I now see as his disinterest in my scars. On the beaches of Italy I saw evidence of bodies ravaged by wars and childbirth and socialized medicine in scarred torsos, steel limbs, keloid cuts, eye patches, exposed without shame. I was just another war-torn body. But the ravages were also inside, where they had gone in several times and cut out the cancerous section of the colon, then sewed it back up, almost precisely enough for me not to notice. Each time they thought they had it all, something would be left behind and in they'd go again, and the scar tissue that grew out from those internal wounds coiled around me, an unstoppable moth vine or creeper, wrapping tightly to all the parts meant to stay open, strangling me on the inside where possibility breathed.

"But what if I want to sleep through this too?" I asked the dark now.

I could hear the cars moving along the highway. I could hear the ice machine cracking in the hallway, the ding of the elevator traveling inside the building. What would my life be like? I wondered, as I had lost my earlier clarity, and with it, my power to imagine. If I could see the face of the child that would be ours, I would know even a little. There in the dark rose the magic pot. I felt Claudine hovering over me, her substantial arm around my neck, the other in front, holding the book, her deep odor of sweat and musk, and the strong timbre of her voice. She turned the thick pages and I can't say I wished for my mother then, but I wished to see her now, as I could see the magic pot drawn in that book, on the ground of a farmer's dusty field at dusk, lacking enchantment. It grew in my imagination, so massive and black, a pot to be stirred by a coven of witches, a cauldron in a forest in winter, cold and oh so empty.

5

—

The next day we were exactly on time. We were the second couple to arrive, and I felt confident and assured as I pulled my chair up to the pretend wooden table, a packet—the yellow logo of a sun beaming along the agency's name—placed neatly at each space, like a table setting.

"Good morning." I nodded to the other couple. "Anita!" I said, because I remembered her name. She was a veterinarian. There has never been a vet I haven't liked or couldn't talk to.

Anita's eyes cracked into whiskerlike laugh wrinkles as she smiled.

"Mornin'," she said.

Ramon nodded. He never remembered anyone's name, ever. And this was compounded by the fact that, though he worked in graphic design and was a visual person, he could not recall faces either. Suffice it to say, it was great fun to go to a party with my husband.

"You guys, you and *Paula*," I said, loud enough so it would somehow imprint on Ramon's brain. "Remember, Ramon?" I asked.

Ramon leaned over and shook hands. "I think we need to put

our name tags back on," he said, after which one of the delicate-skinned social workers hustled over to a table and shuffled through some papers for blank name tags. She sat and began to painstakingly write our names again, the tip of her tongue protruding from her mouth.

Soon the other couples materialized, taking the same places they had the previous evening. And then Nickie emerged from the office with a regal let's-get-down-to-business stance, and the training was thus commenced.

The day was mind-numbing. We were given a wide range of information, including, but in no way limited to, how to create a profile, which includes a letter to the birthmother and photos—with captions—of our lives together. The birthmothers receive these profiles from the agency, sometimes in huge stacks, and this is our way of introduction. We learned the word count for birthmother letters (950 words), what we should communicate in these letters (who we are, where we're from, why we've chosen open adoption, just to start), the sizes of the photos (five by seven for the main one, the one that should communicate visually that we are in love, which should be in front of a seasonless plant), what we should be doing in the photos, what we should be wearing in the photos (bright colors), what we should be thinking in the photos (how much we want to be parents).

There were toll-free numbers to call and be called on, websites to visit and to create, designers to contact, though I saw Ramon scoff at that.

"How will you portray that you're committed to each other, to being parents? How do you want to be perceived?" Nickie said. "Who are you as a couple?"

I looked around at the other couples. Brian, a journalist in DC, was most recognizable to me, with his jeans and a hunter-green wool sweater, the collar of a shirt folded at the neck casually, unlike the blinding white, knifelike corners of his partner Gabe's shirt. Gabe had his hand at Brian's back and together they looked over the sample brochures, bright, sturdy flyers of couples who had come before us and had already measured their photos properly, found foliage to stand in front of in the middle of winter, composed captions that were friendly and informative, and written a 950-word letter that passed muster with Nickie.

Gabe and Brian looked like a nice couple, and so did Anita and Paula, who sat close, rubbing each other's backs. As for the other two couples, each from separate small towns near Raleigh, I was reserving judgment, which is to say I judged them negatively. They made clear that they desired a white child—both claimed the landscape of these small southern towns as motivation for this—before the question had been posed to them. Their concern over what to do with their guns and ammunition when the social workers came for the home visit (store them separately!) made me think of them as the Killers, and I wanted to be sure to remember this term so I could later tell Ramon something droll about our day.

I could see who these couples were on the outside, but what information did that give up about what darkness lay within? What light?

I thought of those late afternoons fading into night in the basements of our American childhoods, the basements we snuck in and out of through sliding glass doors, stickered with rainbows or unicorns, so birds—and drunken teenagers—would not forget the transparent divisions between outside and in, in those basements where we grew up beneath the weight of our homes; it began for me a kind of wonderment that I would carry into adulthood: How would I convey who I am on the inside to the outside? I thought it now: How do we relate what is private about our relationship, a secret sometimes even to each other, to the world? And how would we reveal something so vital and true it would make a birthmother set our brochure aside and say: These two. I choose *them*.

I did not think, then, what would make a woman give up her child. Or any of the factors that might make her have to do so.

We broke for lunch, take-out "Italian," my antipasto salad of canned mushrooms, rolled-up and sliced ham, American cheese, and turkey on a bed of limp lettuce, Ramon's calzone soggy, nearly cold, and, he found upon biting in, nearly empty of its spinach-and-mozzarella promise.

"Good God." I nudged Ramon.

"Stop being such a snob," he said. "Not every meal has to be handcrafted."

I raised my eyebrows at him.

"Hmm." Martin glanced up from his meatball sub to look at my meal. "Did you get the pink raspberry vinaigrette with that? The pink raspberry vinaigrette is awesome."

The training then switched gears from who might want us to whom we might select, as if we had any control in this process. To announce this changed perspective, a large glass bowl of white, black, brown, and yellow pom-poms was placed on the table, and smaller, empty bowls were passed out to us.

"Take the pom-poms based on the color of the various people in your lives, your friends, your neighbors, your family," Crystal and Tiffany told us.

We all stared rather dumbly at the large bowl set before us.

"Even if you are open to adopting a child of any color, you have to think about what kind of role models of their own race they will come into contact with as they grow up," they said. "Think of your families, your communities."

We all went for our pom-poms.

I looked around the room. Martin and James's bowl was very white. So was Gabe and Brian's, though they had some yellow peeking out. I looked down at our bowl; I had taken all the pom-poms. They didn't fit in the bowl, and so I held on to them, my arms widening; I was embracing all the pom-poms.

Ramon looked at the spread before us.

"Okay," they said. "Good! Now we're going to hand out your profile forms."

We were handed a two-page client profile form to select the races and ethnicities of our prospective child, as well as the amount of the birthmother's alcohol and drug use we could possibly tolerate, and the genetics of her family, ranging from physical and correctable issues such as cleft palates and clubbed feet, to mild to severe issues of mental health.

"Be as open on your form as you are both comfortable with," Nickie instructed, tightening the bright-colored scarf knotted at her neck. "Look at your pom-poms but also know that the more open you are, the quicker you will get a child."

Crystal and Tiffany nodded behind her, silent backup singers.

I glanced at the form. And then I watched the other couples looking at the form. For Herman and Alex, the form would be easy. Their pom-poms said: Caucasian. Everything white. Blindingly white. But for us, there were unimaginable combinations of races: East Indian, Asian, and Middle Eastern? Check. Native American, Hispanic, and Asian? I nodded at Ramon and he back at me.

Check!

But what did all these combinations mean? The pom-poms sat alone, a single color. What if the mother of an African-American

Palestinian child (miraculously) chose us? I thought of all the shades of colors that child might be.

Then came drug and alcohol use, and for this portion there were no props to help us decide. Nickie explained that checking no drugs or alcohol included drinking before the woman knew she was pregnant. We had friends who'd had a few glasses of wine before realizing they'd conceived. That had also, we did not acknowledge as we filled out this form, been me. Four years previously, before all the fertility treatments, I had gotten pregnant nearly magically, as we had been told that, due to my surgeries, my getting pregnant would be impossible. I remember being so confused when my period—the only internal process that works in me with Swiss-watch precision—was late. It had been a stressful time—I was finishing my PhD then, studying all day and well into the night for my defense, and—I can hardly bring myself to admit this now—drinking several glasses of wine nightly.

I try not to remember the joy—pleasure combined with that feeling, what does one call it, when one has narrowly escaped something terrible, has made a clean getaway? Is it cheating God? It is certainly more pleasurable than only pleasure in and of itself, I thought when I got that blood test back with the numbers I would come to covet, high beta numbers, strong, irrefutable digits. And then the doctor, with his arrogant face, some stranger, telling me seven weeks later how that pinprick on the ultrasound was no longer a viable prick of a pin. Nope, he'd said. Nothing happening in there.

One moment unscathed, and the next?

The very opposite, of course. Scarred, damaged, injured, traumatized.

I have tried not to think what life would be like now had my pregnancy not come and gone as quickly as gossip. I tried not to think of this also as the indication of how easy it likely would have been to have children of my own had this illness not undone me. Who, then, would I be now? I would be a woman with a child, perhaps two; one might not even notice me at all. But what I asked myself while choosing the box for the tolerable amount of drug and alcohol abuse was, would we have chosen myself as a birthmother?

I looked at Ramon, who shook his head.

"Let's start with the best-case scenario and work backward," he said.

Very quietly I asked, "So many of our friends drank before they knew they were pregnant. Would we not choose them?"

Ramon shook his head again.

"These women are young, Jesse," he said. "You think they're having a glass of Chardonnay with their salmon? If they're drinking, they're *drinking*."

"Ramon," I started. I couldn't think about the one chance I might have had to not be sitting here right now. That baby would have been three in August. My friend Michelle, Zoe's mother, and I had imagined it together; our due dates were ten days apart, and we thought we'd spend long leisurely days at their place on the Hudson, our legs shin-deep in the pool, sighing over all that we were missing, our babies cradled in our arms.

We thought we'd have a double baby shower. We made a list of the friends we shared from the neighborhood, those whom I saw every year at their annual summer party, and others we'd invite separately. And what we would serve. It would be August, and we would be so pregnant, so ickily pregnant and hot and uncomfortable, we'd said, so summer salads, maybe some chilled sesame noodles, shrimp satays.

Now I tried not to think of her face when I told her it would be just her. Alone. I gathered myself up. It is every part of you one assembles, limbs and organs and memories and hopes, every one of your bad choices. Time itself is an imaginary hourglass you carry, lashed to your neck. You straighten yourself against it.

I tried not to think of seeing her in the neighborhood as I walked Harriet, her belly growing rounder. Or at the baby shower, where I had spent most of the afternoon in the bathroom alone with my personal bottle of champagne—listening to the shrieks of Michelle's friends as they smeared microwaved chocolate bars into diapers and bobbed for nipples.

I knew then that soon Michelle would be one of the neighborhood mothers, so exhausted and overwhelmed and cheered by their children that, no longer working, they all got together, the way we had once done as respite from dating in our twenties, cutting out from our jobs early in the roaring start of our thirties, and now, now?, the mothers sat together along a farmhouse table in someone's tricked-out kitchen, sharing war stories of croup and incessant crying, night panics, time-outs or no time-outs, the protocol of the playground, ey wondered when they'd ever go back to being the women ey once were. Once we were such *girls,* remember?, the mothers all said as they picked at their kids' organic chicken nuggets and poured themselves pinots, their children coloring beneath their feet like good dogs, or sucking organic yogurt out of little plastic strips, or playing make-believe in their mother's dresses and lipsticks and high-heeled shoes, or napping, or watching *Bob the Builder* DVDs, or screaming their fucking heads off. Remember *bars*?, they'd say with a giggle as Michelle and I avoided each other. Why not unhitch myself now?, I had thought when I told her. Because I knew that in eight months Michelle would be pushing a child of her very own and the mothers would welcome her. Come!, they'd all say, opening up their front doors, hiding the gorgeous chaos behind them. Welcome!, they'd say. And I'd be drinking alone.

And yet, when Zoe was born, I went to the hospital. And I held her and heard about Michelle's C-section and the horror of what led up to it, and I passed Zoe back to her and watched her bring her to her chest.

I did not know that I could opt out of that visit, or that I needed to. I did not know how to protect myself. I still do not know what will, as Zoe's birth had, undo me.

"Let's just start with the best-case scenario," Ramon said again.

Was there a wrong answer? Martin and James were already done with their forms. They were the ones who turned in their marked-up SATs long before the monitor called for hands up, the ones who set down their pencils and left the testing center, the ones who made us all wonder, as we watched them, longingly, slip out of the auditorium, if they were geniuses, or if they were the mythical students, boys mostly, who would merely write their names as instructed on the top and then shoot the moon.

Leaving the drug-and-alcohol section blank—which meant that if anyone claimed to have taken any substance at all, our would not be sent to them—I continued down the form.

Comfortable with twins?

Ramon shook his head.

It was likely our only chance for siblings. I checked yes.

Comfortable with rape?

I shielded the form from Ramon with my left hand.

Check.

Everything, I remind myself, and everyone, has a story. I am a student—and a teacher—of history. As facts, history does nothing; it merely lies there on a timeline like any number. But a girl's diary, a found scrap of speech, a president's letter, the map of a changed city? These are the ways in which we understand what has come to pass.

How could I choose a child without knowing the child's story? And to know the child's story, one needed to know the story of the mother.

And what, really, I wanted to ask Ramon, was the best-case scenario here?

All I had were questions. What I did instead of ask them, though, was surreptitiously go to Crystal or Tiffany and request the form back. Then, hastily, before anyone could see, I checked all of it—alcohol, methamphetamine, marijuana, heroin—in the first trimester. I would, I reasoned, deal with it later. If someone called us and she explained it to me, and she told me about who she was before she knew she was growing a baby, the baby that could make us a family, if she explained all that to me, it would make more sense.

Because everyone has a story. Even me.

6

—

We were relieved to leave the agency that evening. I'd thought we might ask Gabe to join us for dinner, or maybe Anita and Paula, but as we shut our happy white folders and gathered our collection of papers and books into the cloth tote embossed with the same sunny insignia found on the folders, I knew that Ramon would not want to be with other people that night. This is one of the many ways we're different, Ramon and I. When in front of people, I am cloudless and blithe; I work hard to impress others, to make them feel at ease, and to uphold the notion that I am interesting and charming. Ramon, who is always himself, feels distant and lost when I don't look up from my performance to note him there.

I resisted my impulse to ask others to join and instead, as we were leaving, I asked for a good local place to eat.

"Fancy?" Anita asked. We'd walked over to their Subaru, the back filled with dog beds and bug sprays and a tangle of bright leashes.

I shook my head.

"No, the opposite of fancy. Maybe barbecue?" Ramon asked.

"Oooh." Paula nodded. "We know just the place. Do you guys have GPS?"

I shot Ramon a look. "No," I said. "We do not."

"A, where's that map?" Paula asked.

Anita was already fishing in the backseat. "I know it's here some-where," she said, her voice muffled.

"What kind of dogs do you guys have?" I asked Paula as we watched Anita leaning into the backseat.

"Italian spinones," she said. "Anita breeds them."

Ramon and I looked at each other. "Really?" I asked. Where did I get the idea that lesbians were always bringing in strays and help-ing needy children? I was starting to deconstruct every stereotype I held.

"Yeah." Anita came up for air. "I do a lot of behavior stuff at my practice. And I breed them. I also show some of them, and do agility."

"Wow," I said. "That's amazing." I thought of Harriet's mother, a submissive freckled spaniel who had to be kept separate from her babies while I chose my puppy. I knew who Harriet's mother was. I had a family tree for my dog that went back several generations, all the way to the winner of Best in Breed at Westminster.

Paula took out her wallet and showed me a photo of six dogs, all seated in a straight row on their haunches, their coarse hair wild, heads cocked in different directions, all camera-ready. A family portrait.

Just look at them, I thought. I am in love with dogs. Perhaps dogs are enough.

"That's the mother." Anita pointed to the middle. "Charlotte."

"The birthmother," I said. It just came out.

Everyone stood silent for a moment.

Then Paula shrugged her stocky shoulders. "I guess *so*," she said. "But we're kind of the mothers too. We also have cats. And a few birds."

"We might actually need to be cut off. Here." Anita handed Ramon a wrinkled and stained map of Raleigh and Chapel Hill.

Ramon took the germ-infested map without hesitation, smoothing it out as Anita and Paula leaned over him, tracing a path from where we stood to the best goddamn barbecue we New Yorkers had ever tasted.

"Wait, here?" Ramon asked.

Anita snatched the map. "You know what? Just thinking about it makes me hungry. We'll show you where it is! We're coming too. I mean, it's not like we have kids to go home to, right?"

"Oh, great." Ramon shifted his feet.

"But we have animals, Anita," Paula said. "What about the dogs?"

"We can call Joanie," she said to Paula.

Paula shrugged. "Neighbor," she told us.

"Do you want company?" Anita asked Ramon.

Ramon smiled, genuinely, which pleased me. I could tell he liked them, and when he liked people I took a shine to, it pleased me. "Absolutely," he said. "I don't know why we didn't think of it sooner."

The walls at the Spot were fleshy light brown and pink, beamed with old wood, which gave the effect of being inside the chest of a pig. The restaurant was loud with thrilled voices ordering food and talking about what they'd ordered, and children crying and old people cooing, and it felt good to be part of the bustle of a loved place.

"I'm ravenous." I looked at the menu. "I might just eat one of you," I said.

"He was on the Food Network," Paula told us proudly. Already someone had placed a bowl of corn bread in the center of the table and she nibbled on a piece, leaving a trail of yellow crumbs at the sides of her mouth and down her blue oxford-cloth shirt. She pointed to an enormous man with a sparse salt-and-pepper beard walking around the room, stopping at tables. "He's the pit master. He does this whole-hog thing they featured on that show where that chef tried to beat them at their specialty thing."

"Oh." I couldn't help but be disappointed that we'd been taken to a place everyone already knew about.

"Neat." Ramon broke off a piece of corn bread and popped it into his mouth.

"What's good?" I asked.

"You have to get it Carolina-style," she said. "The meat. Carolina is dry. Not Texas-style, we don't do that here. That's all wet and, well, Texas-like."

Ramon and I nodded, looking at the menu. Whatever we chose, it came with two sides.

The waiter came over and took our drink orders. Without consulting one another, we all ordered whiskey. All but Anita, who wanted lemonade. Women who don't drink get my attention, as I always think they're pregnant. Was Anita not drinking due to alcoholism or religion? I wondered now.

"Look at all the sides," Ramon said to me, eyes bright.

I looked up from the menu, with its drawing of a pig sectioned into parts. I tried not to think about a documentary we'd seen recently on food production. The sound of squawking chickens and pigs sometimes flung together by their curling, breaking tails was still an echo I could not shake. I looked to the section of the menu that said "Everything but the Squeal" and wondered if those pigs were thrown together so tightly they couldn't breathe, if they were given factory-produced slop, which often consisted of parts of pigs that humans wouldn't touch. I thought of those pigs being forced to eat each other, and then I thought of the other alternative: pigs roaming free on grassy land, not unlike the rolling hills dotted with horses we'd seen just yesterday, driving in. Only yesterday.

There was an excessive amount of choosing to be done. Did I want the meat—and who came to a place like this and did not eat meat?—chopped or pulled? Did I want macaroni and cheese or collard greens or black-eyed peas or fried okra or slaw? Well, I wanted everything, of course.

"It's a shitload of food," Paula said as she watched Ramon and me scan the menu.

The multiplicity of choice overwhelmed me, and it became impossible not to think of all the decisions we had made that day.

The waiter came back with our drinks. As always, I had many questions. "Is the corn fresh?" I asked.

I saw Paula look over at Anita, as if to say, *We shoulda known; here we go.*

"Honey, this is North Carolina," he said. "Of course it's fresh, and yes, it's from a farm not twenty miles from here. That's where we get our greens too, and the cheese for the mac 'n' cheese comes from a dairy close in the next town."

I didn't care that he rolled his eyes at Anita and Paula.

"I'm going to have the whole rack," Ramon said.

The waiter tilted his head. "You're not a large guy," he said. "That's a lot of meat."

He nodded. "I know. I'm ready!"

"Baby-back or Carolina-style?"

Ramon looked at Anita and Paula, who both nodded their heads, urging him. "Carolina," he said, with feeling.

"I'm getting the chopped pork," I said. "I think. Should I get the chopped or pulled?"

"Chopped," said Anita. "It's a thing here."

"You all sure you don't want to split?" the waiter asked.

"Let 'em eat," Anita said. "We're hungry as hell."

After the waiter took down the rest of our order and after Anita called him back to order the fried green tomatoes, yet another regional dish we had to try, we sat for a moment, sipping our whiskey.

"Can I ask you guys something?" I said.

They nodded.

"What did you check for drug use?"

They paused and then looked at each other.

Anita traced her finger along the table. "We're gay," she said.

I looked at her blankly, and Ramon lifted his drink to his lips again.

"We know that," I said. Did they think we didn't know that? Should we have told them about all our gay friends in New York?

"No, what I mean is, we live in a rural part of the state."

"It's not rural," Paula told her. "It's twenty minutes from here."

"Fine. We're in Holly Springs. It's a small town. And it's not like a small town in Connecticut. So those guys, I know what they were thinking: just a white kid, otherwise it will draw even more attention to us being gay parents, which is not easy here."

"Is it easy anywhere?" I wanted the fried green tomatoes to come.

"True." Paula rested her hand at the crook of Anita's elbow.

The tomatoes arrived, thick slices in a light batter, on a white oval plate, garnished with long strands of tender basil, a ramekin of vinaigrette nestled to the side.

"Yum." I was the first to stab one with a fork.

"But we are gay women. You know what that means?" Anita carved her tomato.

"I do and then I guess I don't," I said, shoving a quarter of the tomato in my mouth, where it burst with juice and the zing of lime.

"It means that the birthmother? She is dealing with the prospect of two mothers. Did you know gay men are the first to get matched? Because with two men as parents, she will always get to be the mother. Everyone wants to be the mother. Even when the child is being raised elsewhere."

Paula, who hadn't yet touched her portion, nodded at Anita as she spoke.

My eyes widened. Chewing, I felt my throat stitch closed. I couldn't look at Ramon.

"This is delicious." Ramon chewed exaggeratedly.

"This is a roundabout way of saying we're kind of open to everything. We realize we have to be, unless we want to wait until we're, like, eighty for a kid. We have to be open, and so we are open, which means drug use, yes, and race, and all of it. Just whatever comes our way," Anita said.

"We're ready," Paula affirmed.

I swallowed the last of the tomato and batter that had come apart in my mouth, and cleared my throat.

"We've discussed this a lot," Anita said. "Those men in there? We don't think they're wrong to want a white child."

Paula nodded.

"They're realistic. And if they want a white child, having them check a child of color would be wrong for them and wrong for the child."

"That makes a lot of sense," Ramon said. "I don't hold it against them either." He put his fork down. "Look, we're all just doing what we can."

Well I do, I thought. The white gay guys and their guns and their white choices were wrong. I was wrong, too. I remembered Nickie speaking about special-needs children. Think about the prospect of raising a child who has autism or cystic fibrosis, she said. But I didn't want to choose a child who had either of those things, I'd thought when Nickie introduced the idea.

And then the waiter arrived. With a tray of food so enormous, he had a helper with him to lower it. Massive amounts of greens hung off the sides of the plate like wilted streamers. The steaming creamed corn nearly lapped over the edges of the dish, and some of the fried okra tumbled out of the red plastic basket lined with a paper towel before it even hit the table.

Then came the meat.

Shaking his head and smiling—glibly?—the waiter placed about fourteen ribs, food from prehistoric times, in front of Ramon, who gazed down at it, stunned. My chopped pork was piled so high I could have sledded down it. I couldn't help myself; I thought of the pigs in that documentary thrown atop each other into live shrieking piles, cows branded, stomachs seared, and herded in the most inhumane of ways. And then I realized. I had gotten caught up in being around people, in being outside myself again, and of all the things I'd asked, I had neglected the one single most important question.

I'd forgotten to ask about the meat.

I grabbed the waiter by the arm. "The meat!" I said. I could feel the tears hot along my cheeks and I tried to turn away from Paula and Anita, who looked up from dividing up their meals like civilized people. "Where is it from?" I asked our waiter.

He cocked his head. "I don't know what you mean," he said.

"Please," I said to Ramon and to the waiter, pushing my chair out from the table. I couldn't look at the piles of food, the slop of it. I thought of waste and those children in Ethiopia, their bellies distended with hunger, flies buzzing around their heads in the USA for Africa infomercials, "We Are the World" playing in the background, flashes of the video, Billy Joel and Bruce Springsteen baby-faced, Cyndi Lauper, dewy and pudgy—even Dylan was young then.

How had I ever had the right to want?

"Can you just tell me where you got this meat?" I asked again.

"Honey, where do you think I got the meat?" The waiter crossed his arms. "From the kitchen," he said, laughing.

In the bathroom, surrounded by cartoon renderings of pigs and cows, I gathered myself up like so much loose change, coins I had collected on countless other nights, evenings when someone announced their unexpected—and unwanted—pregnancy, or when an acquaintance showed up at a party nine months pregnant, or when my cousin's child answered the doorbell all grown up, offering, in a fake English accent, to take my coat and hat. I gathered myself up, and after I'd splashed cold water on my face and reapplied lipstick, painting on a smile, I went back to the table, ready to hack at my mountain of chopped pork.

"Welcome back," Anita said, patting my leg as I sat down.

Paula bowed her head, slowly and succinctly.

And I was grateful then that we had all dined together. Anita, I had learned that night, spent an inordinate amount of time on the insides of dogs, exhuming objects from their intestines, patching up torn hearts, while Paula mixed up TPN—milky nutrition dripping through an IV for the sick and the elderly. I did not mention that I knew what that was, how I'd lived on it for weeks at a time, but I felt understood more deeply by them than I had been understood in a while.

The rest of dinner was a daze of food, and then the dessert, a banana pudding Anita insisted we at least *taste*. It came topped with marshmallow and meringue, four Nilla Wafers standing in the sugary soup of it. Everyone else tasted, and I ate most of it, and then we slapped two credit cards down to split the cost, which wasn't really fair to Anita and Paula as Anita hadn't had a drink and they only ordered half of what Ramon and I had ordered, and this, along with the amount of food I'd personally consumed, is one of the many things I would feel guilty about as I lay awake at three in the morning.

But I didn't know that yet when they dropped us back at the hotel, where, in our unremarkable room, my husband and I undressed without speaking in the near-dark, two moving shadows in a foreign space. I could feel my stomach distended from the excessive dinner, a stomach not unlike a starving child's.

We got into bed, between the cold white sheets, and we lay there in the dark. I could hear us breathing but I could not reach out to touch Ramon's hand, not even to tell him, tomorrow will be better, or to make a joke about the Killers. Or to tell him I loved him. And I did love him that night.

For hours I lay that way, unmoving, until the strange fingers of an orange-streaked dawn made their way into the room, illuminating the synthetic hotel curtains and then the polyester blanket—the first thing we had done upon arrival was remove the comforter from the bed due to its germs, its semen, its chemicals and killants!—in fuzzy gray light. Finally, in the blurry sunrise, I turned on my side and watched my husband asleep, acutely aware then that I did not know what brings two people together, what divides them, what can possibly let them reconnect. How elastic is a marriage?

Likewise, we could not get back that time wasted on failing. We could not turn around those awful moments of not succeeding in having a child, and I did not know that night and early morning if Ramon's and my relationship had already given out from it, the resilience of our connection worn thin without snapping. I did not know if it would soon split, or if we would manage through this, remain somehow supple, but I rose anyway, and in the glare of the fluorescent bathroom light, I turned on the shower to the highest heat, watched the steam fill the tub, already fogging the mirrors as I stepped in to get ready for the morning.

7

—

The pièce de résistance of that weekend in North Carolina was not the pom-poms or the filling out of the profile form, or even the meat-filled dinner; it was not the sleepless nights in a lonely, sad hotel. It was the film.

Good God, the film.

It began Sunday morning's training session. Nickie wasn't there, so Crystal and Tiffany, now seated at the head of the pushed-together tables, timidly waited for all of us to file in.

When we were all accounted for—public relations Gabe and journalist Brian filing in last and without apology—Crystal or Tiffany stood up.

"We have a movie this morning!" she announced.

The other one, Tiffany or Crystal, also stood. "We usually try and have birth parents come in to talk to you guys. And also some of our clients and the kids they've adopted. But today, we're going to show a movie instead."

I looked at Ramon, my face asking, Why? Another wave of panic: this place is not real. They have no real birthmothers. They have no real people who have adopted real children. This isn't even a real table. We are in a diorama, I thought, like the one depicting Native Americans swaddled in smallpox-infested blankets Lucy and I had seen at the Smithsonian.

Tiffany or Crystal continued. "It's a little out-of-date and it was really for when we started doing open adoption in the late eighties and early nineties. Just warning you! There's some serious hair here."

Crystal and Tiffany giggled, their fine blond hair shining in the light, the pink of their vulnerable skulls peeking through.

James, the volunteer fireman, stood up and flicked out the lights.

Of course the fireman volunteers, I thought as the television went on, a square of blue and then a crude version of the sun shining over the agency logo, flickering across the screen.

I half expected a sex-education tape to come on the display, the film of a dachshund giving birth to puppies, little beings slicked in blood and embryonic fluid, that I'd seen in fifth grade. The boys and girls had watched separately, equally entranced and repulsed by what was happening on-screen. And yet the girls all thought, Will this one day be me? I don't see how that's possible, we all thought, that this is our lot in life, this *grossness*.

Bleary from the previous night's whiskey and lack of sleep, I was grateful to be passive and watch a movie, to not have to think or consider our future. I was tired of deciding.

The movie, a term I use here only loosely, began with a young woman, perhaps eighteen, who had placed her child for adoption and couldn't have been happier about it. She spoke to the shaking camera in the backyard of a large stone house, a child, perhaps three, playing with a woman on an elaborate swing set behind her. "Come to mama," the woman, in her late forties perhaps, cooed to the little girl as the young woman told the camera about knowing she could not parent and yet when she'd had her child, she had become a part of this new family. Through openness, she said. It had been amazing.

The birthmother, who, one could tell when the camera panned out a bit, held a balloon as she spoke—was it a gift for her or the child?—discussed how she saw the family and her daughter often, sometimes five times a year, and always—no matter what!—on Mother's Day.

I admit my heart fell a little. Am I allowed to ask where I fit in here? There is a woman who gives birth and that is not I. And then she is in our lives—Ramon's and mine, *ours,* whatever that life will look like—however she chooses to be. I accept that, but I had to turn away from the screen; when do I get to be the mother?

Perhaps never. This, I realized now, is also an option, even if it is not a box I have checked. Breathless, the adoptive mother— that's what she kept calling herself, that's what everyone but the child referred to her as, and the rumble of a riot began again in my chest—discussed how open adoption had given them a whole new layer to the notion of family. As she said this, the birthmother presented the child with the balloon. The child promptly let the balloon go and at first everyone sucked in their breath, and then, as if becoming aware that this was being filmed, they caught themselves. Let's all wish on it, the adoptive mother suggested. On command, everyone closed their eyes *tighttighttight,* and the balloon floated gently up into the sky.

Then a new couple abruptly flashed on the screen. They looked high school age, and attractive.

"How did you decide to place your child?" an off-screen interviewer asked.

They spoke about being very much in love and also devoutly Christian but not wanting children so early in life. I was cheered by this couple, who sat close to each other and answered the interviewer's questions. One day, she said, taking the boy's hand in hers, we will have a family of our own.

I hoped they would, and I thought about loss and what it can do to love. And how the hardship was really more hers, bodily anyway. Or perhaps that was wrong. Perhaps the birthfather wandered through his days unsure what was the matter, but knowing, profoundly, that something important, ineffable, had escaped him.

"How did you decide on the adoptive parents?" the voice asked.

The couple looked at each other and laughed. "It sounds so silly," he said, "but I'm a musician. I mean, I want to be. And Tony, the adoptive father, also plays music. We both like, umm, Crash Test Dummies, Barenaked Ladies, alternative stuff, and he had that on his profile. It made me feel connected to him. Now we hang out and jam together. It's kind of awesome, and I feel like we chose for our baby what we might have been."

The young woman nodded her head. "Or what we might become," she said. "Now that we have the chance."

"It's true it's the littlest thing that makes you decide," she said. "We chose to live close and be involved, we have Christmas together, and Mother's Day of course, and it is really nice to be able to see our daughter growing up. But before that we weren't sure about near or far, we just knew not in New York City. That was our number one criteria. Not in New York City, people get shot there."

I snapped to attention and looked around the room to see how the others had reacted to this. Martin and James were nodding their heads in agreement. And so were Herman and Alex, and I even saw Paula and Anita smiling a bit, though perhaps this was just to show goodwill toward the couple. Or, I thought in a more sinister manner, they were smiling about the competitive nature of this venture; if no one wanted to place babies in New York, then we were out of the running. Get rid of the straight Brooklyn couple! Which only meant more opportunity for the gun-bearing fireman and his nurse partner.

The only person I didn't look at was Ramon.

After the film, James the fireman flicked the lights on.

Tiffany or Crystal rubbed her hands together. "Let me just say, the New York comment was from a long time ago." She looked at Ramon and me. "I meant to warn y'all about that."

Paula cleared her throat. "So what happened to that couple anyway?"

"What do you mean?" Crystal or Tiffany asked, cocking her head.

"Well," Anita said, and I noticed how often she completed Paula's sentences in a way that made Paula shrink back in her chair, "the musician couple, in college. Are they still together? That was what, fifteen years ago. Do they have kids now?"

Tiffany and Crystal nodded. One of them said, "Well, they broke up when they were in college, not long after this was filmed, actually. And we lost track of them, to be honest. They don't see the adoptive family anymore."

"What?" Brian the journalist said. "I thought this was a film to promote openness."

"It does, and we as an agency do, but, to be honest, many of the birthmothers lose contact. If they move, or have other children, more often than not—statistically speaking, I mean—they fall out of touch."

You catch more bees with honey than with vinegar, but who the hell wants a collection of bees? And so I asked, "If openness is best for the birthmother, and dealing with *her* grief is a large part of this, which I totally understand, but if it's also about the child knowing who her family is so she doesn't have to fantasize about her parents, and doesn't feel abandoned, well, what happens, say, when the child is four, and the birthmother just disappears? What about the child's grief? To feel left twice? How is this healthy for anyone?"

The room was silent but for some head-bobbing in assent, and I could feel myself galvanizing my troops, a trait I inherited from my mother.

Crystal or Tiffany paused a moment before speaking. "The child will know the reality. Open adoption is not a science, but from the research we all know open adoption is best for all parties. It is."

I looked around the table and all of us were nodding, myself included. But how did we know? We didn't, after all, have children.

"But there is no guarantee that it works for everyone or that it is stable at all times," she continued. "This is about people."

I thought of myself as a teenager, those nights I screamed at my mother, who would not let me go to a concert or to a friend's to study. What would that have been like had I known I had another mother, just in the next town or state. I could, in these fraught moments, tell my mother I liked this other mother better, or worse, that I was leaving to find her. What would I do if my daughter left for her biological mother?

The lawyer, with her purple hair, her lost furniture, her fears, made every ounce of sense now. Someone else out there will always be the mother. This is true for the lawyer's children as well—it is the biology of adoption—but that mother will be unfindable.

Better, I thought then, to colonize a country, take the Chinese children, the Koreans, the Ethiopian babies that, yes, I knew would be black than to live through the thought of the mother's arriving, or worse, perhaps, the anticipation of her sure departure. I had no idea what the effect of her going, leaving that teenager only to disappear, would be.

"There's no guarantee of anything with children of your own either, genetic children, I mean," Tiffany or Crystal said.

"That's a good point. Nothing in life is guaranteed. It just isn't." Gabe shared this with the rest of us.

"Exactly," Crystal or Tiffany said.

Family, just the word. Even *second generation.*

There it was: my grandfather holding my hand in the dark movie theater as we watched the red balloon in the film, hovering over the streets of Paris, waiting for its chosen little boy. I imagined it now, my grandfather long gone, the balloon that birthmother held, lingering at my window, and then following me down the streets of my Brooklyn neighborhood, past our butcher and our cheese shop, the yoga studios that weren't there when I moved in, past the restaurants with their local and sustainable food, past the park with the fountain kids run through all summer long. It waits for me at Harriet's favorite grassy hill, where it will meet all the other pink metallic unicorn balloons in Brooklyn, and it will soar up into the sky, far above my brownstone-lined borough, above our city; all the balloons, together, will carry me high into the air, and very far away.

8

—

My mother stood waiting at the door with Harriet like June fucking Cleaver when we reached my parents' house late Sunday night.

"How'd it go?" Her arms were open.

"Fine." I put down my bags and caught Harriet's paws in my arms, leaned in for her smooches.

"So," she said, eyes wide. "Where's our new grandchild?"

I stood up from Harriet and looked at my mother. "You can't be serious." I placed her front legs back on the floor.

That was when my father came out of the living room.

"Hi, guys." He kissed us both.

"It's going to be a wait, Joanne," Ramon said. He turned to my father. "It could be a long wait for a baby," he said.

My father shifted his feet. "Sure. Of course it will be a wait. Of course."

"I mean, Jesus, Mom."

"Honey, I was joking." My mother went into the living room for the spread of cheeses and a tapenade I now saw on the coffee table. "I just hope it comes before I'm too old to get on the ground and play with it."

I let out a sound that resembled the initial escape of steam in a humidifier, the warm steam of illness.

"Sweetie, Mom's been really hoping this weekend went well. Just so you know. We can't wait to hear about it. I made venison!" My father clapped his hands together.

"And I made risotto," my mother interjected. "Right?"

"Your mother made her famous tri-mushroom risotto. The mushrooms are from the farmer's market."

My mother's famous risotto? Famous to whom? I knew I'd certainly never tasted it or heard tell of it. I also knew my mother was not aware of any other mushroom variety than the porcinis she got at the Safeway (did she even know they were porcinis?) until she started reading Alice Waters and talking about the importance of eating together, as a family, though of course by then neither my sister nor I lived at home.

Ramon said, "Well, that sounds positively delicious!"

Ramon was always so sweet to my parents, but the truth is, he has a delicate, catered-to-by-an-old-world-mother constitution, which makes him sensitive to just about everything physical, and we'd eaten so much meat the night before I knew it sounded as revolting to him as it did to me.

I, however, had the energy for only one battle. "Well, we're exhausted and I don't really want to talk about it, okay?" I cleared my throat. "Dinner sounds awesome!"

"Cheese?" My mother swatted Harriet's nose; she was already grazing around the table.

"But hopefully it will be soon." Ramon walked over to the coffee table and cut a slice of Manchego, clearly chosen in his honor. "I, for one, certainly hope this is all over very soon."

Why couldn't he have just said "we"? I clenched my teeth. I am angry at everyone, I thought. How will I stop being angry at everyone? Ramon had opened the door to discussion.

"I understand." My mother watched him eat her proffered cheese. "We are really excited to hear all about your weekend. You know you haven't talked to us much about this at all."

I closed my eyes. How would I explain? About one of those blond social workers—Crystal or Tiffany, with their Johnson's No More Tangles–like smell, asking us, their faint eyebrows raised: Will the adoptive child feel welcome in your home, embraced by all members of the family? Will the adoptive child feel welcomed by the prospective adoptive grandparents?

"We're not against talking to you about it, Mom."

"Thanks so much for taking Harriet." Ramon looked at both of my parents.

"We love having her!" My dad cut himself a big slice of cheese.

"Anyway." I grabbed my bag to go upstairs. "Just so you know, we're dancing as fast as we can."

Up up up to the attic. The goddamned attic. It is a place, but let's be real, the attic is also a metaphor. And so is the woman who lives there. I was moved to the attic when Lucy was born and she, in all her adorable, teensy babyness, took over the room next to my parents' bedroom.

I heard the padding of Ramon making his way up the carpeted stairs behind me.

"Can you believe that?" I hissed, turning toward him.

"Come on, Jesse." Ramon reached the top step. "Your mom's just trying to help."

I rolled my eyes. "Oh, please."

"You have to relax." Ramon put his hands on my shoulders.

I shook them loose. "Seriously? If you tell me to calm down, I might lose my mind."

"I said *relax*."

The last time I'd seen Michelle, Zoe had been playing with some hideous bald doll at the table, and, reaching to pat my arm, she'd told me, as her kid banged the shit out of the doll, It will happen for you guys. Everyone I know who has really wanted a child has gotten one, she'd said. I'd laughed inwardly then, but now, here in the attic, I thought perhaps the problem was that I had not wanted this enough. Perhaps I had, like so many mothers, had my doubts. My wasted wishes, ones I'd made in this room, for boys to love me, for my sister to disappear, for my nightmares to recede and my dreams to come true—perhaps these were responsible for what I now lacked.

"I am as relaxed as I'm going to get," I told Ramon as I lay back on my old twin bed.

"You know, we don't have that many black friends," Ramon said. "A few, but not that many."

I breathed deeply. "What's your point?"

"You took the black pom-pom. You just took them all without thinking."

"Oh, I thought," I said.

"Did you though?" Ramon asked.

"You guys ready for dinner?" my mother called from below.

Up came Harriet, her little brown nose peering over the top stair.

"Harriet!" I threw myself on top of her, willing her to lie down. She licked my face. I lifted up the leather of her ear and whispered to her, and she kept trying to pull away to lick my face, language too much for her to bear.

"I might have liked to choose too," Ramon said.

"We're good!" I screamed downstairs. "Be there in a minute!"

9

—

At the dinner table Ramon talked to my parents with an easy manner he rarely possessed in social situations. For him there was a divide between family and non-family, and tonight he seemed natural in his skin as he chatted casually with my parents about the weekend.

"And then"—he gestured with his fork—"we had to choose colored pom-poms. And deal with a lot of forms. Wait, let me back up. We have to get this eight hundred number. Randy," Ramon said to my dad, "can we do it from your business line, which would then be forwarded to our cell? But anyway, that's a whole other thing, basically, the mothers—"

"The birthmothers." I could sense it gathering itself up in the pit of my stomach, the past, dinner, a tight fist, a ball of hair and bones; I could feel all of it amassing.

"Sorry," Ramon said, "of course, the birthmothers, the birthmothers, well, they call us directly on this eight hundred number and we talk to them. Well, Jesse does. We've decided it will be Jesse."

I smiled broadly and sarcastically. "Yaay." I lifted my shoulders to my ears and kept them there for an extra beat.

Ramon looked at me very deliberately, and I could feel my parents' excitement in receiving so much information. "We did this role playing."

I began shoveling food into my mouth. I had to hand it to my mother; her famous tri-mushroom risotto was tri-fabulous.

"So we had these made-up cards of who the birthmother was— her identity, like where she was from, what her situation was, if she had other kids, which is a good thing as she knows how difficult it is to parent then . . ."

My mother nodded her head knowingly, and I wondered if she was also thinking about the help she got with parenting from Claudine.

"Anyway," Ramon continued, "we had to practice what we would ask the birthmother on the phone."

"If they call." I watched Harriet come out from beneath the table and head straight for my father, always the softie when it came to table scraps. "If."

"They're going to call." Ramon turned first to my father at one end of the table, and then to my mother. "We have a very good chance of being called," he said.

"Wonderful!" My mother beamed. "That just sounds wonderful."

"Wonderful," my father agreed.

"Can we talk about something else please?" I asked. "I am really tired. Of this. I'm very tired of talking about this."

"But, Jesse," Ramon said, "we need to discuss the race of the child with your parents."

My mother perked up. "Oh yes, let's talk about that! I would love to talk about it. What are you guys thinking?"

"Absolutely," my father said. "We are here to talk to."

"No, I'm tired," I said. "And come on, Ramon," I said.

"We need to discuss this," Ramon said. Was he smiling?

The three of them looked at me and I thought of Ramon in the car on the way back from the training, after we'd hugged everyone good-bye and gotten into our car and driven away. As we'd entered Virginia it had begun to grow dark on the highway, and in the gloaming Ramon had turned to me, as excited as he was tonight with my parents, and he'd brought up the issue of languages again. Of legacy.

"The child needs to be Jewish, too," I'd told him. I had looked out at the highway growing so quickly dark.

"No, fuck you, Ramon," I said now.

My parents gently set their napkins down at the same time.

"Stop it," my mother said. "Jesse, please."

"Okay then. What would you like to know? We are open to many many races. We're not totally in agreement, as Ramon seems to think a child born in a meth lab—a white child—might be more appropriate for us than an African-American child because he doesn't think we have black friends. Ramon is very happy with a Hispanic child, though, as that speaks to his origins. My origins, ours . . ." I swept my hands to encompass the dining room with its muted yellow walls and white molding, the African art and the tea set that had been my great-grandmother's, the one my father was always hoping someone would break in and steal so we could collect the insurance. "Our origins do not seem to be relevant. But, as you've asked, we're sorting out the race thing. We're deciding on drug use and mental health and physical deformities and if I have to make one more decision I'm going to pitch myself out of a window."

"We understand," my father said.

"Seriously, Jesse?" Ramon asked.

"Seriously." I turned to my parents. "So, Mom, Dad, how comfortable are you with a child of color in our family?"

"Stop it." Ramon folded his hands in his lap. "This is not the way we want to have this discussion."

Color. What is it? I thought of Ramon adjusting the brightness on one of his designs. Turn it up, tone it down. Color. "Me? You had no right to just bring this up. When does this get to be private again?"

"Okay," he said. "I get it."

"It's okay." My mother picked up her napkin and dabbed at her mouth. "It's okay, Ramon."

"It seems I can't control a thing, can I? Because normally, making a baby is between two people, so I don't really care what my parents feel about a child of color."

"Look." My father cleared his throat. "You guys have been through quite a lot and I just want to say that of course we are comfortable with any child in this house and we will be thrilled to be grandparents to any child you have."

"Absolutely," my mother said. "And remember how much time I've spent in Africa."

"Fabulous," I said.

"You can discuss this with strangers and not your family?" Ramon asked me.

"Yes. Exactly." I realized he was getting me back for all the talking I'd done this weekend. Ramon, it turned out, had felt left out.

"It's a postracial world. Obama has changed everything," my father said, passing some meat to Harriet. Right in front of my face.

"That's not true," I said.

"Oh yes, it certainly is." My father straightened in his chair. "Do you know what it was like before? In the fifties? Yes it is. So I do happen to agree with you that a mixed-race child—in this day and age—is hardly a risky proposition."

"I can't do this."

"Jesse. We want to know what's going on. You're our *daughter*," my mother said.

And yes, even that hurt me. *Daughter.* I wanted to obliterate the very word. In every language.

"We do," my father said. "And frankly, this is our grandchild, our only grandchild, you're talking about. If you don't want us involved, why don't you just keep him or her in New York then?"

"Don't threaten me," I told him, standing, and only after I did so did I feel myself stand. "Don't threaten me, do you understand me? Because I am done. Because everyone has a limit. I have reached my limit."

I ran upstairs to the attic and I sat on my twin bed, my chest expanding and contracting. I heard my father begin to yell at Ramon.

"You go and talk to her, goddamn it, Ramon, you need to fix this *now*," he was saying, and I could hear my mother trying to use her mobilization and managerial skills: *what Randy is saying, Ramon,* and *Ramon might be feeling a little pressured right now,* and *Jesse has been through so much with her illness, too.* I imagined her brushing her silver hair from her face as she enunciated clearly.

I heard Ramon come up the stairs and then he was there, and begging me to go back down. "Please," he said. "Your father is freaking out on me. You have to go downstairs and talk to him," he said, and I did, wordlessly, brushing by him, touching him gently enough to hurt him, and I gathered myself up, the way I knew even then that I would continue to on nights to come, nights when the phone sat silent and the birthmothers didn't call, or the nights they did call and we talked for hours but then they did not choose us, on nights when, if we ever got that child, that child had grown up to hate us, as much as I had told my parents I hated them, as much as I had run from them, as much as I had thwarted them for only being themselves, but I did not know that as I made my way down the steps to talk to my father that night, I did not know that my parents were only human; I had not reached that level of humanness that would allow me to forgive them. For that, I knew, as I opened the door to the den to see my father weeping, for that, and because of that, I knew, I would have to have children of my own.

10

My parents' introduction is an American story. They were set up on a blind date by friends of their parents, who lived in the Watergate building. That American story. On their first date they had dinner in Georgetown—roast beef and potatoes, my father thinks, though perhaps it was chicken cordon bleu. My mother has no recollection of the meal at all.

Ramon's parents' meeting was otherworldly. His father, Ramon Sr., was studying to be a geologist. He was researching the Pontine region, and I believe, though this is merely my historical take as Ramon is vague on the story, it was to assist in the work that Mussolini had begun maintaining the road over the marshland. Did the Italians hire him? Had he come from Spain? Ramon says only "researching the region," but what I can still see so vividly, as if I had been in the brush at Lake Fogliano myself, is Ramon Sr. coming across Paola walking along the lake. Paola, who worked at her father's café, serving espresso and pizza and fried artichokes to the locals, is entirely alone, away from her two brothers, and she stands at the lip of the lake, one toe pointed, dipping in.

Ramon Sr. was filthy from working and he had come to the lake to cool off. The sun was so hot, he wasn't sure if she was a real woman or a mermaid, and, according to Ramon, his father had fallen in love with Paola by the time she'd turned to face him.

Ramon's father later went to work for BP, as a geologist, and he took Paola away from Italy and her brothers and her parents' graves and her life at the café that had exhausted her. The café had closed when she left—I have seen it on the outskirts of the village—and so Paola got on a plane for the first time, and went first to Spain, where Ramon was born, and then to West Africa and England and then South America and then Holland, and later, when Ramon left her for college in the States, they went off to Java, where Ramon brought an American photographer to the jungle and opened an umbrella in a hot cave to protect his face from a throng of bats.

I thought of Paola as we continued back to Brooklyn, imagining how different this conversation would have been at my mother-in-law's house. *Black child? Spanish or Italian would be better, but why not?,* Paola would have said. *Me, I had no troubles with having the babies* (interesting, knowing how much she had tried for a second child), *but if Jessica has the trouble with the babies, then sure, take one from somewhere else, why not. There are so many here, so many young people with the children, but we take care of our children in Italy. Spain too. We don't give them away, acch, anyway. It's awful, America. Just awful. So high up everyone is. And after those buildings fell? Yes, I know, where you are, it's not so high, but, Ramon, why do you live there? Come back to Italia. I have a space for you here, in the house, where you can make your plans for all your buildings. Here, in Lazio! Jessica, too, we have very nice schools here. She can teach in them. Or Rome. Very good schools! Like England! Jesse could go to*

Rome, and, Ramon, you can stay here. And anyway, Ramon, she'd have said, *you are so young to have a baby. Not yet,* she'd say to her forty-two-year-old son. *Come here and stay here and then you will see, the babies will come.*

From where? I wondered, thinking of Ramon's mother. I understood her better after all these years—or I should say I could anticipate her more accurately—but on that first trip, I'd been shocked as I watched her remove Ramon's things from his overnight bag, as if they'd been plated in gold. She placed these items—regular things!: jeans, polo shirts, balled-up socks—on shelves cleared for him alone. The house was cluttered with a lifetime of trinkets from abroad, an accumulation of crud and beauty and memory and the evident compulsion to keep all of it. As I had not been offered my own shelf, I placed my backpack on the floor. When I returned from the bathroom, which was jammed with unopened boxes and porcelain figurines, jars of expired face cream, decade-old bottles of suntan lotion and shampoos, the backpack had been removed.

"Where's my stuff?" I asked Ramon.

He took a deep breath. "That backpack, you know, it's been a lot of places. Dragged all around, you know? It's probably a little dirty for the house."

"So, where's my stuff then?"

"My mother is cleaning it on the terrace." Ramon breathed out.

"Is this you saying this or your mother?" I asked. "That my stuff is in need of cleaning?"

"My mother," he told me. "But, I mean, she has a point. The trains. The hostels. The dust. Anyway, she's wiping it down now. Then she'll put some sort of plastic down here." He spread his hands out on the floor by the twin bed I assumed I'd be sleeping in. "And then you can set it down and use it. On the plastic."

I did believe it was crazy and slightly defamatory. But then! But then. The social responsibility, the need to understand a different way of life . . . I had thought, as I sat for a moment on the mattress, which managed to be an impossible combination: equal parts hard and lumpy. I was in another country, on another continent. I needed, I thought, adjusting myself on this very uncomfortable bed, to be respectful of a differing culture.

Which I was. Even though where I come from, in *America,* the guest usually gets the largest, softest towel, the finest cut of meat, the heartiest slice of cake. Not here in Terracina. On that evening, as we ate inside the cramped kitchen, sealed in tight, removed from the dust and germs of the fresh open air, Ramon received for his dinner a heaping plate of rooster and polenta. I saw Paola serve him the tender breast meat of that bird, and then deliver to my plate something resembling its talon. As we ate, she would not look at me, speaking only to Ramon, who didn't do much translating. Occasionally he gestured toward me or pointed to certain pieces of art on the walls—a series of butterfly wings fashioned into the shape of women, ceramic ticking clocks displaying incorrect times, and my favorite, a portrait of Ramon and Paola together that must have been done when they lived in Indonesia, as they were both painted with beautiful and flat crescents for eyes, which created an Asian cast. As they talked—occasionally saying words I understood, like *Americana* and *New York* and *gelato*—I looked down at my claw and picked around its nails with my fork.

That night Ramon and I slept in the same room, in separate wooden beds short enough for children, windows closed tight, the bedroom door wide open into the hallway and Paola's open room across from it. The hard lumps were difficult to sleep on, and so I was awake when I heard Paola slip into the room. I opened my eyes to see her there, a silhouette in the half-light of the low-hung moon, standing over her son, her hand over her heart.

I had just fallen asleep when the rooster—one we hadn't eaten—called us up, which led to the baying of donkeys, the squawking of chickens, and the barking of neighbors' dogs, jangling on their chains. Dogs on chains! I tried to think of different cultural mores when I stumbled into the kitchen for breakfast with Ramon. I thought of divergent conventions, even when Paola gave me a thimbleful of fresh-squeezed orange juice—from her garden, she said, in nearly perfect English—and Ramon a glass big enough to hold two cans of beer, and I thought of those social mores again when he got his plate of perfectly fried eggs, while mine were both punctured and a little overcooked, my dish chipped.

I knew her husband was working in Indonesia, but who knew if he'd return, and I also knew that Ramon was not here often. I imagined Paola, at the end of her day of obsessive mopping and dusting and ironing—even socks got ironed, to burn away the germs—and watering her garden and going into town for her bread and cheese and milk, sitting down at the wooden kitchen table, her head in her hands. I wondered what she thought about then, what she wished and longed for and what she missed most about her life, and I felt for her, deeply, all alone out here on this secluded farm, cordoned off from the world.

Until the following evening.

This particular evening Ramon and I had come back from an afternoon of drinking coffee and eating ice cream, wandering through the old stone streets, sitting at the port. We rushed home for lunch at four o'clock, which, we had been told by Paola, was the time to be there, and, as I wanted her love and approval—as I wanted the love and approval of most strangers—it was I who, despite my touristic cravings, made sure we did not go to the Temple of Jupiter on the hill or into the duomo in the piazza in order to make this time precisely.

It was just three forty-five (fifteen forty-five Euro time) when we pulled into the gate. Relieved that we were punctual (not, I would learn, a trait shared by most Italians), I then noticed a series of birdlike shadows on the reddish sand and stone of the drive. When I looked up to see what was throwing those silhouettes, I saw that it was my underwear hanging on the line. All my underwear—and it must be said it was an era of thongs—hung out in the sun, drying in the scorching heat. Just my underwear was on the line, mine alone, pinched by clothespins, the crotches exposed and baking in the sun.

As I stood and looked at the wash line of my undergarments, illuminated by the golden Italian light, I realized I did not know the Lazian customs but also I did not know Ramon terribly well. And, as I stomped over to the clothesline and began to pull my underwear down, one by one, unclipping the cruel wooden teeth that left bites in the mesh and cotton, I tried to think about the societal conventions that would make a woman do such a thing, the history of women in what I could see was an agricultural community, that would make one humiliate another in this fashion.

Paola stood on the terrace above me; I could see her out of the corner of my eye, her head pitched down. I could not see her face, but I caught her crossed arms and the wild, loose pieces of her black hair, her bright rustling housedress.

"Ramon," I said. "Please tell your mother that if she doesn't think I'm clean enough for you, perhaps I should leave." My underthings were gathered in my arms, cradled there. I wasn't sure what to do next, as I had shocked even myself; I have always had such an unbearable need to please even—perhaps especially—the people who hurt me.

"Stop," Ramon said. "Jesse." He came up to me, and beneath the clothesline, now empty, he put his hands firmly on both my shoulders. "I'm sorry. She didn't mean it that way," he said. And then? "I did tell you not to bring lingerie."

I stared at him for a moment, speechless, and then I looked up to see his mother above us, a smile of understanding, like sunlight, spreading across her face.

"It's underwear. *Pantalons,*" I said, because I had taken French in high school and somehow this is what came to me. *"Sous-vête-ments,"* I corrected myself.

"Mama," he said, and then he said something as angry and beautiful as anything and everything else they'd told each other since we'd arrived the previous day.

"What?" she said, again in clean, barely accented English, five fingertips at her breast. "Okay!" Now she brushed her hands together swiftly. "She may clean her own clothes then."

"Yes." My eyes, caught in the light, squinted in her direction. "Thank you, Paola. I think that would be best."

That day, I did not get an apology but I did get the larger shank of lamb that evening, and, the following morning, my own full glass of fresh-squeezed juice.

Back in America, in Virginia, my father, when he was all cried out, had told me how troubled he was for me, how he'd only ever wished for us to be happy, that my happiness had been all he'd ever wanted, Lucy, too, and look at us, one of us living hand-to-mouth without so much as a telephone—"I mean, where *is* Lucy?" he'd asked—and then you, he'd said, you so busy with wanting all these things you can't have.

"All these things?" But the rage, it had receded. In that way, the manner in which it arrives and leaves, rage is like love. It is unclear to me what brings it to me, what takes it away, and how I will know if it has permanently disappeared. "Only a child," I'd said quietly. "I only want a child, which everyone deserves."

He had straightened himself up. "Whatever you need us to do, we want to help you," he said. "Not get in the way."

And I had shaken my head, and I had believed him; I believed him as we threw our bags into the trunk and made our way to the highway.

And now, returning to Brooklyn, I thought of the red balloon following our car as we double-parked in front of our building and dumped out all our stuff on the wrought iron–enclosed front stoop, and then circled the block looking for parking, and then found it, and then let Harriet out to pee, and then walked back and up the four steps and in and then up the four flights and then: home.

Harriet wagged her tail. She didn't hate it there, really. She knew—and she did know—that tomorrow she'd be walked and fed and petted and loved, and I knew that tomorrow I would teach for part of the day and I would meet with some students and then I would return home to this place I was lucky enough to call my neighborhood. I looked at Ramon, who was hanging his coat, and I felt so fortunate and content. Out our window, past the square backyards of brownstones on Second Street, past the windows of those brownstones, and into the distance, the back of the red Kentile sign obscured by the F train slowly rolling by, the sun was setting, and I felt light, for just one moment liberated from the reason we'd left Brooklyn. I ducked my head to look out and see if the balloon wasn't in fact hovering above our fire escape on its long white string, waiting to be held.

"We've got voice mails." Ramon held out the phone. "Your parents." He twirled his index finger, a gesture to rush the message along. "And Cheryl," he said. "You have a department meeting tomorrow. Oh." He smiled. "Anita and Paula."

"That's nice."

"They're happy they met us," he said, hanging up the phone. The living room was illuminated in the late-afternoon sun. Harriet lapped up three-day-old water in the kitchen. Everything was cozy and sweet and good.

"I'm happy we met them, too." I sifted through the mail and threw it on the dining room table.

"They want to know if we're going to use the designer the agency recommended," Ramon reported. He went into the kitchen and began opening and closing cabinets. "For the brochure. Which I can do, you know. Easily. Why should we pay someone when I can do it?"

"Hmmm." I wanted to do exactly what the agency said, just follow the plan, down to the designing of the brochure, the right smile, displaying teeth, evergreens behind us in the correct-size photo. There was no room for error here. I could feel my heart rate speed up, running toward something or away from it; what is the difference if it's all just a circle anyway?

"We need to make an appointment tomorrow with social services for the visit," I said.

"We will." Ramon stood in the kitchen doorway. "We just got in. Relax."

"Don't," I said.

"It will get done." He went to the couch and tipped his head back, touched his head to the exposed-brick wall.

"By magical fairies? We need to get on it."

Ramon closed his eyes and sighed.

I looked at my watch. "Look at the time," I said to Ramon.

Neither of us moved. In the hallway the scream of our downstairs neighbor's child shot through the house. A car alarm went off on our street.

I sat down on the couch next to my husband, my elbows sharp on my knees. "It's so much later than I thought," I said, and just like that, the afternoon light slipped out of the living room, and the gray of winter crept in.

Part 2

THE APPLICATION

11

Winter 2010

If everything about being a mother is a memory—the memory of your own childhood evoked by the sounds and smells and touches of your child and the air and water and substance that surround her—then working hard to become a mother is about the imagination, an unknown future. All the mothers have wondered: What will it be like? Who will I be if I become a mother? What will be gained and what will be lost? Will I be the same woman to myself? To the world?

My mother's water broke while she was shopping for coats on sale at Garfinckel's. There was a small dark spot in the outerwear department until I was three years old, and my mother used to take me there to show me the history of my birth, evidence that it had taken place, that the story she had told me held truth. Then one day the carpets were changed, and that little spot—substantiation of my birth story—was gone.

But still I have this story.

What story will I have to tell? When one doesn't know if or when or how or from where a baby will emerge, the questions change. Where will my baby come from? Who will grow him first? When? How will I know she will be safe until I find her? It is all invention, and the endless possibility of it—all the things one cannot know, and so cannot *un*know—can make for a world of fantasy, thought with no end or resolution.

Which is why details can offer comfort, however cold. The week after returning from Raleigh, I was relieved to be busy with work and meetings and grading student papers on Elizabeth Cady Stanton and the suffragette movement. *Men say we are ever cruel to each other. Let us end this ignoble record and henceforth stand by womanhood,* she'd said at her address at the Seneca Falls women's convention of 1848, and this appeared, largely without attribution or analysis, in nearly every paper.

I called social service organizations to secure yet another training session at the earliest date possible because we were required to use a New York agency to do all the local paperwork, including the home study, a major event in the adoption process. Other particularities offered refuge from my own invention. For the home study, a social worker was to come to our home and interview us, to ensure that we were both suitable parents and lived in a satisfactory home.

After securing the earliest date—January!—I nudged Harriet, who was asleep beneath my desk, gently in her soft stomach with my slipper.

"Want to go for a hike, H?" I asked.

She slept on.

"Harriet!" I knelt down. "Want to go for a walk?"

Her eyes shot open. And then closed again.

Eventually she rallied and I packed up water and a few snacks

for us both, and we got into the car. After some pawing and sighing, she settled herself in, and then we were off to hit traffic on
the Brooklyn Bridge and on the West Side Highway, before we
were in more traffic on the George Washington Bridge. Ramon
and I had once biked uptown from Brooklyn all the way to the
George Washington Bridge the autumn after we'd met in Italy,
and I remembered the exhilaration of getting to the bridge and
riding out over the glistening river. And then: sudden, paralyzing
fear. I could not move, not forward or backward. We had walked
our bikes off the bridge and cycled back to Brooklyn, where we
wolfed down burgers and too many beers as the sun went down,
and it was the kind of day that I recognized as a salient memory,
even while it was happening.

Finally, Harriet and I crossed over and onto the Palisades, the
Bronx across the river to my right, as glittering and shining and
bright as any jewel I'd seen.

The local news was on NPR, and soon a story about a young
woman abducted as an infant in a Bronx hospital came on the radio.
After twenty years, she'd been reunited with her biological mother.
There had not been one day, her biological mother said, that she
had not thought about her daughter and what had happened to
her. What had happened was that the woman, the *kidnapper,* had
had several miscarriages, disguised herself as a nurse, and took the
child. She then went on, the piece said, to abuse her. Now the FBI
was hunting her down.

As the city fell away, and Harriet and I made our way to Har-
riman State Park along Seven Lakes Drive, toward the trail that
snaked around and up from the water, I wondered if I understood
any of the players in that drama, the child, the woman whose child
was taken, the woman crazed by loss. I felt I had been all of those
things; but I knew exactly which one I was now.

———————

At Lake Askoti, there was a large flat rock that Ramon and I would sit on and eat chicken sandwiches as Harriet flung herself into the lake, then, trembling with joy as she shook water all over our food, she would attempt to eat our sandwiches, and lick our faces, before jumping back into the water.

Ramon and I came here on weekends, when the rock and other places to hang out comfortably around the lake were crowded with boys guzzling beer and smoking joints, and the trails were filled to bursting with families and hikers. But occasionally it was still and quiet but for the lapping of the water, the creaking of trees, and the swooping of small birds.

When we arrived, Harriet leapt out of the car and made her way to the familiar trail, jumping in and out of the water along the lake before I even got to the water's edge. We passed by our rock, and I stood for a moment as she hurled herself in, and then I hauled her up when she couldn't make her way up the smooth, wet surface. The lake was a brilliant blue, a mirror reflecting a cloudless day, the remaining foliage browning. I turned from the lip of the lake and Harriet followed, pushing ahead of me, her energy boosted by being wet, and we made our way up along the rocky trail that led to another trail higher on the ridge.

I could feel the moss and pine and dirt beneath my boots, the give of earth, and also its resistance to my steps, the way it protected its boundaries, and I felt filled up as I walked in the crisp air, across streams and up switchbacks. I felt the singing in my legs as we climbed up, passing only a German or Austrian or Dutch couple, in lederhosen, carrying crooked walking sticks, their long white hair pulled back, as they hiked the Appalachian Trail, which intersected here with our local one. We nodded hello and then Harriet and I walked along the perimeter of the hilltop, in the sun, occasionally stopping to sit and look out onto the lake and the lakes beyond, the rise and fall of the uneven trees.

Hiking gave way to thoughts of being in that upstate town for graduate school, all the time I spent alone there in the woods with Harriet, growing stronger again after my surgeries, and with it that feeling that I might not be a stranger to myself forever. I remembered my mother seated next to me in the hospital, holding my hand. It is one of the few memories I have of us touching. I thought about the mothers as I drove onto the bridge, toward home, and I remembered Harriet, just today, running down the hillside, bounding ahead of me, the splash of her entering the water, and then smiling as I came upon her, so happy in all that blue.

12

———

Winter came on suddenly. An icy draft I hadn't remembered from the previous year curled around my ankles and wrists; a raw numbing cold filled up my office as I tried to plan the following semester's classes. Gearing up for the new semester, I had every intention of creating innovative, mind-blowingly wonderful classes, courses where students would learn about feminism and women's diverse and global histories in creative ways, which would somehow reflect all the research I'd been doing on women's activism in rural communities. And yet, the deadlines came and the deadlines went, and I found myself sending off the same syllabus I'd used several semesters in a row, the same books, the same supplemental reading material, my ingenuity sapped.

How had this happened to us? my friends and colleagues asked one another, not the mothers, but those of us who had never left our careers, not for a single moment. Perhaps it was poor strategizing or lack of proper planning, or the ignominious notion that we were always on the very cusp of our most significant work, an opus that would be widely recognized, placing us far above the standard academic fray. Whatever had caused it, we marveled at where we were, midlife really, up for varying contract reviews in non-tenure-track jobs, our futures terribly unsure.

But life, my grandmother had always told Lucy and me, is what happens when you're busy making other plans. Sure enough, Ramon got laid off, along with the rest of his department. He had begun freelancing for what at first seemed like more pay, until work appeared to be something he was doing little of. I was still appointed on a contract basis, just when money seemed like it could be the answer to so many of our problems. I had visions of defying those beneficent Hague laws and just showing up in a developing country, throwing a bag of cash at someone who would run behind some bush—perhaps an African wanza tree—and return to me with a child.

I don't know if my grandmother knew she was quoting John Lennon, but she said it again after my grandfather died, and she said it when I got sick, and then we said it without her when she died, just before my final surgery, the one that attached what was left of my intestines together.

My poor mother. She wept when I went in for that surgery; she wouldn't let go of the gurney they wheeled me away on, and I know she was thinking of her mother, too, and all that could be lost.

In the time between the training in Raleigh and the information session in White Plains, we worked on our birthmother letter. Oh, the birthmother letter. The editorial suggestions that came from the offices of Crystal or Tiffany were endless and nonsensical. As I made each correction, I longed for the editors at scholarly journals, whose comments I often laughed at as I read them aloud to Ramon. But we believed now that Crystal and Tiffany held the secret to what would "work," the key that would unlock the doors that led to what these birthmothers, these magical earth women, wanted, the key to our own houses of happiness.

For the birthmothers, whoever they were, wherever they were, however we would come to meet them, please please let us meet them, we would write about my pie baking and how we could not wait to watch our child squish berries in her fingers. We would write about my mother-in-law's recipes (You want rooster claw? She's got it) and our happy visits to her village each summer. We would write about our diverse Brooklyn neighborhood, about my family's celebrations at Christmas, where my father, in a fit of submitting to the dominant culture, dressed the house in candy canes and mistletoe and framed the fireplace with poinsettias. He placed the Christmas cards carefully along the mantel, noting who had not sent one this year and who would now be added to the list. We would address our birthmother letter to a "special person," which we certainly believed this hypothetical woman was, though it was not how we would have chosen to express these sentiments.

This brochure of our life featured an assortment of pictures. Our friends' children embracing us, Ramon and I eating at large tables with our families. Here we were holding on to other peoples' children tightly, everyone smiling brightly. These photos were chosen over those we might have picked, of Harriet and me looking out from a hilltop, Ramon crouched and smiling in the branches of one of Paola's lemon trees, the two of us leaning into each other, beaming, before a table in Capri all those years ago, wine and bread and tomatoes and sardines set out before us, the sea winking behind us, tiny glittering whitecaps breaking. No wine in photos, we were told. Never.

Just after the New Year, Anita called. She was attending a conference at the vet hospital where I'd gone to graduate school, and she wondered if we would meet her.

I imagined that town in winter, the cruel weather effect of the Finger Lakes, the way—before I had gotten Harriet—that I had walked the neighborhoods, stooped, freezing, barely able to carry the brutal weight of my coat and scarf and mittens.

"Do you want to go?" I asked Ramon.

"To go to a freezing town for a freezing weekend in the middle of freezing winter? Not really," he said. "Is Paula going?"

"Just Anita. You like Anita," I told him, as if he needed reminding. "And Harriet will have such fun going back." I wondered if I would enjoy this return, or if it would spark some deep vulnerability that had not been excised with the surgeon's cut.

I thought of Harriet springing through a blanket of snow. It is a fact that dogs are like humans in that they make long, deep friendships; they recognize places they have loved, and I pictured her bouncing through the high snow along the creek, running into some of her old pals from puppydom, though most of those dogs would be gone now.

"I have all this work." Ramon waved toward the dining room, the large glass table strewn with papers and contracts. This was his new default position. As a freelancer, he could always be burdened by deadlines and future projects or trying to acquire such things.

"You do?" I asked. "Like what?"

"Several things," he said, very specifically.

"I think I'm going to go up," I said. "I've got another ten days until school starts. I think it might be fun."

"If you think fun is freezing your ass off, by all means, have at it," Ramon said, cracking open his laptop. Sometimes he looked so out of place here. In the dining room, and also in New York. I thought of him at a café in Terracina, idly ordering the sardine pasta and muscat. As I clomped awkwardly around the village, heavy with my Americanness—my clothes, my books, my decidedly un-Italian shoes—Ramon's gestures were elegant and effortless.

Now I got up to go to my own computer, and passing through Ramon's new office, our dining room, I could see him begin a game of some kind—involving mice, or perhaps it was little hedgehogs—rutting around underground and digging a system of mazes.

"I think a trip will be fun, Ramon," I said. "I can show you all the fabulous places where I hung out in grad school: the hippie restaurant, the really lame local bar, the place where people fling themselves off bridges and into the gorges. The little hospital where I stayed for days before going to the cancer center in Baltimore." And there it was too, the hospital dark, the slip of light beneath the door, the sound of nurses, the squeak of their shoes, the beeping of machines, the weeping of visitors, the click of my professor's knitting needles, Lucy in a dark corner, rising to leave. The body really does remember what the mind long ago let fade.

Ramon looked up.

"We need a break." As I said this, I realized it terribly clearly. "Something to get us out of here." I looked around the room. We had been held hostage by our wants.

"Another time, okay?" He turned back to the computer and, I assumed, to his hedgehogs channeling their way aboveground for air.

I nodded, but he did not see me. "Let me know if you change your mind."

Three days later, I headed upstate alone.

Driving into town was just as I remembered: rolling hills and wide expanses of snow, a low gray sky that gave way to the town, overcast, gloomy, blighted. I pulled into the lot at the Holiday Inn, where the rooms were practically free as students were not yet back to school, and I checked in with Harriet.

An hour later, we were at the mouth of the trail with Anita and two of her spinones, Madeleine and Toby. Harriet sniffed at their asses, and they sniffed at hers, and, for the first time in over a year, Harriet got down on her haunches and barked, ready to play.

"You brought two dogs with you? Wow."

"I'm a vet," Anita said. "We collect animals for a living. At least these monsters aren't sick. I can't tell you how many vet friends we've got who have birds with broken wings and cats in kidney failure, dogs lumpy with tumors."

"Really." I could see the small wooden bridge that led to the trail through the woods and then a path along the frozen creek.

"It's what makes us vets," she said.

"I used to come here in graduate school. When I first got Harriet."

Anita stepped ahead and we crossed over the footbridge. "I think you guys will love it," I said.

"It's cold as shit here." She rubbed her arms.

I laughed. Ramon had not been wrong about that. Anita was dressed in several layers of hair-covered polar fleece. I wore a parka that had sat in the trunk of my car since I'd left this frozen town.

I had been in school here after the second surgery, alone in a winter so brutal even the students were isolated from one another. After recovering at home in Virginia, in my sister's room, as I could not walk the steps to the attic, I went back to school just as soon as I had the vigor to open a can of soup. This was before Harriet, and I walked the streets of that town on my own, to build up strength. My weight had dropped to just over one hundred pounds. My hair had begun to grow back slowly, in clumps. Even my coat felt heavy, too much to bear. My scalp and face flaked and itched. I remember picking my way along the snow and ice, like an old person, fearful of falling.

The math I had been doing was different then: it only counted backward from the moment. Nine years earlier I had watched my sister slam the door in my face, refusing to say good-bye, as I drove away to school. Seven years: my college roommate and I by a campsite in Utah, sipping wine and reading Jack Kerouac. Three years: a breakup with a classical Greek scholar I'd met at a party in Tribeca. But then the future stopped; the math no longer moved in front of the present. Even my imagination, the foil of memory's powerful muscle, ceased.

Anita and I were silent as we walked through the woods, and I could hear the crunch of branches and the hard earth beneath our feet as I watched Harriet bound up the small hills and then return, leading Madeleine and Toby through the snowbanks and fallen trees. There is little as beautiful as dogs running free through the woods.

We walked for an hour or so, until our extremities were uncomfortably numb, and then Anita and I agreed to meet for dinner.

In the hotel, as Harriet curled up on the bed, exhausted, snoring—a bug in a rug, my grandmother used to say of any contented creature—I checked my e-mail. Notes on the birthmother letter. I went to make the corrections right away, as we were losing time.

We were always losing time.

Under the section "Our Interests," I had written: *We really enjoy the country, where we can all run around, pick blackberries behind our friends' house upstate, and kayak in the pond.*

Here were Tiffany or Crystal's editorial suggestions: *After the blackberries is a great place for an example, something like, "we look forward to our little one giggling as they squish the berries in his or her hands as we bake our blackberries into yummy pies."*

It is? I thought. Really? But I did what I was told, minus the *little one* and *yummy*. Time was of the essence, yes, but Ramon and I had agreed we would try to be as true to who we were as possible, even if we might still be discovering what that meant in this unending new phase of our lives.

Anita and I met at the famous hippie restaurant I had hated in graduate school. I hated it still. The waitress smelled of patchouli and armpits, and she told us about the special lasagna made from house-made soy cheese and spinach, picked under the shamanistic light of the New York State moon and stars, and also a special ancient grain medley of amaranth, spelt, and millet served with maize and beans.

"For the love of God," I said, "We'd like a bottle of the Shale-stone red." It was the name of a local winery I still remembered from a trip I took there with other first-year graduate students when I had just arrived at school.

Anita snorted. "What is Shalestone?"

"Everything local," I said. "It's their thing."

The wine came and we ordered our food and then we both sat back and relaxed in earnest.

"How are you guys doing?" I asked.

She raised her eyebrows and nodded her head slowly. "Eh. This whole thing sucks. Have you done that fucking letter yet?"

"In process," I said.

"We just finished it. It's approved."

"Are you serious? How?"

"Just did what we're told. We love ponies and puppies and bun-nies and unicorns. We have flexible schedules and a three-bedroom house. Got the home study done, too. We are very good at getting stuff done, Paula and I."

"That," I said as I gulped at my wine and watched several locals enter the restaurant, "is awesome.

"So being a vet . . ." I changed the topic in order to quell my growing panic that Anita and Paula might get a baby first. "Tell me all about it."

Anita talked about clicker training and animal obesity, and I talked about Harriet and how perfect she was—like a person almost. Anita nodded in assent and then we discussed their home in North Carolina and what Ramon and I liked to do in Brooklyn. We'd had two glasses of wine by the time our meals, two heaping piles of mush, arrived. I dug in, and despite the disagreeable presentation, the food was comforting and delicious.

We ordered another bottle of wine, and after we got deep into that came the emmer and raisin pudding and flourless dark chocolate cake. Then we went out to the new "cocktail place"—and by cocktail place, I mean a dark room with a couch and vodka that was not dispensed from a gun—across the commons, where I ordered us martinis.

After, we made our way, rather drunkenly, out to the street. We were padded up with scarves and hats and mittens, human teddy bears, as we hugged good-bye.

"Thank you so much for inviting me up," I said. "It was a good thing for us to do."

Anita placed a lint-covered, lumpy fleece glove on each side of my face. "So good to see you!"

I don't know who went in first for the kiss. I think now it might have been Anita, because it was I who pulled away. As it was happening, though, I felt her soft lips and her warm tongue flickering against mine, and it was delicious, for a moment, to be kissing on the deserted street of a deserted college town.

"Hey." I pulled away. I licked my lips and instantly they froze.

"Goodness," Anita said. "I didn't see that coming."

"No." I touched my lips with my mitten. *Swish swish* went my jacket. I had never thought I'd kiss anyone new again. "Me either."

Anita cleared her throat.

"It's okay," I said.

She nodded and looked down.

"Well," I said. "This *was* fun. I'm going back to the hotel."

Anita looked up and nodded. "It was," she said. "Thank you."

We both turned away, then, and headed in different directions, Anita to her car—which I should have prevented due to all the drinking—and me to my hotel at the other end of the commons. My parka, moving against itself, hissed at me as I walked away.

The next day I woke up late, with a hangover, and I dragged myself out to walk Harriet. It had snowed again during the night and the town was covered in a blanket of white, concealing the cars and garbage cans and streetlamps, and also further defining them.

I thought about Anita then, as I had during the night, when I'd woken with a start, zapped awake. Then I'd felt horribly guilty, and I'd wondered what Ramon had been doing on that night, and also on any number of occasions we left each other to our own devices, relieved to be apart and not to be confronted by our lonely coupledom.

Driving home, past the hills, the clapboard houses set beneath the horizon line of trees and over the hanging green bridges that cross so many upstate towns, I wondered why I had done that.

There had been other drunken evenings, with other people, on many other nights, so why had this happened with Anita? It was nothing, a quick kiss on a frozen night, and then the rescinding of that kiss. I thought of Anita all bundled up in her layers of fleece, her dark wavy hair and her ruddy skin, and how her eyes squinted just at the outside corners of her eyes, like pulled spiderwebs. But in that moment, despite being wrapped in all of winter's effects, I felt my costume undoing, as if I was unzipping my outer casing, stepping out of the livery I now wore. I was getting closer. To someone. Recently it seemed everyone I had loved was receding.

I wished for Lucy. Or for what I wanted Lucy and I to be to each other as adults. When I went to college my sister would call and report on all our parents' usual activities. Mom's away this month, she'd say. Dad's taken up cooking, she'd report. Italian.

Once, she'd called sobbing. This was when Claudine left. Did you know she had children of her own? she'd asked me.

I'd had no idea that Claudine had children, that she tended to us and then went home to her own. And who watched them by day? I wondered what they looked like, what they wore, if their beds were made and what they were covered in. If they were girls, or boys, or both. If they cried in her lap, head on her breast, little fingers reaching to the shining, synthetic hairs of her wig, the way Lucy did. Or if they kept away from her as they aged, watching her from hulking shadows, as I had. It is a historical fact that African-American women have raised a considerable number of white American women's children. I know this now, but how did I become part of a dialectic and not notice it, not even later?

She was practically my mother, Lucy had said.

Several years later, Lucy visited me in graduate school, before I got sick. I had dragged her to classes with me, introducing her to professors whom I called by their first names. Jean, I'd said, oh-so-casually, meet my sister. What was Lucy doing then? Waitressing, I believe. Did I say, Jean, meet my sister, the waitress?

While it is likely true that I did speak more that day in my classes in an effort to show off to Lucy, I was shocked when, after class, at the bar around the corner from my house, a place where I proudly knew the bartender, Lucy downed three whiskey sours in quick succession and turned instantly dark.

"Such a showoff." She looked straight into the mirror behind the bar, blackened in spots, as if the reflective parts had been rubbed out.

I smiled at the bartender, Charlie, who made me excellent old-fashioneds when I needed them, like on those late afternoons in the premature upstate winter dark, those short fearful days when I thought the worst thing that would happen was that I would remain insecure in my work and so would not find a place in the academy. And then I looked at my sister in that bar mirror and laughed. Because I thought she was joking.

Her eyes grew small. "You always try to be so goddamn smart," she said, sliding off her stool. "When does it end?" she asked as she went toward the door.

I watched her slam out of the bar, and then I paid up, apologizing to Charlie, and followed after her. I found her on my front stoop, waiting for me.

"Lucy," I said. "Come on."

She closed her eyes and shook her head. As I unlocked the door, pushing the warped wood open with my shoulder, I heard her stand and follow me inside.

I put the teakettle on and then came out to the living room, where she sat, brooding, in the dark. I took off my coat and smelled the cigarettes from the bar in my hair.

"Lucy," I said. I sat down next to her. "I'm sorry."

It was the first time I had realized it: I have always been looking ahead. I rarely saw my sister because she was always behind me.

I watched her remove her coat in the blue dark. The kettle whistled.

"Okay?" I stood and moved to turn on a lamp.

I saw my sister nodding, shyly, as the room filled with delicate light.

And now, if I were to call Lucy to tell her what had happened with Anita, how I had done this strange and horrible thing in that same town, all I could imagine hearing between us was the sound of the surf or the caw of a foreign bird.

When I arrived home, Ramon was playing his hedgehog/mouse game, several beer bottles on the table.

"Have you even moved?" I asked, dropping my bags.

"Barely," he said.

"Living it up, I see." I bent down to kiss him on the cheek. I should mention Anita. Say something and make it go away, I thought.

"I don't know." Ramon stared straight ahead at his computer. He didn't even greet Harriet. "Sometimes I just think I'm living it all down."

I looked over at my husband. It was not worth repeating, I thought, nodding at the five bottles of beer on the table, lined up in a perfect row. I took off my parka. He was far away. "Sorry," I said.

Ramon looked up at me. He smiled. "Oh, by the way," he said. "Lucy called."

13

——

In the two months that had stretched out between Raleigh and the information session in White Plains, there was Anita upstate and then, as always, there were pregnancies. Three of my friends informed me—some gingerly, as sensitively as they could, some in mass e-mails to avoid telling me directly—that they were pregnant. One friend gave birth to an eight-pound boy, and another had to have a surgical abortion at six months due to a rare genetic disease. She already had a child, but I don't think this made it easier for her when, in the supermarket, old ladies put their hands on her stomach, not knowing that inside was only a ghost.

That was when Michelle let me know Zoe would have a sibling.

"You're pregnant?" I said when she called with the news.

"Yes! Yes. I'm so relieved, you know? Thank God," she said. "You just never know if it's going to work out. Of course, you know what I mean."

"Congratulations, Michelle!" I was in my office/closet trying to get organized. I looked out onto the street, where two women walked together, both about to burst, one's stomach taut and rounded, a fanged snake who'd eaten a bowling ball, the other's belly torpedoed, as if she'd inhaled a missile.

"Maybe we'll get to do this together again. Like we almost did before. Ugh, you know what I mean. You just never know; you just have to believe," Michelle said. "Stranger things have happened."

I was silent and I continued sorting through my piles of paper.

"Okay, I'm just going to say this," Michelle stated. "And if you're mad, you're mad."

There was a Mother's Day card in one of these stacks. It was given to me. By Ramon. We'd been dating almost a year, and on Mother's Day he had made me a card he'd created on the computer. "Maybe you shouldn't say it then," I told her as I fingered the card. "Because I'm not in a great mood."

"What else is new!" Michelle said, falsely cheery.

"I realize I've been in a bad mood for like four years now," I said. "I know."

"I know. That's the thing, Jesse. Being a mother, it's not like it's all good. It doesn't solve everything. You can't do everything. As a woman, I mean. We have all these roles, still. Nothing's changed since our mothers, really. As you know, I have a fairly liberated husband, and he still tells me, 'Just bring Zoe to your meeting. We can't afford a sitter for your meeting.' He would never do that! Bring a child. Your job isn't taken as seriously—no matter what you do, you will always be seen as the mother. You will always be seen as caring more about your children."

"But you will," I said, "care more about your children than your job." Also, Michelle's husband was not so liberated, but I let that go.

"No, I won't," Michelle said. "Not every moment, no I won't. I was a person before Zoe. I am still that person."

"I get it." On the front of the card was a photo of Harriet seated at a formal table set with a white tablecloth and golden china, a white napkin at her throat.

"Do you really want to be part of a conversation about babysitting and organic carrots? Do you?"

"Yes!" I said, opening the card. Inside was the same table utterly changed, food strewn about, stuck to the walls, noodles hanging from the crystal chandelier. Harriet was still seated, her expression the same. "I do," I said.

"No you don't, Jesse. If this had been easy for you, having kids I mean, we would be sitting here bitching about what all the mothers are discussing—the five-hundred-dollar boots they deserve to get for themselves, their strollers, the new line of organic toys, attachment parenting. We'd be saying, 'What happened to discussions of art and politics?' You would be so pissed."

"I get it," I said again. Were the complications of motherhood more than just history's slow arrow? "You can't really think I don't know all this, Michelle. And yet here you are, somehow managing to have another," I said.

To Mutterly Love, the card said on the inside, below the great mess. And written in, beneath the print: *To my favorite mummy. I love you, Ramon.*

"Yes," Michelle said. "I realize that. Yes. I suppose I am."

While striving to become a mother has been unnervingly bewildering, actually being a mother seems even more complicated. It occurs to me how little time I've spent thinking about the care and feeding of children. Where will it play and sleep? What will it eat? There is the faceless, raceless child: skinless, bloodless, hairless, featureless. The child is only organs, a map of arteries and veins, wrapped in transparent glass. How will I make sure it lives and that I do not shatter it? And if, right now, I order books on this matter, or go to a website, take a class even, what heartbreak have I set myself up for?

For this reason, all our tables still have exposed glass corners. Our knives and cleaners and bleaches and open windows are in easy reach. Why prepare for something that could never arrive? Why safety-lock cabinets and bar the windows, store a stroller in an overstuffed closet, a dismantled crib in the trunk of a car? There is no reason, and yet still there is the constancy of my own internal reminders: an incessant ticking clock, the calendar, its days ripped by unnatural winds from its pages as in an old movie, marking time, seasons revolving like planetarium moons, circling Jupiter.

Not long after I got Michelle's happy news, along with her lecture, Ramon and I took the train to Coney Island. It had not been our intention. We had gotten on the train headed for Park Slope to see friends, including one of the newly pregnant couples, for brunch.

"I so don't want to do this today," I said. I looked at my boots, scuffed from winter. The leather was worn thin; I could see the shapes of my toes wriggling inside them.

"Me either," Ramon said. "I hate brunch. I have never liked—"

"Don't," I said, anticipating his tirade against the American tradition.

"I just don't like it." He looked out into the dark tunnel. "It ruins a perfectly good day."

Our designated stop was approaching and Ramon slid closer to me. "Let's do something fun." He hooked his chin over my shoulder.

"Okay." What would that be, I wondered.

The train stopped; the doors opened. Neither of us moved.

"Let's go to Coney Island," Ramon said as the doors closed and the train groaned to a start.

I felt his chin move against my shoulder as he spoke, and I smiled.

Once we had ridden our bikes there on a sun-filled path along the water, New Jersey rising across the river. When we had gotten to the Cyclone, Ramon had looked at the wooden structure and balked. He cited reading a piece about it, the only wooden roller coaster in America, and how years previously someone had died on the thing, as reason to avoid it. But I'd insisted. I remembered being a kid: Kings Dominion, Six Flags, Hershey Park, my mother refusing to go on any of the rides. She waved to Lucy and me from outside the fence and I thought that I never wanted to grow up, never wanted to become an adult who was too scared to get on a roller coaster.

As the coaster creaked up the tracks then, Ramon's face blanched beneath the hand-painted REMAIN SEATED sign, flanked by American flags. The beach sprawled out before us; we could see out into the ocean, over the horizon, and his palm was sweating as he held my hand tightly. Going down, Ramon screamed and I laughed maniacally, breathless. We caught our breath around the bends, then journeyed up and then shot down again. The Wonder Wheel was more Ramon's speed. We rocked in our seat, our feet dangling in the sky, like the kids at the end of *Grease,* like Julie Harris and James Dean in *East of Eden,* as we tipped toward the boardwalk and the beach, teeming with people far beneath us.

That was years ago, when we biked all over the city. It had been summer then, but today it was winter. As we walked from the subway I could see that the Cyclone and the Wonder Wheel were stopped, their cars empty, as if they'd been frozen in mid-ride. It seemed that all we had to do was switch the correct lever to "start," and we could access that day again, a day when we had just gotten back from that first time together in Italy, when we walked the boardwalk amidst the girls in short shorts, smelling of coconut, passing by the arcade and funnel cake stands, the bumper cars and the strongest man, and Nathan's, and the spinning carousel, all the remnants of the stuff that Coney Island once was, a day when Ramon screamed on a roller coaster for the first and last time, when we were at the beginning.

Today the winter light was dazzling and clear and heart-stopping, and we headed out into the sand, toward the sea. Two shirtless men with bushy gray mustaches, their chests and cheeks a furious red, walked by us vigorously as gulls swooped around us, cawing. We walked along the sand, the sun behind us, toward Brighton Beach, the steel parachute ride, also empty, rising at our backs. We turned up to the boardwalk and sat for a moment, watching the ladies in their furs parade by, and for a brief moment I thought of Anita, bundled up against the cold, the way my lips had frozen as soon as we'd pulled apart.

Behind us, there was a splash. Ramon grabbed the sleeve of my coat and turned me to watch several men in the water, screaming from the horror of cold and from the joy of it. We stood and waved and walked along the boardwalk. Ramon put his arm around me and I leaned into him, and the honey sun poured down on our backs, and the wind blew sand across the wooden planks, and the gulls swept in and around, and I could feel the sand beneath the worn soles of my boots as we walked, nodding to the old people who ignored our smiles as we passed.

Your people are Russian, that lawyer had said.

"Let's get dumplings and borscht," I said to Ramon.

We walked a block to a café one of my colleagues had told me about, where the borscht is green and sour, the pickled watermelon, loaded with vinegar, and the dumplings are stuffed just right, served with a gravy boat of sour cream.

My people—the Russians—did not seem to recognize me as such, perhaps because they were Ukrainian. Despite the many available tables, we were not seated for fifteen minutes. But we waited patiently, as we would in a foreign country, until finally we were seated at a table for two. Then we ordered all those things, and pickles, and a fruit compote juice, and we took off our coats and sat back and listened to the families screaming in Russian or Ukrainian, leveling our gazes at the people who stared at us without kindness, and then the food arrived, steaming and swimming in butter, all delicious, and I felt like we'd traveled somewhere together again, that we had left Brooklyn and New York and the States altogether for a place where neither Ramon nor I spoke the language or could claim the culture as our own.

On the F train back, it all grew incrementally familiar again, each of the eighteen stops bringing us closer to home, the language shifting from Russian to Mandarin to Spanish to English. The factory buildings whipped by and the train left the outdoor track and dipped into the station. Ramon and I shivered and for a brief moment we knew we had traveled together, again, to another country.

When we got back, we were both invigorated and in a good mood. Ramon rushed Harriet out, and I phoned Lucy for the fourth time, at the new number she'd given Ramon.

"Lucy?" I screamed into the phone.

"I'm right here," she said. "Right here in the twenty-first century."

And yet, Lucy had no computer to video-call, there could be no visual telegram between us, and so it did remind me of the past century, the few strained conversations we had with our mother when she was away on a special occasion. Hello? she'd shout. Hello! The shouting was necessary then. In addition to the exorbitant cost, lines were often crossed or suddenly cut, and her serrated voice made me feel the panic that the conversation might end with each sentence. I stepped on the place that divided the earth in half, she'd said once, calling from Kenya. At the equator, she'd screamed. I had imagined my mother walking the line I saw drawn across all the maps my father pulled out of the *Encyclopaedia Britannica* to explain to us where our mother was. Upon her return there'd be a grand showing of her slides of the trip, and sure enough, there was our mother smiling alongside a yellow sign with a crude black silhouette of Africa, EQUATOR in red, like a warning sign, slapped across it. And then the words: THIS SIGN IS ON THE EQUATOR. Just a crappy sign along a road.

"Where are you?" I said.

"El Salvador," Lucy responded.

"What?" However long it has been—nearly twenty years now—I will never not associate that place with a war. "What the fuck are you doing in El Salvador, Lucy?"

She paused. "I'm here with some surfers. In Punta Roca. It's actually kind of touristic."

"Touristic. You're being a tourist in El Salvador."

"Kind of," she said.

I was silent.

"There are a lot of surfers here. This is a famous place for surfing."

"Well, I've never heard of it." My good mood was dissipating.

"Jesse, did you call to berate me again? Because honestly, I'm tired this morning." She was silent.

"Are you okay?"

There was a brief silence.

"Lucy?" I said.

"I just haven't been feeling great."

I closed my eyes. Latin America. She probably had some worm, a bug, some terrible disease. "Have you been taking, I don't know, anti-amoeba pills? Whatever it is you're supposed to take?"

"Please, Jesse," Lucy said. "I've been traveling for a long time. I know what to do."

It was true. It had been over two years since I'd seen my sister. Where was she staying? I wondered. In what kinds of places did she sleep? How did she get around? Was she still strapping on that REI backpack I watched her leave with? She had tried to look so assured, so grown-up, but she had gotten caught in the doorjamb and Ramon, who had come home with me for the weekend to see her off, had pushed her through it.

"Tell me about Punta Roca."

"It's fine," she said. "I'm fine. I was just calling to check in."

Did she sound weary? Perhaps, I thought, she was almost finished with this part of her life. El Salvador, though war-torn and gang-ridden, was at least a bit north, was it not?

"Thanks," I said. "That's sweet. Your Spanish must be awesome." I should tell her about the baby, I thought. About the Hispanic baby we might one day get to parent.

"It's good. I mean, Ramon says it's pretty good. How are you?"

"You guys speak in Spanish?"

"Sometimes. How are you anyway?"

"Fine. You know Ramon and I are doing our paperwork to adopt."

I could hear Lucy breathing. "That's great, Jess. That's so great."

"You didn't know?"

"No, I did."

"Who told you?"

"Ramon."

"Ramon? When?"

"A while ago, I guess, a month or so?"

"Oh," I said. "Well, you never said anything." I wondered if he told her in Spanish and suddenly I thought of my sister and my husband and my hypothetical child all sitting around and having a blast in Spanish as I ran back and forth from the kitchen bringing regional snacks and trying to understand.

"I haven't talked to you much." Lucy cleared her throat.

"There's also e-mail."

"I thought we'd be able to talk," she said. "There's not a lot of e-mailing here."

"Anyway."

"I think this is good news, though."

"You think?" I asked her. "Well then it must be!" I was becoming furious, but I could not say why that was.

"Yes," she said. "I do. All those hormones, after everything you've been through, I just don't know if that was good for you. Being pregnant could be difficult too for you, I mean, if all that stuff had worked."

"Stuff."

"Okay, treatments."

"Hmm," I said. The sound of judgment. I guess I didn't like it much either.

"How are you feeling? Can I help with anything?" she asked.

"You mean physically?"

"Both," she said. "Are you feeling okay?"

"Yes," I said, tensing up. "I feel just fine."

"How's your stomach? Are you able to eat okay?"

"Yes." But I no longer wanted to discuss it with her.

There was silence.

"And how about the adoption? Are you excited?"

"Excited? No. Feeling hopeful," I said. "Cautiously optimistic,"

I told her, though this was just something I had read that I was supposed to feel.

"Being positive is important."

I didn't respond. People were always telling me such things. Had this all happened because I had been negative? Like Ramon and I just had fantastically awful karma? I made another mental note not to send my hypothetical child to school in California. "Yes," I said. "It is. Anyway, you're surfing in El Salvador, right?" El *Salvador*. It might be a fascinating place. Our future baby could have biological parents from there.

More breathing. But I noted that it seemed quiet, in Punta wherever. I tried to picture my sister, tan, her legs smooth, the color of Bambi, and easy on a board. Instead I kept picturing her at her eighth-grade dance, a huge corsage strapped to her wrist, waiting for her date to arrive. Now I didn't hear the sounds of people or traffic or the sea breaking hard on the shore. "I'm not surfing, but yes, there is surfing here. It's actually the largest break in Latin America."

"I don't even know what that means."

Lucy laughed. "It's good is what it means. People come from all over to catch the waves here."

"Okay!" I said. "Dude."

She laughed. "In any case, all's well. Seems like we're both fine! I should get going, but maybe we can talk again soon."

"Okay," I said. "Talk to you soon then."

"Kiss Harry for me," she said before hanging up.

I smiled when she said this, but I had the worst feeling, when I hung up, that I had missed the purpose of our conversation, that we both had. We had been apart for so long and no longer knew how to speak, other than as strangers. How are you feeling? we said, but what we meant was, Where are you? Who are you now? Are you still in there?

The next day, Ramon and I were back on the road—albeit this time just for a forty-five-minute jaunt to White Plains—for our information session with the organization that, as our agency did not have an office in New York, would be handling our local paperwork and doing our home study. The moment we got on the Brooklyn-Queens Expressway, we hit traffic.

"About tonight," Ramon said now. "Let's try and let other people talk a little tonight, okay?"

"What do you mean?" I asked.

"Other people need to talk," he said.

"Well, I'm sorry." Wounded, I gazed longingly out at the road.

"Me for instance. Or anyone. You could really just let anyone talk."

"Oh sure!" How easily can hurt become anger? Far too easily. "Sure. And why don't you try and not say something completely stupid then. Okay?"

"I said *let's*. I did not say you. God, Jesse."

"Yes you did," I said. "I know what you meant. I know exactly what you meant." I felt the anxiety filling me, water poured over ice, crackling, in a tall glass. Please, I thought, let us just not be late.

"Of course you did. Because you take over every conversation we ever have. Stupid?" Ramon was incredulous, his hand thumping the wheel. "What, may I ask, do you find that I say to be so stupid?"

"Let's see." I placed a finger to the side of my cheek, replicating a person deep in thought. "Calling people who are in charge of getting us a child the wrong name? Stupid. Telling the entire group that we didn't agree how we were going to raise our children with regards to religion? Also stupid."

"We agreed when we signed on for this," Ramon said, "that we were going to be ourselves. Isn't that what we agreed? It's the only way I can do this."

"Let me explain something to you." I turned toward Ramon, whose hand rested on the gearshift, waiting for traffic to abate. "This?" I pointed from myself to him and back to me again. "Not therapy. We are not here to explain everything. To understand ourselves. We are here to present ourselves in the best possible light."

Ramon grunted. "We said we were going to be honest."

"To each *other*!" I curled my hands around an invisible giant bowl, playing to an invisible audience. "And yes, in the letter, we didn't want to misrepresent ourselves, absolutely. We want to be natural—and this is hard because there seems to be a format for it all—but not so that people *question* us. As parents!"

Ramon stared ahead. More traffic.

"You know what?" I sat back in the seat. "I'll just try not to talk too much."

"That would really be best, because sometimes you're exhausting," Ramon said.

We were silent. I had lost it then, the memory of Ramon, beautiful Ramon, coming toward me in that café in Rome; his whole body silvery and smooth and filled with light in the dark cave of the Grotto; seated across from him in the restaurant in Brighton Beach, his cheeks red with steam and winter. How susceptible I was to the way good memories can slide away.

I turned up the radio. Today's news: a woman had recently been incarcerated for throwing her baby into a Dumpster. She'd given birth in a bathroom, unaided and alone, and had then thrown her baby out the bathroom window.

We wondered—I know Ramon did, too, because we were for just one moment not cruel to each other—why that couldn't have been our baby. Why couldn't the baby in the Dumpster have been our Grace? Perhaps, we thought, that infant, thrown into the air and landing in a cushion of New York City garbage, had been the baby meant for us.

When we arrived in White Plains, we parked in a mall, in front of a blazing Bed Bath and Beyond.

"Hurry *up,* Ramon."

He fretted. Tonight, leaving the car involved a series of inspections. Were the windows secured? The sunroof shut? (It had not, as I reminded him, been opened since September.) Was the moon roof that covered the sunroof also closed tightly, its shroud pulled over the smoked glass like an eyelid? Was the heat set to off? The radio? Best to turn it on and then off again and then on and then off, and the lights too. There are countless dials and knobs and switches to check before leaving an automobile, should you be the obsessive-compulsive person Ramon had become.

"Look," he said.

I sighed loudly.

"The car has to be left correctly." In order to enrage me and prove his point that I did everything in a negligent and cavalier fashion, his inspection was more drawn out than usual.

"Seriously?" I could feel my jaw clenching, my hands curling into fists. "Why are you *doing* this?" Again we would be late and all the babies would be taken by the sane and the prompt.

"Hmmm." Carefully he rose from his seat, looked again inside the car, running his hands along the driver's seat—feeling for what? A time bomb? Did he not know he was looking at one right *here?*— before he straightened and then leaned over the top of the car toward me. "Jesse," he said. "You really have to be more patient."

I was like sound. I was faster than sound; I was light. I was not aware that I was at his side of the car until I was there, and once I arrived, I pushed him by the shoulders, hard, slipping on black ice and then catching myself. "Are you kidding me?" I screamed. "We're going to be late. Again!" Already I felt our possibilities diminishing, candles on a birthday cake, burning out.

Ramon looked up at the nameless, faceless office tower we were headed toward. The building was dark except for a large room about six floors up, bathed in warm light. Several people moved around inside, pouring coffee and greeting one another.

"Nice." Ramon shook me off. "I hope you realize that everyone can see you. Everyone just saw you." He smiled.

I closed my eyes. Then I turned away from my husband and made my way to the building. I pulled open the door and stepped into the cold, sterile, and empty lobby, where I waited for him so that we could take the elevator up to the sixth floor and enter the agency office together. Led by the sound of chatter, we walked toward a conference room with a wall of windows that looked out onto the black parking lot, nearly empty but for a few scattered cars, including ours.

"Hello?" I said.

Ramon walked past me. "Hi!" he exclaimed to the room. "I'm Ramon, and this is Jesse! Did we miss anything?"

Everyone smiled at him. "Everyone" included a social worker— dark hair escaping in curled tendrils from a scarf she'd wrapped around her head—and her assistant, who, pudgy, with white-blond hair and watery blue eyes, looked uncannily like Tiffany and Crystal. They both stood at the front of the room by a dry-erase board and before them were two couples and a woman seated alone.

I smiled shyly and pulled out a chair.

"I hope we haven't kept you waiting," Ramon told the room.

"Not at all," the social worker said. "We're still waiting on another couple. We were just introducing ourselves. I'm Lydia, and this is our newest addition to the White Plains family, Marie."

Ramon flashed me a triumphant grin as he sat down. "So nice to meet you, *Lydia*!" he said.

Lydia smiled. Her freckles twitched and she straightened her head scarf. Marie waved wanly.

I cleared my throat and looked around the room. One couple was Caucasian, easily pushing fifty, and the other was an Asian woman and an African-American man. There was also a woman alone, also black, with short, cropped hair and bright red glasses. I sat back. I love New York, I thought as another couple walked into the room.

When everyone was settled around the table, Lydia stood at the front of the room.

"I'd like to just take a second to speak about the history of adoption, if you don't mind. I'd like to give some context of where we are now."

She had me at *context,* and already I liked her for her attention to scholarship. And also? I could tell she was Jewish. I registered this, as I registered all the ethnicities we had discussed, because Lydia was likely the first Jewish person I had encountered in this adoption process. I also wondered if the birthmothers were making their decisions to bring a child to term based on their religious beliefs, would they ever give their child to a Jew, even if her mother-in-law, a strict Catholic, went to mass each Sunday and stood in line at the Vatican for seven hours in order to be the proud possessor of rosaries blessed by the Pope himself? Even if her father loved Christmas? Lydia's presence created and alleviated that anxiety, simultaneously.

She shuffled through her disordered stack of papers, as if she were giving a paper at a conference. And I was waiting: for a lecture on how we got here, as a *people*.

"So, adoption in this country," she began, her voice gravelly and deep, tremulous, perhaps from nerves. The best listeners get the best babies, I thought, rapt.

"So the first law recognizing adoption and its regulations was in 1851, in Massachusetts. In the next twenty years several placement agencies were established, and soon adoptions really began to climb." Lydia scratched at the side of her head and looked out at us. And then she continued. "A new culture in America started to place a premium on the innocence and vulnerability of children, and helping them, which was at odds with the more dominant idea that a poor person's child would disrupt a superior gene pool. So began the rise of eugenics," Lydia said, looking up from her notes. "You know eugenics?"

Five out of seven of us knew eugenics.

"It was a 'science.'" Lydia used her fingers as air quotation marks. "It was used to 'improve' genetics. When the Nazis used it, well, then it really fell out of favor."

I smiled. She said *Nazis*.

"And so, soon homes for unwed mothers became safe places for pregnant women, and often an adoption could take place just after the child was born, especially as the use of formula was becoming quite common," Lydia told us.

Everyone in the room had a physical reaction. The single woman bobbed her head furiously, as did I. Of course the invention of formula would have this effect, just as one small thing—the zipper, for instance—can alter history's meandering course. Perhaps this process could become interesting to me so that I might get through it, heart intact, I thought. I imagined building a class around this material—"For Safekeeping: A History of Women and Adoption in America"—as Ramon sat back, legs spread, head tilted in listening position.

"Also during this time," Lydia continued, "there was something called the orphan trains."

"Oh yes," someone said. "I read about these just the other day."

I glared. I did not care what anyone but Lydia had to say about the orphan trains.

"Well, these trains brought children from the industrialized East Coast out to the plains, the dust bowl, so they could be placed in foster homes. Some of these children, mind you, were not orphans; their parents simply could no longer care for them. Some were street kids. The fortunate ones found loving families, older couples that could not have children. Others, though, were thought of more as cheap labor and were treated very poorly, almost like indentured servants. As attitudes in the country began to change and move toward keeping families together, new laws began to prohibit out-of-state placement, and the orphan trains stopped in 1929. Now," Lydia said, "what else in this country affected adoption?"

We all looked at one another. "The Great Depression?" someone offered.

"Well, yes, that's true, the economy always has an effect, but that's not what I'm thinking about," Lydia responded.

"War?" Ramon said.

Lydia nodded.

Go Ramon! I thought.

"War always affects adoption, as it affects families so profoundly. And war orphans in the fifties really set the stage for international adoption. But in regards to domestic adoption, which I suppose is more our concern tonight, what happened later?"

"Roe v. Wade." I did not ask it. Because I *knew*. I sat back, professorial, all my fingertips touching.

"Absolutely. Abortion was legalized. When?"

"January 22, 1973." I practically screamed the date.

"Yes, that's correct. In 1973 abortion was legalized. And with that, maternity homes began to decline, and adoption was presented less as an option for women. Two Supreme Court cases increased legal rights for birthfathers and a few states enacted laws requiring birthmothers to name the father of the baby. This made things very complicated. And so international adoptions increased well into the eighties and nineties."

The invention of formula, the pill, a wire hanger, a court decision—we are all changed by it. This is why I love history. We are a living, breathing part; it affects us and we affect history. Even the word—*history*—is beautiful, I thought, remembering that brief period in college when I insisted on calling my history of the enlightenment class "Enlightenment Herstory." *Herstory,* I insisted, would be passed down through the mothers of Diderot and Descartes and Kant and Spinoza. It was the mothers, and not their sons, who made herstory.

"But now, with the Hague Laws, international adoption is terribly complicated. Those in a queue for international adoption can expect to wait about four years."

We all nodded gravely. I did the math and a sack of butterflies let loose in my stomach.

"Most adoptions—international and domestic—up until about the nineties were closed. The research shows how negative this has been for the children who have been adopted, as well as for the birthmothers, even the adoptive parents, who want more information about their children's backgrounds, their medical histories." Lydia paused to look around the room. She smiled. I could see a space between her two front teeth. Before it closed naturally, I had this space too, and everyone told me that it meant good luck. "You are all here because you believe in some way in open adoption—and how open it will be differs with each situation—but now over eighty percent of all domestic adoptions have some degree of openness."

Lydia looked up, her minilecture complete. She asked us all to introduce ourselves, by way of how we came to adoption, if this was something we were *comfortable* with.

Ramon sat up straight and tall, which seemed to indicate that he was going to speak.

First.

"I was *not* a fan of IVF," Ramon began.

As he started to speak my neck and shoulders grew tight and I gripped the sides of my chair to calm myself.

"It was Jesse who really wanted to do these treatments, and so I relented. But so many times! I really didn't want to, I felt that it was wrong, when there are so many children who need homes. Also, it's just not healthy and I felt it was terribly bad for her, for Jesse, and, to be honest, I'm not sure how all those hormones and drugs affect her and these children."

Inside, I was a crazed lunatic. This was not the beginning of our story. It was not the beginning of *my* story anyway. Inadvertently I placed my fingers, ice pack–like, over my left eye.

"That's not really the beginning, though," I said, removing my hand. Would he mention that we were out of money? Because that could preclude us from getting a baby. Would he mention that word—*cancer*—because that could very well do it too. I couldn't remain silent. "I mean, that's not really exactly why we came to adoption, because you didn't want to do IVF anymore, is it?" I asked Ramon.

I could feel the temperature of the room change as people shuffled their feet. Lydia looked at us with unconcealed interest.

Ramon scanned the room. He swallowed hard. I watched his Adam's apple move along the knobby spinelike track of his throat. "We are so happy to be here." He looked around the table, eyes glistening. "And very relieved."

My limbs loosened, the tension in my body draining. Perhaps this would not be a mutiny after all. I nodded my head. "We are really really relieved."

"Everyone here is coming from a different place," Lydia told the group. "But I think we can all recognize that adoption is not always everyone's first choice. That's the reality, and everyone's journey here is different. Even those in couples often feel differently about it."

I nodded. The tone was so all-encompassing that I could see us dabbing patchouli behind our ears, joining hands, and breaking into "Kumbaya." And while I was grateful Ramon did not mention our finances or my illness, I understood his urge to discuss them both. Ramon was making less money now, and we owed an irresponsible amount for doctor and hospital bills. My job was not secure. I was a cancer survivor—it was only because the cancer had been in remission for almost fifteen years that we were even entitled to pursue domestic adoption at all—and I wondered if that could be considered an ethnicity of some kind, if there could be affirmative action for the almost-died.

I remembered it then, that moment just before I was to have my first and rather sudden surgery. My mother led the surgeon by his elbow, out of the room. Doctor, she'd said—I could hear her, and she was so plaintive, my mother, who up until that moment, I had always seen in charge—will she be able to have children?

Yes, of course, he had said, and even through the haze of pain medication I'd thought he was one of those doctors who can close a woman down with a mere nod of the head.

My mother had come back into the room. You can still have children, my mother told me, taking my hand.

Jesus, Mom, I'd said. I don't give a shit about children right now. I remember that I said this.

You will, my mother had said, patting my hand. I know that you will.

"Thank you." I dipped my head to Lydia. I looked across the table at the single woman, so that she might continue the introductions, ensuring our story would end there, for now, willing myself, just this once, to be silent.

"Well," the single woman began. "I had to make a decision. It was now or never . . ."

The last person to speak that night was Lisa, of the white couple. I learned she was, in fact, in her early fifties. She was tall and thin, and pinched and plain and nervous and sad. The man looked younger and more dapper in his tie and hat, and he was fidgety as his wife spoke, gazing around the room with a glazed expression. I did not like him in the least.

"I'm Lisa and this is my husband, Danny. We are here because we want to foster a child again," she began, clearing her throat. I watched her long bony fingers work themselves. "We are older, I know, and Danny already has a child, a girl, who is grown." She looked down at her hands.

Danny's legs were crossed and the top one kicked vigorously, rocking his upper body. He looked at his watch.

"We were fostering a boy until a little over eight months ago." She took a huge breath and stopped suddenly, as if her heart had caught in her expanding chest. "He died!" she said, with more emphasis than I know she'd intended. "He was four years old. We'd been fostering him for two years. He had congenital heart failure."

I closed my eyes and opened them again. And I could feel Ramon do the same.

"We are ready"—Lisa looked down at the table—"to do this again. Adoption is just not an option for us. We're older now. So we would like to foster again. I would. Danny's daughter, she never lived with us. She's all grown up, you see."

My throat was again tied, as if with a large needle and coarse thread. Everyone in the room nodded, our wobbling heads an affirmation that this woman should—*please*—be able to foster a child again. I placed my elbows on the table, and my hands, together, pressed at my mouth, and I swallowed hard through that rough, prickly embroidery. I heard Ramon breathing, hard. Like images of dogs suffering at the hands of cruel humans, wounded birds, an old woman alone on a crowded street, I knew this story, too, would undo him. Because about all the things that mattered we were the *same,* and I was grateful and ashamed.

How many ways can a person feel shame? That night, after hearing Lisa's story, this unremitting shame was for me like the Eskimo words for snow: varied, numerous, precise, particular to any one aspect of the thing itself. I was ashamed for our behavior in the parking lot out front, for my behavior, and I was ashamed for the reckless way I had often treated my marriage, for my disregard of Ramon, and how I'd buried his want of a child in and beneath my own. Were it not for me, Ramon could have had a family. I was physically in the way of that wish, and I was lucky that he was willing to go through this with me, lucky that the family he desired was the same family I wished for. I was ashamed of my self-pity, and my glibness, the privilege of my relative youth. I was ashamed of kissing Anita beneath a frozen star-filled night. I was ashamed that I had not told Ramon, and now time had passed, and I could not. I was ashamed of the boxes I checked on those forms, of my wishes for a healthy child, for an infant, someone we might bring up from infancy and somehow call our own. I was ashamed of the boxes I had not checked, and I was ashamed of capitalism and this country that fueled it, and so my need to own, for my unwillingness to give that proprietorship up.

The room stirred first with stunned sadness and its effects—cleared throats, shifting seats, the rustle of clothes being pulled and straightened—the sounds of the humbling of humans who had previously had the privilege of shaming others with their own dismal plights.

Then Lydia stood up. "Thank you all for sharing your stories," she said. "I know it's hard to do. Now, let's take a look at the paperwork we'll need to do for the home study aspect of your process."

Relieved, we stared at yet another packet of paperwork. I pushed ours toward Ramon. It sat between us for a moment, until, with the tips of his fingers, he slid the folder toward himself, and then, slowly, as if he were creaking open a rusty old door, Ramon turned to the application.

After the training session, we sailed home, no congestion on the road at all. It was a bright, clear January night, still very much the beginning of a new year. Perhaps this would be our year, I thought; don't we get to have one? I looked up at the stars that punctured through that deep night blue, piercing, glinting, even this close to the city.

I will be good, I thought. I will be positive. I will try to get the life I had before all this happened back. I will hold on to my memories that are so quickly lost but can return as well at any moment, evidence of love. I apologize for my self-pity, for my obscene wanting. I will think about Lisa.

I watched the susurration of the swaying treeless branches in the moonlight, and I had this thought: I am getting closer to you. Closer and closer. I can feel it. I can feel you out there, I thought. Truly, I did.

14

—

March 2010

"O kay, ready?"

"Yup."

"You go."

"No, why don't you read yours first?"

"Okay, okay, Jesse." Ramon ran both his hands through his hair. "I'll go, but I'm not done with it yet."

"Just read what you have then."

"Okay. So. 'I was born in Madrid, Spain, in 1969,' Ramon read from his laptop. 'When I was two years old my father, who is Spanish and a geologist, got a job working with BP.' Can you believe it?" He looked up at me. "BP of all things." He shook his head. "'We moved to the Netherlands, where we stayed for two years. From there, due to his job, we moved every three to four years. We lived in Gabon, Africa; England; Argentina; Colombia; and back to the Netherlands, where I finished high school and from where I came to the States for college.'" Ramon looked up. "What do you think?"

I shrugged. "I guess that's as good a place to start as any."

"I'm using the guidelines." He rubbed his fingers over his chin, with the dimple I have always believed to be the imprint of his mother's watchful finger.

"But it's the autobiography part."

"Yes, but I want to be sure to address all the items in the guidelines. I'm doing it in one go."

"Okay," I said. "Go."

He cleared his throat. "'Growing up I remember my father working long hours and also helping my mother and me adjust to the new countries we moved to. He was a great resource. As an avid reader, he'd tell us tales and the history of the countries we were about to embark to. Moving and adjusting to new countries and cultures was hard and I remember these moments with my father. They subdued the apprehension that the moving always created. My mother, who is Italian, and had never left Italy before meeting my father, had great anxiety each time we left somewhere.'"

"I didn't know that," I said.

Ramon looked up from the screen. "That my mother had anxiety?"

"No. That I am well aware of. I didn't know that your dad read to you about the places you were headed to." He nodded and then began again. "'All this moving forged a very strong bond between my mother and me. She was my guardian, and often, my best friend. She was a stay-at-home mom and was always around when I came home from school. Maybe even overly protective at times, but understandably so, as a lot of the environments I grew up in were quite dangerous.

"'Because of that, my mother kept me home a lot. My hardest times were adjusting to the new schools and making new friends with children that I often had nothing in common with. I remember moving to Venezuela and attending an American school after

145

three years of living in England, where I was enrolled in a strict private boys' school. I wore short trousers and had a British accent. That was a tough adjustment and something I wouldn't necessarily want for my child, since young children can't always understand why someone is different. Sometimes children respond with cruelty. I will always make sure that if we do move to a new environment that the transition for my child is as seamless as possible.'"

"Cruelty?"

Ramon swallowed. "Yes. I was bullied a great deal."

"I didn't know that," I said.

He nodded again. "Sometimes I had to stay home from school. There was this kid who waited for me every day to beat me up. He beat me several times, but I didn't want to alarm my mother, so I just said I fell while running track, or this kind of thing. I'm not sure she believed me, but she never asked anything else about it."

"I'm so sorry!" I pictured my husband as a boy in little gray wool shorts, scared and vulnerable, which affected me strangely. Pity is not love, but it can feel just like it sometimes.

He continued reading. "'My parents came from a different time and place in the world. Both grew up in postwar Europe and so had difficult upbringings where the focus was on the basics of existence. In raising me, I see now that these basic needs like food and shelter took precedence over my emotional and psychological health. I was taught right from wrong, and I listened well, but with my own children, while I obviously want to care for their physical needs, assure their safety, I'd also like to be a father aware of their emotional weather, too.'"

"I like that part," I said. "'Emotional weather.'" I wondered whether our child would be sunny or stormy. Emotional weather. It can change so quickly.

"'After I moved to the U.S. to study, my parents continued mov-

ing around the world until, after four years in Indonesia, their marriage ended. My mother now lives in her birthplace, Terracina, Italy,
and my father lives in Java.'"

"Are you going to explain?"

"No," Ramon said.

"It's kind of abrupt though."

"I don't think it would be good for us to discuss it."

I nodded. I had inadvertently learned what had actually happened to Ramon's father on that first visit to his mother's. It was the
middle of the night, and I had woken up to the sound of chanting
and the distinct smell of smoke, something burning. I tiptoed by
Ramon's bed and out into the marble foyer, which led to Paola's
room.

There she stood, stooped, her white fleshy arms waving in the
dark. Her hair had come unfurled, her face was draped over a
lighted candle, and she waved incense around the room. The wall
was strewn with crosses and golden icons, and candles, the kind
they sell at bodegas in my Brooklyn neighborhood, surrounded her.

Paola was spellbound—almost possessed—and before she
could look up to face me, I ran back to Ramon's room and shook
him awake. "Ramon," I said. "Something is wrong with your
mother!"

He sat up and threw the covers off, instantly vigilant, a cat poised
to make his own kill. He paused this way, all bone and sinew, senses
alert, and then he let out his breath, closed his eyes, and relaxed his
shoulders. "She's okay," he said.

"Oh." I sat on his bed, readying for the story.

"Don't sit here!" he said. "She might see!"

"Are you kidding me?" I stood up. "Your mother is having a fit
or experiencing the rapture and you're worried about her seeing
me on your bed?"

"Okay, okay." His hand made a circular gesture in the air, Italian-style. "Calm down."

"Do not tell me to calm down. A word of advice? Don't tell any woman to calm down. Ever."

"She's putting a hex on the woman who stole her husband," Ramon said.

"Your father?"

"The woman who stole my father."

"A hex."

He nodded.

"Please, Ramon."

He leaned back on his elbows. "I'll tell you in the morning."

"No." I stamped my bare foot and it made a slapping sound. "Tell me now."

Ramon sat up again and rubbed his forehead. "Okay, so my parents were living in Jakarta and my father disappeared and then he returned a month later married to another woman. She was a Muslim woman and he had just become a Muslim, just out of the blue. He invited my mother to stay with them, and of course she refused, so she had to leave and come back to Italy. She believes the woman was involved with black magic." He ducked his head so he could see out the window. "She does this on nights when there is a full moon. Okay?"

"My God," I said. "That's awful."

"Now you know."

I sat across from Ramon and as I nodded, gradually, his face began to shift. I turned around, slowly, and, as if summoned, Paola stood in the threshold of the door. Moonlight fell over her long black hair and her black eyes, which made the crevassed terrain of her face a ghostly white. I screamed, and then placed my hands over my mouth, to stop myself.

"Paola!" My heart went out to her, left all alone on the other side of the world. Her husband married to another woman. A Muslim! Her son bringing home an American Jew! This woman from this little teensy Catholic place at the unstable heel of Europe's torn shoe.

She crossed her arms. "You!" she said, pointing to the other bed. "What are you doing here? Get in your own bed."

My eyes went wide. I had wanted to talk about her life. I had wanted to place my hand softly on her forearm to tell her I was sorry for what had happened. I will help with this hex, I wanted to tell her. Can I light some candles for you?

"Get to your own bed, now!" Paola said.

Speechless, I scurried across the room, scrambling under the sheets. I pulled them up to my chin and watched the moon hanging over the fields—a harvest moon, huge and round and trembling and white.

I could hear Ramon follow his mother into her room and reprimand her in Italian. I could smell the candles, snuffed out, the smoke of the extinguished incense. But I didn't move. Not when Ramon returned, mumbling an apology. Not when he crawled into his bed and went instantly to sleep. I stayed that way, my hands shaking beneath those vinegar-scented sheets, until the moon faded into the sky and, finally, it was morning.

"Yes," I said now, to Ramon. "Best just to say he's with a new family now. That you are not too terribly in touch."

"That we talk but don't see each other. Just if I'm asked," Ramon said. "If." He adjusted the screen again, scanning the document for the place where he'd left off. "'I was alone growing up,'" Ramon continued. "'I felt really alone. My schools were initially hard to adjust to, but due to my athletic abilities—I held most of the track and field records in my class and was on most of the sports teams, soccer being a sport I excelled in—I was able to find my place.'"

"What?" I said. "Track? Come on."

"I did! You know why I had to walk around like this?" He got up from his chair and hung his head and his shoulders low, his back stooped, as if he was imitating an elephant for a child.

"Why?"

"So many medals!" He sat back down and crossed his arms. "It's true. So many medals it was difficult to stand up straight."

I clapped my hands and laughed. I pictured him running through some ribbon on a dusty track in a country I'd never been to, waving his arms in victory.

"'My favorite subjects were art and geography, yet I was very good at math and physics, and until about halfway through college I wanted to be an architect.'"

"Is this how your mother got the idea for you to build the house?"

"Are you going to let me finish? It's my autobiography, stop interrupting!" he said, but he was smiling. "'My friends through tenth grade were for the most part the "outsiders," kids who, like myself, had come from other countries, as well as the geeky kids.'"

"I can't believe they ask that—about what kinds of kids we spent time with in high school."

"I think it's interesting. I think who we are in high school matters. Because people don't really change, do they? I mean, really, fundamentally? Not so much." He turned to read again. "'My friends and I spent a lot of our time playing Dungeons and Dragons and video games. It was only when we moved back to the Netherlands for the end of high school, where everyone was from another country, that I finally found acceptance and got along with everyone. I also finally dated a girl.'"

"Ooh," I said. "A girl." But people do change. I thought of Lucy.

From horseback rider to fake ID–bearing, white-faced, red-lipped clubgoer, to solo traveler. But that's only the outside.

"Yup. Magdalena Cortada. She was quite something." He looked back down at the screen.

"Well, if the name is any indication . . ."

"'It was when I got to college, though, that I was finally able to accept who I was and even appreciate my uniqueness. What had been a curse till then finally became an asset.'"

"I can imagine." I liked my husband's difference, and the way it turned into ease when we traveled, how he shifted effortlessly from English to Spanish and how we received different treatment in the world—shelter from a storm in Costa Brava, special tapas in Barcelona, an upgraded hotel room in Madrid—because of this.

"'My mother is a wonderful cook who grows all her produce on her farm in Italy. Jesse gets along great with my mother, whom we visit every summer. We spend two to three weeks with her and enjoy every minute of it.'" He glared at me, his head cocked to the side.

"Absolutely." I nodded vigorously. "I can't get enough of Paola's farm." The truth was I had grown to like it there: the town, the proximity to other towns, and the food and the sky there and the way the lemon trees smelled, the way the wine tasted, all of it sun-kissed. As an extra bonus, a few years after that night, Paola even allowed us to close the door to the bedroom.

"'My mother and my extended family in the village are an important part of my life. Having grown up all over the world, Terracina, which I've visited for almost every summer of my life, has been the one constant place I've gone to.'"

"Umm, Ramon?" I interrupted. "Just say your father lives with a new family in Indonesia and you don't really speak as often as you'd like."

"Okay," he said.

"Be careful." What if it seems like your family is broken? I thought. Perhaps it is broken.

"Okay. Where was I? Oh yes, here. 'Jesse and I met in Italy, too. It was a strange confluence of events—I was early to meet friends, and I just stepped into this church on a whim. I had not been inside before and I saw Jesse standing there. It was magical. Her hair was pulled back and I could see just the very tip of her profile and she looked both familiar and other. I knew that I would marry her.'"

"Really?" I remembered Saint Apollonia's skull lighting up, and then fading out, a heartbeat, and how Ramon told me that the relics were not real. None of them, he'd said. You didn't know that?

I had not. I had believed that the relics were real. Part of me still believes that all the relics in all the churches have been real.

"That's sweet, Ramon. Did you really know though?"

"I did. Even then. I do love you, Jesse."

I looked at my husband. There he was. "I love you too."

We were silent a moment.

"That was really beautiful," I said.

"Now you." Ramon pointed at my papers.

I took a deep breath, but I couldn't catch it. Then another.

"I'll start here," I began. "'My sister, Lucy, and I are three and a half years apart. I remember her always as a baby. One of my clearest early memories, cast in this fuzzy light, is her coming home from the hospital on a warm November day, my mother bringing her out of the wood-paneled station wagon to show her to me. My sister lives abroad now, and we talk as often as we can.'"

I stopped again. "That's not really true though. We have to be truthful."

"Like with my father?"

"Well. Let's not do ourselves in here, Ramon."

"It is true, though. You do talk when you can. We both do. I love talking to Lucy."

"You do?" I asked.

"We spoke the other night when you weren't here. She told me that some restaurant she started with her boyfriend in Panama City went under, which was why she left, I guess. She seems like she's doing great."

"Her boyfriend?"

"Yes," Ramon said. "That kid Greif."

The restaurant had failed? With her boyfriend? Greif? She hadn't told me that. She'd merely said she was moving on. Was he still with her? I didn't know this because I hadn't asked her. "Oh," I said to Ramon. "I didn't know that."

He looked at me funny. "The guy she's been traveling with for the past six months. Her boyfriend. The one from that wealthy family on Ojai."

I thought of my sister now, watching the largest break in Latin America. I saw her on the sand, knees curled into her chest, her chin on her knees, and I remembered walking in the woods by our parents' house with Harriet, several years previously, before Lucy had left the country.

Look what they've done to the high school!, we said to each other as we passed it in the car on the way to the park; the building where we'd spent those years now had a structure of steel and glass connecting its red brick wings.

It was a crisp, sunny day and the park was crowded with dogs and their owners, couples leisurely strolling along the paved path that led in and out of the woods. Old leaves crunched beneath us.

"Mom seems older," I said, as the high school, so sleek and modern now, had surely made me think about the passage of time. "Don't you think?"

Lucy turned to look at me, her face framed by long, tousled hair, as if she'd just risen from bed. "I think I'm going to leave," she said.

I had nodded and we continued walking in silence.

"Did you hear me?" Lucy stopped on the path.

"I did." I watched a golden retriever gambol in and out of the creek that ran parallel to the path.

"Do you want to know where I'm going?" she asked me.

"Sure," I had said, but I recognize now I hadn't thought she was going anywhere. I had lost sight of Harriet and so I called her name and soon she came bounding back to us, tail wagging. "I hear you, Lucy."

"Are you going to ask me then?" Lucy still hadn't moved.

I looked at my sister, her hands on her hips, incredulous. Behind her, the retriever leapt for a small branch his owner threw from the other side of the low-running creek. "Lucy!" I exclaimed sarcastically. "Where are you headed?"

"I don't know yet," she said.

I had laughed at her then, shaking my head and rolling my eyes.

Lucy walked away from me. "Somewhere far away," she said, continuing on the path toward the woods. "You'll see."

Now I looked at Ramon. "I didn't know any of that," I said. I felt my face redden. I could feel it, the way I do sometimes in class when I am really into a point I'm making. "So do you think it's okay we're doing this as a whole piece? Not answering the questions all individually? Like: my first memory was this, and so on?"

Ramon smiled.

"What?"

He rubbed his forehead. "Can I just say? You are going to be such a good mother."

"Thanks."

"And?"

"And you will be a great father." I pictured Ramon again, bending down, guiding a toddler by the thumbs.

"Thank you."

"Maybe going through all of this will make us better parents," I said. "Together."

Ramon closed his laptop. "Together."

I watched Harriet open her eyes and wobble awake.

And then I read Ramon the rest of my story.

15

———

I was "advising" a student, a term I use loosely as the curriculum requirements continually change without my knowledge, in my "office," another approximation, as several of my colleagues banged on their computers nearby, when Lucy called my cell.

"Well, hello!" she said.

I put my hand up to the student to signify it would be a moment, and I moved out into the hallway.

Lucy was in Belize now, in a place called Sweetwater Key, where, I gathered, the surfing was no good, but the fishing was amazing.

"The country's mostly reef," Lucy explained. "There's this place, Glover's Reef, where the surfing is decent, but it's super expensive. What's the point, you know? There's so much else to see."

"And anyway, how much surfing can a person do?" I asked. "Especially someone who's not a surfer."

"Jesus Christ," she said. "I am a surfer and the answer is never enough! But I'm not surfing now. Anyway, Greif has been doing lessons and stuff. It's how we've had money to travel."

"Greif of the Greek restaurant?"

"That was just an experiment. A failed one, admittedly, but we thought people would like that in Panama. The food can get so monotonous when you're traveling in a country for a long time. Anyway, there's reef everywhere here and I've gotten kind of into saving this bird sanctuary. There's a nesting site for wading birds, like the roseate spoonbill, for instance. And herons. I met someone here in Sweetwater through Greif who was involved with advocating for this sanctuary."

"When did you get so into birds?" I walked slowly along the bridge, flanked by windows, connecting the two main liberal arts buildings of the college. On one side, I could see into an inner courtyard, where students stood sulking and smoking. Along the other side was the city street, where, on the sidewalk, a woman walked by with her daughter, who in turn pushed a stroller of her own.

"I've always been into birds," Lucy said. "Always. Since I was a kid. I love birds."

"I'm your sister. I grew up with you. I know who you were and you were not into birds."

"That just shows how little I was understood in our family," Lucy said. "I have always loved animals fiercely, most particularly birds."

I did not know if Lucy was being serious, though she seemed to have lost any sense of humor she'd had, due to, I was sure, those misspent years in Santa Cruz. "Okay," I said. "Sorry."

"In fact, I have a bird tattoo."

I laughed. "Well, that must make it so. Where?"

"I know. I know. I can't believe I said that. The small of my back. Of course." She laughed. "I also have a tattoo of a horse. At my hip bone. Did you know that?"

"A horse? No, God, I didn't know that." I thought of my sister's body, its folds and ripples, her blank page of a stomach but for this ridiculous horse in some low quadrant of her belly.

157

I too had a risible tattoo, also on my hip. Dolphins. I am that age. But I didn't say anything.

"So are the birds going to keep you there? Your love of them, I mean. Because we have birds here, too."

"Not going-extinct birds."

"I'm sure we do have those. I'm sure they're around the almost-extinct mangrove forests."

More silence.

"When are you going to just stay put is what I mean. I mean, we're not kids anymore, you know? Like when did you get that tattoo, Lucy?"

"Over ten years ago. I guess you just didn't notice."

"Oh," I said. I could not picture it, my sister's bird tattoo. Mine—two dolphins, entwined, ridiculous—was now faded, blurred. It was nearly twenty years old.

"But I know what you're saying. I've been thinking about coming back a lot," she said. "Coming home."

"Great!" I was very surprised to hear this. And also? I felt inexplicably happy at the thought of it. The kind of happy that, at this point, brought bright jewel tears to the corners of my eyes. "Any thought as to where you might do this?"

"I don't know." She hesitated in a manner indicating that she did know.

"Are you coming alone, Lucy?" I asked.

"No."

"But I mean are you, like, with someone?"

"Yes."

"Greif? Are you happy?"

"Yes. And I don't know. Are you happy?"

I thought of the last time I'd been happy. Hiking alone with Harriet made me happy. Happy. Lying on my stomach at the beach with

Ramon, turning the pages of a Victorian novel, the sound of the sea at our feet. Research. Eating makes me happy. And being right. "I have a lot of happy moments," I said. "Fleeting though."

"I know what you mean," Lucy said. "Just moments. I've been traveling for so long. I think I've been searching for happiness and really, I've been only having happy moments. Perhaps that's just it, you know? I mean, perhaps that's all we can hope for."

My student passed by on the breezeway. "I'm sorry!" I whispered to him. I pointed at the phone. "Long distance!" I said, as if we were living in pioneer times.

I did know. But our parents had raised us to achieve and be committed. That was happiness: success. And Lucy had bucked that, so shouldn't that have made her happy? "Well, I've been staying put here and doing kind of the same thing."

"Happiness." Lucy laughed. "I don't even know if that's what I've been going for. Like is happiness even a goal? Maybe it's just not one of my larger goals."

"I want a child." It just slipped out. I had lost any semblance of control over what I said and how I behaved. "But anyway, I don't know if I associate it with happiness. I suppose that's strange."

"I know," Lucy said. "I know that you do."

"Hey!" I said. "Come to New York. We've got a semi-comfortable uncomfortable couch."

She laughed again. "Maybe. We'd kill each other if I lived with you."

"I didn't say live!" I said. But briefly I imagined us with mugs of coffee, the blanket she'd cover herself with to sleep thrown over our legs as we talked into the afternoon. There we are, Lucy and me in my attic room. We are the ages I remember us as most often: I'm fourteen and she's eleven. I've just learned to put on eyeliner and mascara, and I'm leaning in, toward the full-length mirror. I've also learned to curl my hair, which I try to do so that it feathers out. Lucy leans on her elbow, watching intently from my bed. I'm getting ready for adventure, a night out with new friends. I put down my eyeliner and I look at Lucy, on my bed, leaning her head against my fading poster of James Dean.

Everything is stopped. When I turn back to the mirror, my face, now with makeup, framed by this strange hairstyle, looks foreign to me, and I both like that and fear that distance from myself. Everything is about to happen.

Lucy has been gone on this trip over five years.

When she told me that day in the woods that she was going away, I had not even thought to ask her where to, or when, why, even, and I see now I hadn't believed her. It was my mother who left. Lucy and I, we stayed. We were the stayers. I lived in New York and she lived in California. We saw each other only at moments of unusual intensity: our grandmother's funeral, where I tried to give a eulogy but could not, and where my sister had guided me, shaking, away from the bimah. At our cousin's wedding, where we sat at our designated table drinking champagne and watching everyone else dance. Look at that one, we said, laughing. We never danced at family weddings.

We had not lived together and fought for the bathroom or more mashed potatoes or space in the backseat of the car since she was fifteen.

"Well, offer's open," I said. It would be different this time. Now we were the same.

"Thanks, Jesse," Lucy said. "That's nice to know."

"Come home." I looked out at the students filing out of the courtyard for class.

And then my sister and I said good-bye.

Meanwhile, the photos. We were told we needed to take the main photo by foliage, preferably of the "seasonless" variety so that our profile would not be tethered to a time of year. We were to face front, our teeth exposed. This is what you need to know: if you do not smile with your teeth showing, you are not really smiling, not according to our adoption agency. You can be smirking, you can be leering, simpering, but you cannot be smiling in a way that a birthmother will interpret as joy, unless you are smiling teethily. Also, you must be touching.

This is what Ramon and I did one Sunday. We left Harriet at home and walked around our neighborhood, looking for trees that were not bare, bushes that were not brown, and hedges that were not dead. This is harder than one might imagine in Brooklyn in the lion part of March, but we found a solution. In the front gardens of several of our neighbors' was the coveted timeless foliage, large evergreens in one, trimmed hedges in another, a holly bush (was that seasonless?) around the corner. We opened and then closed gates, and ran inside. Ramon would find a stoop on which to place his camera, setting it to automatic, and then he'd run back to place his arm demurely around me as we flashed the camera our toothiest grins. Mostly, the camera shot too soon, as Ramon was reaching around me, which registered in the photo as if he were about to strike me, or too late, our smiles faded or forced, and we'd have to take the photo again, before the old Italian woman straight out of Terracina parted the curtains and sent her young beefy son out to shoo us away.

We might as well have waited until spring, when the crocuses pushed up through little boxes of wet earth, when the tulips, petals open like throats, black tongues wagging, were out in full force, as the text of that "Dear Birthmother" letter took ages to be approved. It needed to be revised again after it had been edited and re-edited and edited again, each time by a different social worker or branch director whose concerns negated the edits of the previous, which in turn needed to be edited. I felt I was in a Dantean sort of hell, where my students gathered to taunt me. Revising is an important aspect of our work, I'd tell them, and here, as revisions of our revisions were repeatedly returned, I felt all those chickens roosting. When all was said and done, it had taken approximately five months, and four different social workers and a director, to complete.

In its finality, this sacred text—more holy than the Dead Sea Scrolls—would appear in hard copy and digital form in both English and Spanish. Who would edit Ramon's translation was unclear. The holy text included our first and last names—a testament to our commitment to holy openness—and already the idea of my students finding this document online, reading this earnest text about our admiration for each other and my love of baking pies, which, in the end, was not as true to us in voice and tone as we'd once pledged, kept me up many nights.

What is opened and what is closed, I thought on those nights when I remembered Ellen Beskin, and my father pushing my sister and me on our wooden Flexible Flyer down the snow-covered hill at Shepherd Park, and also the earliest days of life with Ramon when just the way he smoked a cigarette made me want him. What is time moving and what is time standing still, and what will I do with all my memories, of everything that is finished? If you don't see the past growing in the future, do you lose them both? All I pictured on those bleak nights, my husband walled off by sleep, was sand spilling from the hourglass.

We were even hemorrhaging sand.

16

Lydia, who had spoken to us at our session in White Plains, turned up for our home study visit in a torrential downpour at the end of April. I had hired a professional cleaner to prepare for the occasion. When I called to book someone from a woman's co-op, I said to these strangers on the phone that we were having a home study visit, where a social worker comes to your home to make sure it's suitable for a child and that you and your partner are adoption material. It needs to be very very clean, I said. These women were expensive, but I was willing to pay extra for their days off and health insurance, so as not to be exploitative. When the woman came to clean, she said, You can't have babies? Her palms moved in circles over her stomach.

I looked at her hands, her short fingers, the bitten nails, circling and circling. Just make it clean, please, I told her.

I bought daffodils and set them in a little vase we keep on the mantel. We have several vases there, but rarely are they filled with flowers. I baked banana bread. In our birthmother letter there was the bit about the pies, but it was morning, and there was no reason for pie in the morning. Also? I don't really make pies. I could. I could absolutely bake a pie. And I would.

Magical thinking: the cleanest house, the best banana bread, the prettiest flowers, will yield the healthiest, most beautiful baby. I knew this was not true. This visit afforded a simple "approved" or "not approved." Couldn't it be, though, "highly approved," or "extremely approved," or "*significantly* approved"?

Lydia arrived dripping wet, and Harriet came out of the bedroom to greet her at the door, tail wagging.

"I don't like dogs." Lydia straightened. "But this one doesn't jump up, which is nice."

"She's amazing with kids." I took Lydia's raincoat, hanging it carefully on the rack behind the door.

"Old dogs usually are," she said.

Ramon stood, smiling broadly with teeth. "Well, she is. Hi, Lydia."

She smiled at Ramon and then she smiled down at Harriet in that distant way that people who are not dog people smile for dogs they are trying to make the owners think they like. "Good."

"Have a seat." I pulled a chair out from the dining room table, normally strewn with Ramon's papers and folders and invoices, but today wiped completely clean. "Coffee?" I asked.

"Sure." Her eyes wrinkled at the corners when she smiled. She had a batik scarf on her head that was shot through with gold and silver threads, tied at the nape of her neck, the way I used to wear a bandana in college. "Black," she said.

I went to the island by our dollhouse kitchen and poured her coffee in the china cups I'd set out. Once they had been my grandmother's. "Would you like some banana bread?" I unsheathed it from the tinfoil and Saran wrap I'd swaddled it in last night so it would retain its freshness. I wished I'd had the wherewithal to bake that morning so that now the smell of sugar and cinnamon—the smell of motherhood—would permeate the room, warming it on this rainy early-spring day.

She shook her head and looked up. "Just coffee."

My heart fell. I looked at Ramon, who had not moved from his position in front of the mantel, but was now starting to shift his limbs, as if his batteries had warmed up.

"None for me," he said. "Not now." Ramon looked at me and shrugged.

"We got your application, and I've read it, and you seem like such wonderful people."

"Oh, thanks," I said.

"Thank you," Ramon said.

"This is really a time for me to get to know you." We all leaned in around the table. "It should not be stressful at all. I'll just go over the forms—the employment history, your family information, the autobiography—and this will serve as a starting point for our discussion. Then I will quickly look around the place so I can draw a map of it for your home study document. We do not go through your drawers or open closets. It's really just to see how you live and if it would be appropriate for a child."

"Great," Ramon and I said.

He reached for my hand, and I took it.

Lydia saw this and smiled. "I am an advocate for you," she said. "I just want to get it all right. I hope you can see it this way."

Over the course of four hours we discussed our lives with Lydia. We went over it all again. What our parents did and didn't do, what they wanted for us and what they got and did not get for us. We discussed our jobs and why we wanted to adopt. How we came to adoption. It was an enjoyable conversation, talking about our lives together. It felt natural, helpful even.

Until the word came up.

"Let me just ask you about the cancer. It's a word that frightens many people."

I laughed. "With good reason," I said. "As it says on my physical forms, I have been cancer-free for almost fifteen years."

"That's wonderful." Lydia sipped her coffee from my grandmother's teacup.

"Would you like some banana bread now?" I asked. I had also bought a very beautiful hand-churned local farm butter at the farmer's market over the weekend, which I'd hoped to put out with an olive-wood knife I'd purchased in Italy several years before, made solely for the purpose of spreading soft butter.

She shook her head and continued on.

"Ramon?" I asked.

He also shook his head. "No, thanks."

I could not believe the betrayal.

"Now, to religion," Lydia said. "I understand that, Jessica, you're from a Jewish family, and you're from a Christian background, Ramon. What are your plans for raising children?"

"We're not religious," Ramon told her.

I imagined Paola, stealing our child away in the middle of the night to be baptized in the church where I'd seen Ramon's cousins' children, held up to the golden icons, dripping in oil. "But we plan to expose our child to both traditions." I cleared my throat. I knew I had interrupted.

"We did meet in a church though," Ramon said, turning to me.

"Well, yes, but I was just visiting one. As a tourist, I mean."

Lydia nodded, her pencil on her yellow pad moving with comic speed.

"My father loves Christmas," I offered.

Lydia cocked her head at me.

I shrugged. "I know. But he does. And, as Ramon's mother is so far away, we spend Christmas with my family. Chrismakah, we call it."

She nodded at the paper and continued to write.

Ramon shot me a sideways look. Was that wrong? I thought. Did that somehow dilute both religions? Was it disrespectful? I thought of my father setting poinsettias along the fireplace and hanging mistletoe. Who's going to kiss me? he'd scream, and Lucy and I would squeal away as my mother ran to stand beneath it, exaggeratedly puckering her lips.

"It's nice to make your own family traditions," I continued. "We went to temple at the high holidays too, of course, but I hope Ramon and I can find creative ways to integrate our upbringings, both religiously and culturally."

"Yes," Ramon said. "My mother took us to church, and I have that religious training, if you will, but I plan to be less rigid about this."

Lydia looked up at Ramon and smiled encouragingly. Every time my husband spoke he got some kind of golden star.

"You talk a good deal about your mother, Ramon." She leafed through her papers. "And I see your father lives in Indonesia. What is your relationship with him like? And yours?" She turned to me.

Cancer, religion, and now Ramon's father. We are going to fail the home study! I thought. Do not panic, I thought. Do. Not.

"My father married another woman, a local, and he stayed there. Because he sort of left the family, we don't have a lot of contact with him. Just e-mail and the occasional phone call."

"When did this happen? Do you have stepsiblings?"

"About twelve years ago. And no," Ramon said. "I remain an only child."

That word. Only. Lonely.

"Have you met Ramon's father?" Lydia asked me.

I shook my head. "No." I said. "Unfortunately I have not."

"Look," Lydia said, and as she did so I realized that it is the social worker's practice to offer comfort. Not to judge, but to understand. Even though Lydia was not, for some reason, eating my banana bread—was this some kind of a mandate? Do not eat the food of the people in the homes you visit?—she was not being critical. In fact I found her encouraging. Or, I thought, watching her search for the right words, perhaps this is a trick! It's a scheme to suck us in, allow us to reveal our lives openly and honestly, and then, because we are so clearly insane, revoke our rights to a child. "Families are very complicated. We all understand this."

I nodded. But Ramon Sr.'s story disarmed me: someone who could just walk away like that, and not look back. Is that passed on from father to son? And how does that get passed on? Nature or nurture? Perhaps Ramon too would one day just bolt.

Ramon looked down at his hands.

"Let's talk about your choice of child. Is this correct, you are requesting the placement of a healthy infant of either gender, aged zero to six months, of Caucasian, Hispanic, African-American, or Middle Eastern descent, or of any combination of Caucasian, Hispanic, Middle Eastern, Asian, Pacific Islander, East Indian, African-American, or Native American descents?"

It was dizzying. "Yes," I said.

"Now, am I correct that you also prefer the placement of a healthy child?"

"Yes," I said.

"You might want to consider a child with special needs," Lydia said. "You will get a child more quickly, if you are as open as you can be."

"No," I said. "I don't mean to interrupt you, but we are not equipped to raise a child with special needs. We just are not."

We were not here to save the world. Unfortunately we were only here to save ourselves.

Lydia bobbed her head as she wrote. "Well, it's something to think about. I do see that you are open to a child with a family history of mild mental illness, and a child whose birthmother has used alcohol or other substances in the first trimester of her pregnancy."

Ramon looked at me. I had not yet mentioned how I had gone up after the meeting all those months ago and changed the form, another deception.

I nodded. "We were told that even if a birthmother had gone to counseling just once, about being pregnant even, this would constitute mild mental illness, and if we didn't check 'mild mental illness' we would be precluded from that child. And that even if she had a beer, say, before she knew she was pregnant, this would constitute drinking in the first trimester, according to our agency's criteria. So."

Ramon sat back and crossed his arms. I willed him to be silent.

"This is correct," Lydia said. "I think you are making the right decision. You can always say no to a situation. And I can send you some reports we've been gathering—drugs are a lot less detrimental to a fetus than alcohol. Heroin does not enter the placenta. Smoking cigarettes is the worst," she said.

Ramon closed his eyes for a moment longer than a blink. I admit I did not care what he was thinking.

"Great!" Lydia said, both hands gripping the glass table. "So. Do you mind if I have a look around?"

Lydia made her way—tentatively and yet with authority—into the kitchen and along the living room and dining room, and then, as if to acknowledge the terrible awkwardness of the situation, she walked quickly through our bedroom. My closet/office was last.

"This will be the baby's room?" she asked.

"Well," I said, "we're not sure. I work in there now. For the first year we thought we'd have the baby in the bedroom with us."

"Babies come with a lot of stuff. You'll be a lot happier if you make that the baby's room," she said. "It's not a requirement, but I'm telling you, I don't see how else you'll do it."

Where will I go? I thought. Where will I work? "That makes sense," I said. "I have an office at school." I would never work there. I had tried it recently, when Ramon started working in the dining room. But the glare of the lights, and my colleagues with their student meetings, their phone calls, their *typing*—I found it impossible to concentrate.

"Okay!" Lydia said when she was done. It took her a grand total of three minutes to get through the rooms of our estate. She sat down again and began to draw a crude map of our apartment. "We work with your agency a lot. They are always so confused by New York apartments. I have to explain how not having a baby's room, say, or a playroom, is typical of all New Yorkers."

Ramon looked at her blueprint of our apartment. He cocked his head as she moved her pencil and I know what he was thinking: Why *didn't* I become an architect?

"Thanks so much for sharing your life with me this morning." Lydia glanced outside onto our fire escape. It was still raining in great sheets. "Ugh," she said.

"Wait! Let me give you some banana bread for the road." I got up and cut a hunk off and wrapped it in wax paper. Then I put it in a sandwich bag, which I sealed tight. "Thanks for taking the time to talk to us today." I handed the package to her.

"Yes." Ramon stood. "Really. And when can we expect to get the home study document? I imagine you are busy and these take a while to write up."

"Too true," Lydia said. "But I understand that time is passing. I know everyone's anxious to get their profiles up and running and available. I should have this in a few weeks, maximum. I'll do my best to get it to you sooner."

I turned to get her raincoat and heard a squeal.

"Oh, I'm so sorry!" Lydia said.

Harriet went cowering into a corner, and Ramon headed over to pet her.

"I didn't see her," Lydia said.

"It's okay," I said. "She can get underfoot."

Lydia stuffed the banana bread into her bag and went to leave.

"Let me walk you out," Ramon said, opening the door.

I heard Ramon chatting easily with Lydia as he sent her out into the rain. Would she throw my banana bread away, or would she eat it, enjoy it even, back at the office? Would it be moist and sweet and delicious? Would it change everything?

Seeing Lydia made me think, as I often had, about Lisa. Whether she and that hideous Danny were fostering a child now, and if they were, would they be able to keep the child. Forever. I could not bear to picture gaunt, timorous Lisa, her hands marked by the attenuated, welt-like bones of her fingers, gripped tight around a steering wheel, driving her child back to social services. Honestly, I could not.

I wondered what happened to many of those people whom we'd talked with up in White Plains. I was curious about the ones in

Raleigh, too. Unless we scanned the couples on the agency's site, constantly watching for who had been matched—an activity I could not do for the stress it caused me—we had no news of anyone but Anita and Paula.

I am moving closer to you, I thought. And then Harriet walked over, wagging her tail. "Pea," I said. "Poor Pea." Mutterly love, I thought, kissing her and receiving several licks in return. I remembered bringing Harriet home from the vet after she'd been spayed; her belly was shaved, and stitches bisected her abdomen, not unlike my own.

Dogs could be enough, I thought as Ramon came back in, shutting the door quietly behind him. I imagined, not for the first or second or third time, giving up this ridiculous idea of New York City, the hum of the fluorescent light in my shared office, the apartment that affords such gifts as roaches, belly-up, when it rains, the scratch and shit of mice when the weather is cool and dry. I saw hills and grass and a backyard filled with dogs. But I could not picture children playing there.

"Weren't we going to start with the best-case scenario? Mental illness?" he said. "Drugs and alcohol use?"

I rubbed Harriet's ears and stood up. I turned to face my husband. Dogs running free and wild in my own backyard. They jumped out of the hair-filled car, leapt with joy from it, when we went for weekend hikes. The seasons were changing. "Yes," I said, crossing my arms. Suddenly none of this felt like it was Ramon's choice to make. "Bring it on."

17

———

Just after classes ended in mid-May, and before our annual trip
to Italy, our home study was approved. The letter stated: *We
are very pleased to recommend Ms. Weintraub and Mr. Aragon as
adoptive parents and believe that any child placed with them would
receive the benefits of a stable and loving home life. They meet the
standards of this agency and the preadoption requirements of the
State of New York to be adoptive parents.*

On a Post-it attached to the document, Lydia wrote: *The banana
bread was delicious!*

It could have been what did it, I thought, tearing the note from
the document. My banana bread.

In Terracina, just as we were recovering from the jet lag that made
us sleep too late, waking up groggy, dehydrated, and hungry, I
grimly turned thirty-nine.

The day was not unusual for us. We stepped into the kitchen,
where our fresh-squeezed orange juice awaited us, the tops of our
glasses covered in tinfoil to keep out bugs and germs and microbes.

As I removed this protective cap, the story of the agony of the oranges began. They had to be picked from the trees; they had to be hand pressed; it was not easy, not at Paola's age. Look! These calluses from so much work. Then there were the farm eggs fried in olive oil and topped with a farmer's cheese, served with fresh bread, each with its own tale of woe in how far the special bakery only the locals knew of was from Paola's house, and how the eggs from the farmers are very special, practically gold. Liquid gold, I thought, as I pierced the bright orange yoke, and I agreed then that these were special eggs, very very special eggs indeed.

Ramon and Paola fought as usual on my birthday. Today Paola wanted her blood pressure taken at the special pharmacy, where her friend worked, before 10 A.M.—10 A.M. was the cutoff—and Ramon did not want to make that trip, not that morning. I finished my breakfast—delicious, yes, but what's the point of it when there is no talking, no discussion, no *conversation* while consuming it?—and made my way out of the kitchen.

I could still hear Paola screaming in Italian, accusing Ramon, even I could tell, of trying to kill her, of wanting her to die so that he could inherit all this—there was silence as I imagined her arm sweeping over her small kitchen. He was refusing to help her with her blood pressure before the designated deadline so that he could also inherit her art, her mahogany furniture, and the two sets of ivory tusks, illegally bought and sent here from West Africa, now wrapped and stacked in the basement. *You want all this because your job is no good!* she said in English. *Why did you not become an architect? Why oh why,* Paola began to wail, and I heard Ramon thump the table with his hand and tell her: *Mama! Ho già abbastanza preoccupazioni.* Enough is enough. This, I understood.

In the bedroom, I gathered up my purse, my laptop, and my book on why there would never be women artists, an anthology from the seventies I was using to write a new paper for a conference in early fall. Still we slept across from Paola's bedroom and her altar to the past, her rosaries laid out like clothes for a child, her candles floating in oil, and her incense sticks, for spells. I changed into a skirt, because God forbid I go to town looking like the American strumpet I so clearly was and had been accused of being by Paola on more than one occasion when I left, in the stifling midday heat, in shorts. Even though many Italians wore shorts and jeans in the village, I paid heed.

I headed down the marble stairs to the gate, creaking it open, and then out—free!—onto the dirt road and then the paved one that led into town, to the café at which I had been sitting summer morning after summer morning since I'd met Ramon, where I could read a *Herald-Tribune,* check my e-mail, and, today, look at how many people had wished me well. I took a seat at an outside table that looked out onto the ancient piazza still waking, light illuminating the old stones, famous for having been taken from the Roman Forum. My parents, in their usual effusive way, screamed *happy birthday* out of my computer. They sent off-center, low resolution, barely readable photos of Harriet. And, despite the early hour in the States, several friends had already sent notes.

Also in this mix was an e-mail from a friend who regularly fostered dogs. Every week she housed what seemed like at least fifteen of them in her Upper West side Apartment, and she spent much of her waking life trying to find these animals good homes. Today she sent an image of a collie-spaniel mix, just to me. *A sibling for Madame Harriet?* she wrote.

I did not delete it as I flipped to the next e-mail, from Lucy. When I clicked it, a mouse in a sombrero played a manic happy birthday to me. I looked around the café, embarrassed, and deleted it before the mouse had finished his song.

And then, turning to Facebook, I looked at the early birthday wishes from former students; colleagues; peers I'd gone to high school, college, graduate school with; friends. Since I was here at the café anyway, I thought, why not take a quick look at Michelle's page to see if there was evidence of her pregnancy. And yes! There, in a photo, was her round, full belly, Zoe with a child's pretend stethoscope pressed to it as she professed to listen. A mutual friend in this photo looked a bit bloated around the eyes and cheeks, and sure enough, her page announced boldly: *I'm told we'll have a little one in November!*

Why not, then, look at the baby status of my colleagues and acquaintances, distant relatives, friends recently married, women I'd met on those hateful cold dawns in sterile doctors' offices? One or two of their status updates shrieked with happy, blessed, beautiful news, photos posted of their faces, dazed and sleepless, with that postcoital look special to those who had recently given birth, teensy loaves of bread swaddled in soft blankets in their arms. I scanned Anita's page for any kind of update but found only evidence of yet another spinone puppy. No baby news from her or the eighteen other women I investigated. Still, I went farther in, now to the bloggers, their links offered from acquaintances' walls, writing extensively—for whom I could not say—about every aspect of their pregnancies, from how they felt (*Big as a whale! Icky!*) to what they bought (*baby food makers, German breast pumps, organic strollers*). I read these exhaustive accounts all morning, looking at all the mothers. Spending the start of my thirty-ninth birthday in the beautiful coastal town of Terracina, Italy, running away from my mother-in-law and her farm eggs and her just-off-the-boat squids and fishes, her rising blood pressure, and my husband who tended to her.

Ramon found me seated at one of the small wicker tables, trying not to finish my second coffee in three gulps. I watched him amble up to my table in an easy manner he wore only here.

"Hey," he said.

"As much as I love the screaming, I thought I'd get a break from it today," I said.

"You're hardly a stranger to screaming."

"Too true."

"Why didn't you tell me you were leaving?" Ramon pulled up a chair and in one swift movement had the barista's attention and a coffee already hissing.

"I just can't deal, Ramon." I opened the paper. There had been an *E. coli* outbreak in Germany due to Spanish cucumbers and Paola had been screeching about it all the previous night. As a result, tomatoes were, for some reason, banned from our diet, a tragedy, as there was little I enjoyed more in life than a delicious Italian tomato, with fresh mozzarella, and basil from Paola's garden.

"Look." I turned my computer toward him. "Jackie sent me another dog in need of a home."

"Oh! So sweet."

"Should we take her?" I asked. "She's part spaniel."

"Don't you think we've got enough on our plate?"

"No!" I said. We didn't have enough, remember?"

"We could get a baby at any time, just as soon as the profile goes up. We have a good shot. Compared to a lot of those couples, we're young."

"Not the ones at the training session," I said.

"Yes, but the ones online. And I have the Spanish. We translated every goddamn line of that letter into Spanish. We could have a birthmother in just a few weeks. I don't think we want a puppy and an infant at the same time, do we?"

The dog, Jackie said in the e-mail, was named Daisy. She was adorable. "I suppose you're right." I turned the computer back toward me.

Ramon's macchiato arrived, and the waitress smiled at him, her long nose dipping down into her flowering mouth, as she set the teensy cup surely on the table. His legs were crossed, and the top leg kicked slightly, a navy cloth espadrille dangling from his toes. He sipped at the coffee and he looked nothing like he did at home, where he seemed caged, stalking our apartment, unsure, his movements jerky and new, skin sallow.

"It's your birthday, Jess, let's do something fun today."

"Ecch. Birthdays." I thought of myself this time next year, in this very café I'd been sitting in for the past ten years, still without a child. Only on that day I'd be forty.

"Want to take the boat to Ponza? Or go to the beach? Take a nice walk in the hills?"

My husband does not hike. He walks. And this walking never involves any kind of *gear*. In fact it involves little in the way of preparation—looking up trails, say, places of interest that might be passed along the way—just leather sandals and perhaps a bottle of water if I fight hard enough about the perils of dehydration.

"Whichever," I said. "It's not going to be much fun anyway."

I knew I was in a sort of paradise and I knew that I could not appreciate my good fortune.

"You know, you are really something." Ramon lifted the coffee to his lips and then placed it back down on its chipped saucer. "Do you know how many girls would love to take a trip to a coastal Italian town with their husbands?"

"To come stay with their mother-in-law? Not so many."

"You wanted to be away for your birthday," he said.

"I know. I know. And it is so beautiful here. But I wish we'd done something different."

"Like what, Jess? We have so many expenses right now and this is free for us."

"I know this." I imagined us on a lounge chair by an infinity pool, a drink with a pink paper umbrella popped into a tall glass dripping with condensation, on a holiday we would never take even if we had the money. "I wish you'd just plan something for the day."

"Okay." Ramon stretched with catlike grace. "Here's the plan. Let's go to the beach. In a coastal town in Italy. Together. Let's go to the beach, and let's just this once be thankful for what we have."

We did go to the beach that day and we swam in the cold, salted sea and we lay back on the sand, and watched the Italians with their racquetball, and their ease, and their elaborate packed lunches, and I read in my book about how women, living in a man's world, have been cut off from education, culture, life, and Ramon sat beneath his umbrella reading *The Spy Who Came in from the Cold,* and then, after a glass of beer by the ocean, we went back to the house because Paola was cooking dinner.

And then that birthday was, thankfully, behind me.

We stayed in Terracina for two more weeks. I read and made stabs at an article in the mornings as Ramon and Paola divided and conquered, each other and the world, and then, in the afternoons, Ramon and I took a few hours to ourselves in town or at the beach or at the lake, and often we'd come back along the canal after dinner, to drink wine and eat strawberries and fresh ricotta. Once a routine was established and I was able to work, the trip somehow became more relaxing.

Until the moment I realized I was a week late getting my period. There it was: that familiar *pingpingping* of my heart, the sign of dread and longing. Could this *be*? I reached, Pavlov-like, for my

breasts and squeezed: Had they grown? And had we actually managed to have sex at the right time this month? I had peed on sticks
each month to pinpoint the coveted LH surge—the onset of the
hormone that indicates the start of ovulation—for so many years,
I'd had what I had come to call ovulation syndrome. We both had
it. Ramon and I had become two trapped, frantic, desexualized animals, unable to mate. While most months we still managed to have
sex when I was ovulating, by my own calculations, it was hardly
with much of the gusto of our earliest endeavors.

Oh, the times we thought we were having sex for children in
earnest! After, I stood on my head. And then, in those first few
months, I was so good! Not a drop of alcohol touched my lips. I
ate organic kale and brown rice sweetened with sushi vinegar. I did
not jump up and down, not even for joy, lest I risk destabilizing
the possibility of implantation. And yet my period still arrived each
month, unerringly on time.

Within a few months of this tedious process, sex was trans-
formed into something unrecognizable. I peed on sticks, and we
did it on the nights the blank white space was slashed bright pink,
but it was the very opposite of those first tries. We were completely
lost to each other now; worse, perhaps, we lacked hope. When I
began to feel that remove, I wondered what Ramon was thinking,
or about whom, and then, at some point later still, I did not care;
he could think about whatever he wanted to think about if it would
end it sooner.

Which felt like the worst thing ever until it got even worse, as
on the high holy days of my ovulation we began to rattle the bars of
the cage of our apartment, the chains of our marriage, most fiercely,
as we tried, helplessly, hopelessly, to turn our marriage of two into
a family. We would fight about who would clean the bathroom or
pay the rent or wash the dishes, and in the middle of my yelling,

I'd think, Great, how am I going to get my husband to have sex with me now?

Which is why so many women become pregnant when they decide to make that leap from relying on their own bodies to conceive and give themselves over to the bodies of strangers. How many stories—life lessons, really—had been retold to me of the infertile couple who decided to adopt and then, *boom!*, they became instantly pregnant. Too many of these tales, but now I clearly saw their worth: could that be us? Day after day, moment upon moment, in Terracina, waiting for my period to come and hoping for it to stay away, I thought, This time, it is us. This time, we were the lucky ones. If, however, this was so, had I drunk too much frascati the other night as the town cooled and the moon rose? At four glasses, I knew the answer was an unequivocal yes.

I did not tell Ramon that I was late in an effort to keep expectations to a minimum. Alone, I envisioned my scar tissue unraveling from my insides the way I pulled ivy from the wooden fence surrounding my yard upstate. I thought of swaddles printed with giraffes, the texture of cheesecloth, lightweight city strollers, the safety of car seats. And the more I did not tell him, the more anxious I became. If I were pregnant, complications were likely. My chance of an ectopic pregnancy—where the egg implants in the fallopian tube and so cannot create a viable pregnancy—was about 85 percent. And if, miracle of miracles, that did not happen, there was a good chance I would be in pain from all that scar tissue stretching—those weeds, again, clawing in, forced undone. And yet, still, each month, I lay back and had a go at it, with gusto or without.

Because I never believed it. Still. That any of it, or none of it, was possible.

I decided if I did not have my period by the next day, which would be seven days late, I would just take a pregnancy test and be done with it.

That night, I refused wine at dinner, which Paola noted as she served her rigatoni with offal with an exaggerated raised eyebrow. I was not a fan of this dish—I am an adventurous eater but the frisson stops for me at entrails. I felt a wave of nausea as Paola heaped an enormous serving—my mother-in-law had, in fairness, come to understand my American love of a large portion—onto my plate. Surely, I thought, picking my way through the sauce, this nausea was due to my secret pregnancy.

"This is how you take care of a man," Paola told me, not for the first time, as she cleaned up the dishes. "You cook for him; you clean. You *iron*."

"Got it!" I said, bringing in the plates for her to wash in a special process so complicated—there was vinegar and a miniature dustpan and brush, and several different containers of soap—that it was impossible to get involved.

"You iron?" She looked at me sidewise, wiping her hands on her apron.

This was the three hundred and forty-seventh time she'd asked me this. "Of course," I told her, looking away. We didn't even own an iron and the last time the conversation had turned to the washing machine issue—when she discovered we did our laundry en masse with other Brooklyn villagers—it had ended in tears. Hers. I feel sorry for you, Paola had said. *Pacch.* Me? I lived all over the world and never have I shared a machine in this way. "I iron all the time," I said. "Actually, I enjoy it. I find it extremely relaxing."

She nodded her head happily over her dishes. "Goot," she said through her smile.

Why ruin it for her, I thought as I went to clear the rest of the table. Why ruin it for any of us.

Utterly exhausted—from that ancient, scorching Italian sun, perhaps, I thought, trying not to consider what I knew to be the real reason: my surreptitious pregnancy—I turned in early, the way many pregnant women's bodies force them to do. I could hear the television at a volume that must be used to signal boats from the sea—first the news and then some kind of talent show resembling *American Idol*—as I lay back, alone, and I wondered if this would be what it was going to be like for the next nine months. I was very excited to complain as I attempted to adjust myself so the bump in the mattress that hit just at the tip of my spine and the one at my right shoulder would somehow hit my body's fleshier parts.

When I woke the next morning, the first thing I remembered was that today was a day I could be pregnant.

I still had not gotten my period! And instead of eating with Ramon and my mother-in-law, I explained that I needed to take a walk on my own. I left to their indifferent shrugs and headed into town, to the pharmacy in between Paola's and the village, and as I made my way in, a friend of Paola's looked up from behind the counter. Though she did not wave at me, she nodded her head in assent, and so I bought some sunscreen for an obscene amount of money and then left. It struck me then that Paola knew everyone in this town, the gelato makers and the jewelers, the bakers and the sandal makers. And most especially Paola knew the pharmacists and the people who worked there, as this is where she spent her mornings getting her blood pressure taken. I imagined all the pharmacists calling one another in a game of wicked telephone. It was like being sixteen again, slipping in past curfew, hiding condoms, everything about my life contained and concealed.

But I was very far from sixteen, even farther, perhaps, from

Northern Virginia, and when I entered the other two pharmacies within walking distance, a thick-lidded woman would look up, her head moving an infinitesimal amount in acknowledgment, and then she would return to her paperwork.

My bladder was uncomfortably full—I was holding on to the morning urine, which I knew gave the most accurate reading—and I had not yet had coffee, when I returned, exhausted, to the house.

"Ramon." I pulled him aside. I could see Paola standing in the threshold of the kitchen, holding a spatula, her head cocked to listen. And I explained.

"We'll be back, Mama," Ramon told her, grabbing the car keys, and I watched her part the curtains as we drove out of the gate.

We drove twenty minutes outside of town, toward Fondi, not far from the lake, to go to a pharmacy that would not house a woman who would ask my mother-in-law, with mock sincerity, when she would be expecting her first grandchild. I used the bathroom at this anonymous shop, to find out what I had always known. Had it been positive, the story—my story—would be that I had always known it, but this story ended here: I was not pregnant.

Ramon had only been aware of this promise for half an hour and its brokenness had not damaged him, not visibly anyway. Back in the car, he chatted on about going into the hills today for some lamb for his mother. He knew I liked these excursions out of town, and I was aware that he was talking over the layer of my disappointment, a skin forming across the surface of hot milk.

"Everything good comes from the mountains." Ramon yammered on and on. "Everything healthy and important, none of those diseases, like those cucumbers—my mother was just so upset about that! We do know the best places here. It's not like New York either, so rarefied."

I was not listening. "Ramon," I said. "I have to get a coffee. Can you just drop me in town? Not the old town."

"We have coffee on," he said. "Filter coffee! I know you like that and there is no filter coffee in town."

I looked at him. I was not, for the first time in a long while, angry. "Please. I just want to sit and have a coffee on my own, okay? I can't deal with going back and sitting at that table right now."

"Do you want me to come?" he asked. "I'll come with you."

I went to roll down the window, carefully, with that same piece-of-shit manual crank I had inadvertently torn off on that first visit. Warm air rushed in through the open window. It smelled of salt and berries and the sea. "I'm just going to take a few minutes and walk back on my own," I said.

Ramon dropped me off and I walked away from the piazza, where, I reasoned, I would not be recognized, even though no one identified me in Terracina with anything but dismissiveness.

Now I walked along the stones of the street, facing the sun, and I could see my shadow stretched out long and flat behind me. I remembered Ramon and me at the warped picnic tables outside the bar by our first apartment in the West Village drinking pints of frothy beer and pulling at greasy onion rings. The waitress knew our names and we tipped her well then. We would go home and push my stacks of papers off the bed I worked on, and we'd make love and then fall asleep and we would wake up and do this again. In any number of countries, I had lain in bed with Ramon, a window open onto a street, a breeze rustling long curtains.

Now I saw a café in an alleyway out of the sun, and I stepped toward it, my shadow disappearing beneath the cool shade of the high stone walls.

Perhaps, I thought, this was also the end of desire.

Part 3

THE BIRTHMOTHERS

18

———

August 2010

Here's the thing: there's no getting a break; there's no respite from breathing. Everywhere we go there are children and the mothers who birthed them. They are outside my window, a mother pushing a double stroller, shielding both heads from the sun. I make room for them on the street, in stores. I hold the doors open and the mothers walk straight through, so absorbed with their children that they do not even thank me. I see the mothers on playgrounds, of course, at restaurants during brunch, a meal ruled by children. And at the ob/gyn, where I went after Italy, as my period was late again, and the following month as well, and the following month, again.

I entered the cool reception of the Soho office, out of the blasting end-of-August humidity, and was confronted by a lobby filled with pregnant women, some about to pop, others in newer stages of pregnancy, but each rubbing her rounded belly as she sat, legs spread, on one of the oversized chairs, an array of parenting magazines—*Parenting, American Baby, FamilyFun, Fit Pregnancy*—fanned out before her. Where the hell was *American Infertility Today*? Where was goddamn *Vogue*?

I sat down in the sliver of space left on the large leather couch. "We." I saw it clearly that each of these women was already a "we" and I was an "I." I can have a husband and parents, a sibling, but I am still an "I." My body, I mean. Even how those letters look: *I. We.* I pictured them. I saw all our bodies.

The women smiled at one another—when are you due, how far along are *you*? Is this your first? Oh, your third, can you believe it, we thought we were done!—but no one made eye contact with me. I recognized I was being ignored, as overlooked as poverty can be, and also I sensed that I was feared. These women who fidgeted and cleared their throats as I sat beside them seemed scared of catching what I had, or more, what I lacked.

The technician eventually called my name, and I practically ran into the examining room. I changed into yet another hospital gown. Then I was weighed (facing front, weight gain was the last thing I needed to worry about) and measured (was I shrinking? Please, God, tell me I'm not *shrinking*!) and blood pressure taken, the *ziip* of the blood-pressure cuff's Velcro as familiar a sound as traffic to me now. My vitals.

I sat on the examination table, my bare legs dangling between sock-covered stirrups, waiting for the doctor to arrive.

This is what I saw: along with the array of gynecological tools, each with its own look and gleam of an instrument of torture, was a fetal monitor laid out on the counter. On the cupboards above it, signs were taped, colored sheets of paper offering: INFANT CARE! BABY PROOFING! CHILDBIRTHING CLASS! BREASTFEEDING CLASS! Beneath each oblation was a list of dates, mostly by month: August 8. September 12. October 3. November 15. Some of these dates had come and gone, but when one is pregnant there is a different notion of time. For me even the future was passing.

But forget all of that, because the worst thing about waiting in that room was the thin walls. I could hear talking—a man and a woman's voice and a third chipper voice that I assumed belonged to the technician. Then there was silence, and then a thumping noise set against a sound not unlike the calling of the ocean. Bum *bum* bum *bum* ba *bum*. I closed my eyes. It was a sound I had only heard by the sea.

"There it is!" that technician-like voice said.

"Oh my God!" the woman gasped.

"Hmm, hmm," the technician said. "That's the heart!"

"Wow." That was the male voice. "Wow."

"Look! Look!" said the technician. "That's eighteen weeks," she said. "And there," she giggled, "is the penis."

I kicked my feet. CHILDBIRTHING CLASS! I looked at the dates again. This woman in the next room might take this class. And at the end of it, or maybe somewhere in the middle, she would have her baby.

I, however, did not need the childbirthing class.

"Bye!" I heard from the next room. "We'll see you in a few weeks!"

There was a rustling and then ripping of paper, and the shuffle of clothing, the squeak of shoes—sneakers—on linoleum, then someone exiting the room.

"I'm so excited," the woman said. "Are you excited? Are you as excited as I am?"

I didn't hear a response.

"Oh," she said. "Are you crying, honey?" There was another brief pause. "I know," she said. "I know. Aren't we just the luckiest people in the world?"

This is the way in which we were lucky: our birthmother letter, our home study document, and our online profile were finally approved. Shortly after this our profile went up online with our toll-free number and our special designated e-mail. The day it went "live," my ob/gyn called to tell me that my results were normal, in regards to my extended cycles. I had thought perimenopause, she said, but that's usually when the periods get closer together, but you're good, she'd said. And I see you're thinking of fertility treatments. Any more thoughts on this?

Set the stunned rage aside, I thought, hanging up. Because now we have pre-menopause to consider. I was in a new state of alert and so the day our profile went online, I took my phone from the shower to the bathroom to the coffee shop to the grocery store. This must happen now, I thought, before I go into *menopause,* and so I resolved I would not leave my phone's side; I pledged myself to it. Until we were matched with a birthmother, I vow, Phone, I will never leave you.

We were told this process could play out in one of several scenarios. One scenario was we could get no calls, until, several months or a year or so down the line, we would be contacted by a birthmother who would be the right match for us. In scenario number one, there is a lot of waiting without any calls, which can be stressful. Or, in scenario number two, we could get several calls and e-mails from several birthmothers, who might, in the end for any number of reasons, end up choosing other prospective adoptive parents. Whatever the case, we were told that this process could take a year, on average, but for some it was much quicker, for some far longer.

Since when did average apply to me? The one time I came home with a C—in algebra!—my father nearly lost his mind. When I told him a C was *average,* this made him more distraught. Let me tell you something, my father said to me, a fury in his eyes I had thought previously saved for my mother, I will not have mediocrity in this household. Average, he'd said, incredulous. I will not have it, he said.

When it came to adoption, Ramon and I were not really a C couple, I reasoned. For one we were heterosexual. In the South and the middle of the country, the red states, where many of the birthmothers seemed to hail from, where our agency had offices, it seemed, heterosexuals might have an edge. Though my Jewishness might wear that sharp blade smooth, we did have what I had begun to refer to as the Ramon Advantage, his Spanishness. Our letter was translated into Spanish. *Queremos agradeceros por vuestra valentía y generosidad en su consideración de la adopción abierta,* he wrote. Thank you for your bravery and generosity in considering open adoption.

And while some in these parts had the false impression that New York was where people got shot, many people living outside of cities might find our lives rich and exciting. In this way, we were told, adoption works in the same manner genetics might. A birthmother who wants her child to live in diverse, culturally-minded Brooklyn is likely to be more similar to Ramon and me, who struck out for the city and all its rewards and frustrations.

Why didn't anyone call the first day? Was it New York, or that we lived in an apartment, or that I was Jewish? Could they tell that we were not wealthy? That we were renters?

In the beginning of the second week, though, we did get a contact. Someone at the agency office in California—Allison—called to tell us there was a Carmen, a twenty-year-old in community college who lived with her parents in Los Angeles. I was told she was shy, and so she didn't speak with me directly, but, Allison said, from her experience, as long as she'd been doing this (from her high, seventeen-year-old-sounding voice, how long could that have been?) she could tell Carmen was serious—the real deal—and though it was quite early in her pregnancy, she would be contacting us soon.

I intensified my relationship with my phone and did little else but sit and wait and watch it. I thought of Los Angeles, where I had an aunt in Pasadena, a cousin in Silver Lake, a friend in Los Feliz who once had taken me surfing in Santa Monica. I thought of Venice Beach, and Rizzo from *Grease,* her schoolbooks held close to her chest, just like Carmen, I imagined. This waiting was familiar; I had waited for the results of our embryo transfer, from petri dish to womb, for my period to not arrive and the strip to be darned with two pink threads. I had waited for the ultrasound results to be conclusive the one time a fetus did for a moment grow. But every kind of waiting, like each Eskimo word for snow, like shame, has a different facet, a new slant of light.

While I cannot say that Ramon was unmoved by this development, he did not have the obsessive attention to the possibility of Carmen that consumed me. He had a meeting in the city, which he did not cancel. He even met a friend for a drink afterward.

I thought, This adoption process has been so easy! Finally we have gotten through something relatively unscathed. Waiting on someone else's body is nothing. Some couples have been waiting for years! Not us. Not this time, people. We were called and we are about to be matched with a birthmother in the second week. We'd been unlucky in many ways, but now good fortune was smiling upon us and all our wishes—the important ones, prayers, let's say—would soon come true.

But of course the call did not come. Nor did the e-mail to our special designated JessandRamon Gmail account. What did arrive was Ramon, in the evening, smelling of beer. He shook his head when I told him and he got into bed with the pillow covering his face.

I did not sleep well, not that night or the next, and each time I woke from a fitful sleep, my hands were at my sides, clenched into fists, half-moons impressed in my palms. For three days I sat in my office refreshing my e-mail and having Ramon call our 800 number to make sure it worked properly.

It works, he'd say, staring at his computer. It fucking works. Could you stop being so compulsive?

By the end of the third day, I had revised my theories about this particular moment of waiting being effortless. The worst state a human can be in, in fact, is in the state of waiting, I decided, and so I called California Allison.

"Carmen has not called," I told her. "We're waiting and waiting."

"Oh she will," Allison assured me. "I know she will. Sometimes," she said, "birthmothers are scared. They're unsure. But I know she was serious about placing and serious about you and Ramon when she called."

It was August, and while I was supposed to be writing and preparing for my new classes, I didn't have to be anywhere, per se, and so I waited some more, languishing around the apartment like a bored housewife. I turned the television on and off. I opened and closed the refrigerator. I baked cookies, as the mothers, I reasoned, once again, are always baking. I spent inordinate amounts of time trolling the Internet, where I checked our profile. Unable to control myself, I went to those pages of the pregnant women I'd looked at on my birthday in Terracina and who had, by now, given birth, of course they had, time was passing.

Three days more of this and again I called the agency.

"Oh, Jesse," California Allison said. "I was about to e-mail you. It looks like Carmen went with another family here, in the next town. She wanted to be nearby."

This is part of openness, being close, perhaps, close enough to visit often, like the girl-holding-the-adoption-balloon movie. Still, I was stunned. I was silent.

"I'm sorry. It happens," she said. "But that you got this call so soon, it's such a great sign."

"A sign of what?" I said.

"A sign that someone else will call again soon. It will happen," she told me. "Believe."

Believe in what? When I hung up the phone, I felt a crushing sensation, a physical feeling that I can't say I didn't recognize. I felt flattened by everything. By illness and financial stress, and childlessness and disappointment. I thought of those used-up wishes—for decent dry cleaning, a sleek couch, a country house—and I tried to comfort myself with the thought that I had not known that I should store up my wishes like a squirrel stores nuts. I did not know that a cache of dried berries in my puffed cheeks was one of my essential wishes. Babies happened to every creature. They *happened*.

When Carmen—a woman whom I had never spoken to but whose life, if given the different flap of another butterfly wing, could have been intertwined with mine forever—did not choose us, I felt I would not be able to get up from bed, not ever. The weight of the past and the future, both, was devastating, and without my knowing it, Carmen had become the key to life. And now the key had gone missing. The door to happiness was locked! I could not get in.

The opposite of happiness is not unhappiness. The opposite of happiness is waiting. The opposite of happiness is panic, that the future held no one but Ramon and me. The panic that this—my husband and me, alone at a table, moving our forks to our mouths, the cups to our lips—would not be enough. The panic that Ramon and I had chosen the wrong agency, one that specializes in southern gay and lesbian couples, an agency that promotes the idea that where we live, in New York, is where people are murdered. And who's to say it isn't? My friend Liza had been mugged at gunpoint the previous year, when she emerged from the F train, not far from the school where our child—should we be lucky enough to get one—would go to school.

I imagined Carmen; she was caramel colored with black hair. Her back was against a wall and she sang, "There Are Worse Things I Could Do," the diffuse Southern California light behind her. I saw her burgeoning stomach, rising like bread. Like my stomach, from the tumors that wouldn't stop. I saw Carmen as clearly as anything I had turned to watch disappear.

Who is a birthmother? What we were told by Crystal or Tiffany that day, almost a year ago, is this: a birthmother is eighteen to twenty-five years old. Fifty percent of birthmothers are in relationships. The birthmothers are scared. They fear the unknown. The birthmother might have wanted to terminate her pregnancy, but it is too late. Or she might not believe in terminating a pregnancy. The birthmother has love for her unborn child, big big love, which is why she wants to make a plan for that child. But at the same time she is detached from the child, to protect herself from the sorrow to come. The life of the birthmother, this rare bird, tends to be chaotic.

In other words, the birthmothers are only women.

What we were waiting for now was the birthmothers.

I did not move for forty-eight hours, but to drag myself to the table to eat. And while extreme emotion—depression, wild happiness—often puts people off food, this sort of thing has never, ever, made me lose my appetite. I am not one of those wan, depressed people listlessly wandering drugstores; I am the depressed person listlessly wandering the aisles of the pharmacy with a rosy plumpness in my cheeks that comes from sustained good nutrition.

I heard Ramon's moving about and working in the dining room, so much weather. He peeked his head in to check on me.

"You alive?" he said.

I nodded into my pillow.

"This is the first one." Ramon sat on the bed. The weight of his body, how it moved the mattress in the slightest way, hurt me. "We were lucky to be called so quickly," he said. "Sometimes it takes months and months."

"Not helping," I said. "And remember. We were not called."

Had I had the opportunity to speak to Carmen, perhaps my very charm would have made her forgo California and choose us. Was being picked over—scenario number two—better than scenario number one, not being contacted at all? Was it better to be bludgeoned with a club or assaulted with a cleaver? Which, I wonder, would you rather?

I heard the landline ring and I heard Ramon speaking into it and I heard him and Harriet come and go for her walks, her return signaled by the *click click* of her nails on the wood floors. She arrived to check on me and then departed quickly—was she skipping?—to get to her meal or her biscuit, depending on the hour. She always gave a little yelp before her meals, cries, I imagined, of uncontainable joy.

After two days, Ramon came in and dragged me up by both arms and, as if it were my leg, not my spirit, that had been broken, he placed my arm over his shoulder, gripped that hand hard, and helped me into the bathroom. He shoved me into the shower and I held my face up to the spray of water and washed up and dressed

198

myself and then we were in the car heading upstate to Fishkill on the Hudson for Michelle's annual family summer party.

Going to that party started out as a good idea, a sure diversion. It was an hour-and-a-half drive out of town, and just leaving my bed, and the apartment, felt pleasant and fresh and like a brand-new day. I turned on the CD player. Our car had one of those old players where seven CDs get loaded up in, of all places, the trunk. It defies explanation and logic, and because of this, the same seven CDs had been in this contraption in the trunk since we purchased this car, used, five years previously. Despite this, each time I turned on the CD player, which was rare, I was surprised and grateful to hear the first few electric bars of *Blood on the Tracks*. I reflexively skipped "Tangled Up in Blue" and went to song number two: *He hears the ticking of the clocks / And walks along with a parrot that talks . . .*

Fishkill was Harriet's second-favorite place, after my parents' house, with its abundance of food and love (not the same thing, I tried to show Harriet, but how do you teach a dog this lesson?). Michelle and Jacob used to invite us several times a year, and often, during the week when it was empty and I wasn't teaching, I would go up with Harriet and stay alone to work. Harriet could spend the day in that pond, flinging herself jubilantly off the dock, chasing a stick I'd throw for her. When I tired of this repetitive exercise, I would often turn to find her swimming the pond in circles, her little tail a propeller, her paws paddling her along. She looked like one of those old ladies in the community pool I belonged to as a kid, the ones who emerged from the lounge area during adult swim, hair tucked into rubber bathing caps with straps under the chins like gaping smiles. When the pond bored her, she'd step out to shake herself off, always as close to me as possible, and after she'd dried in the sun, often we hiked up to the summit of a small mountain.

Now, as Ramon and I drove north, I put out of my head that, because of the spotty cell service, I would have to take a break from my phone, and as we pulled up to the house, as if to reinforce this point, the *SOS* came up in red. Indeed, I thought, this ship is sinking. Send flares.

Ramon snapped Harriet on her leash and she hopped out of the car, ready for her day of fun. He pulled the six-pack out of the backseat, and we all headed out to the backyard. First we passed the pool and the sounds of screaming and splashing and laughing children. I looked timidly at Ramon, who did not look at me, but swung the beer in his right hand.

"Hello!" we both yelled when we saw Mrs. and Mr. Sanders standing, wide-legged, on the deck.

Down below, Jacob manned an enormous grill that they rented each year for the party. I could see chicken and sausages and hot dogs and burgers already done and placed in front on platters, dripping with blood.

"Hello!" Mrs. Sanders hugged me.

I expected to hear the splash of Harriet, freed now from her leash, running into the pond, and when it did not come, I looked out at the lawn that sloped down to the water, just over from the clay tennis court. Harriet stood tentatively at the edge of the water. Several friends with their new babies, people from the neighborhood, friends of Michelle and Jacob we'd met here over the years, were all spread out on blankets, already eating and drinking. Every blanket held either an infant in someone's arms, an infant splayed on the blanket, a toddler whom someone was trying to contain, or a kid who kept running from their parents to their screaming friends and back again.

Some kids threw a Frisbee, and the tennis court was packed with kids and two adults who had clearly tried to have a game but had given in to the screams and cries of the children, who now held rackets bigger than they were. They swatted at the air, their bodies spinning around, as the balls went by.

Behind me, Ramon cracked open a beer and headed down to the dock by the pond. There he stood, beer bottle in the air, drinking it down, his Adam's apple lurching along his stretched throat. I came down to meet the two of them, nodding to several other families we knew, including Belinda, who'd had the surgical abortion at seven months and who appeared to be pregnant again.

"Go on, Pea," I said.

She wagged her tail and made this growling sound in the back of her throat that signaled she was excited. Once she would have leapt off the dock, body outstretched and beautiful, but now she stepped into the water almost tentatively and pushed off.

I watched as she made her way around the pond, and when I turned, Zoe and Michelle stood at the edge, Michelle's belly full and round, but the rest of her slim, her legs smooth in her short jersey sundress.

"Hey!" Michelle went to hug me. "Harriet still is such a good swimmer."

I nodded. "You going in?" I asked Zoe.

She shook her head and scrunched up her nose against the pond and its non-chlorinated waters, its algae, and the slimy squish of its bottom. Even I knew she only went into the pool, with its gleaming blue floor.

"Hi, Ramon," Michelle said.

He saluted her.

Zoe looked up, and then, she took my hand.

"Guess what, Jesse?" she said. "In four days I will be three."

I smiled at her. "Oh my God, what a big girl you are! Soon you will be driving! And swimming in the pond."

She laughed and let go of my hand.

I did not think then that Zoe's birthday meant that in two weeks I would have had a three-year-old. I only remembered this after I looked down at Harriet, shaking herself dry, and when Zoe squealed with delight at Harriet's spray, and then she and Michelle began loping up the hill toward the barbecue, that we had nearly escaped everything. I didn't care if all I ever spoke of again was mashed carrots and day care and how long each and every woman should breast-feed. I watched Zoe bound up the hill scissoring her arms to assist her up the slight incline. I had to look away. But look where?

There were so many layers of the noise of children screaming, it was hard to think, but I chatted with a bunch of Michelle's friends—two of them pregnant—as I watched Ramon drink beer after beer on the deck. We ate a lot of meat and some of the salads the guests had brought, and I sat on the blankets and oohed and aahed at the children; I tickled their bellies and made funny faces as I tried to keep Harriet from stealing unfinished hot dogs from plates, or worse, from an unsuspecting child's hands.

Children were proliferating year by year, and so were the mothers. Our friend Helen, with Ryan, whom she'd had the past December, breast-fed her child as she asked me about our prospects.

"How is it going for you guys?" she asked, with meaning, looking up from Ryan, who was pumping away, grunting at her nipple.

"It's okay," I said. Sometimes I wanted to talk about it all the time, like there was nothing else I could bear to discuss, and so was angry—outraged—when people did not ask me, and in other moments, like this one for instance, I wanted to zip my mouth closed and just lie back and watch the clouds pass over. "Not much to report."

"You know," she said as her son sucked on, "holding babies really helps."

"Holding babies? Helps what?"

"With getting pregnant. When we were trying, I couldn't get pregnant for like six months and in addition to acupuncture, I just held a baby whenever I saw one. They say it helps for some reason. Do you want to hold Ryan?"

It took me a moment to register this. I closed my eyes. I opened them and checked my phone. *SOS*, it said. Helen popped Ryan off her breast, which for some reason didn't make him howl, and she held him out to me. I had no choice but to take him, cradling him in the crook of my arm, as I looked out at the party.

"You know what else helps?" She popped a pacifier in the baby's mouth and it moved comically in and out as he sucked.

A new addition to the chaos of the lawn was a woman about my age, spooning food into the mouth of a child in a stroller. I cocked my head and watched her, leaning in and smiling close to the child's face.

"No," I said, "what else?"

"If you go to a bris and if you are the one to give the baby to the rabbi. That helps. It's good luck. Just do it. It can't hurt."

I rolled my eyes and shifted Ryan toward my chest as the woman took her child out of the stroller and rocked him to her. I watched Helen look at this mother we didn't know.

Helen turned to her husband. "That's the kid from Ethiopia, right?" she asked.

He shrugged, shoving food into his face quickly, before his baby was returned.

"I think it is. I think one of Michelle's mom's colleagues or something adopted it. In any case, she's single." She reached out and let Ryan grab her index finger. "And she went to Ethiopia three times or something."

"That's great!" I wanted to know what agency she went through and how long this woman had to wait. I wanted to know what the age of the child was when he or she arrived.

Helen looked at me. "That seems hard."

I cocked my head. "What does?" I asked. "Which part, I mean? The going to Africa three times? The singleness?"

She nodded after a moment. "Mm-hmm," Helen said. "Both."

"Huh," I said. I remembered the single woman being forced to leave that meeting at Smith Chasen and I felt happy for this woman who subverted those rules.

But I don't think that was what Helen was referring to.

I looked out to the lawn filled with white people and white babies. And two or three Asian girls, each over ten years old. And then I saw Harriet sniffing around in a pile of dirty plates next to several mothers and children I didn't recognize. I handed Ryan back over and stood up. "Gotta prevent a disaster here," I laughed. "I'll be back!" I said as I went to remove Harriet from the food.

Just as I had pulled her off of a plate of chicken legs, I saw our friends Carolyn and Michael, who, Michelle had told me, had placed three embryos—that joined donor eggs and Michael's sperm—into a surrogate.

"Hey," I said, trotting up to them, pitched sideways, as I held Harriet by the collar. "How are you guys?"

Carolyn was beaming. Michael too.

"Good news?" I asked, sitting down. I forced a wet Harriet, who wanted only to have a go at every plate of food on each blanket, to lie down next to me.

"Our surrogate is pregnant." Carolyn straightened her lean tanned legs out in front of her and shook them. Her red patent flats flashed in the sun. "Eight weeks."

"Oh, great!" I leaned in on her legs for a moment, emphasizing gladness. "I'm so happy for you guys."

And I was. There is, after all, room for everyone. Maybe there is a magic pot after all. As Carolyn proceeded to discuss the drugs that this donor, *her* donor, had taken to stimulate her egg production, and the spas Carolyn had sent the surrogate to in order to prepare her for pregnancy, I thought, first, about how Carolyn was married to a man who worked in finance, and second, that she and I were really the lost generation. Because soon, technology would be perfect enough to tell us which of our eggs would work, and soon it would be efficacious and cheap enough for all twenty-year-old women to freeze them. It would become a rite—a right—of passage, and soon these women would be stomping through boardrooms and trading floors like warriors, unconcerned with that thirty-five-years cutoff our gynecologists began to warn us about when we were still in training bras. Single young women will freeze their eggs, and suddenly their clocks will tick as steadily and calmly as anyone else's. They'll start drinking whiskey and smoking cigars in back rooms. We'll grow a pair and we will not be afraid to use them.

We will be cowboys.

"Twins," Michael said.

"No way!" I hit him on the arm. I looked around for Ramon, but I couldn't see him. "I can't wait to tell Ramon," I said, though that might have been a little bit disingenuous.

"Thank you," Carolyn said. "I appreciate that, Jesse. And tell me what's going on with you. Michelle tells me you've moved on to adoption. I hope it's going well." She looked into my eyes, to show me just how much she meant this and hoped I had good news.

"Don't ask." I rolled my eyes. "We're up with our profile and now it's a lot of hurry-up-and-wait-a-while. Anyway." Hers was the magic pot. Mine had been taken by the king after the peasants had all been slaughtered.

I still could not see Ramon, but I could hear the splashing and yelling and crying at the pool. I realized that, aside from Jacob's assistant, who was single and in her twenties, and the older couples here for Mr. and Mrs. Sanders, Ramon and I were the only childless or unexpectant people here.

I went to stand up, groaning. "I'm going to find Ramon," I said. "I'm hoping he's not already passed out in the barn."

I scanned the lawn and saw him holding a beer by its neck, chatting with Jacob at the barbecue. Seeing my husband there, from this far away, I could detect his unhappiness. It was physical. He slouched. His hair was too long. His eyes looked tired, and a little sad. He had lost weight—I could not wait for the next time Paola saw him, for her to shriek that he needed to be in Terracina at all times or he would die from starvation.

Ramon and I first had come here ten years ago. We all were here then, Michelle and Jacob, Ramon and me, and Belinda too, before she'd ever had to terminate her pregnancy. She had a different boyfriend then, and the six of us would grill and drink margaritas and roll joints, and Belinda and I would sneak away to smoke cigarettes and talk about presidential biographies and British novels by the pool in the pitch-dark, our feet dragging in the cool water. Someone would always streak naked into the pond and pretend to be bitten by the massive koi that somehow stayed alive in there. Harriet was the only child then, and in the mornings, hungover, we'd all drink coffee on the dock and languidly throw her sticks in the early sun.

Now Fishkill was a place I couldn't get airlifted out of soon enough. After Harriet dried off, and after I ate my weight in chili and sausages, and held enough babies to make me pregnant—by Helen's calculations anyway—for a lifetime, I'd had enough. I could feel the weight bearing down, but I had lost sight of Ramon.

"Where is he?" I said to Harriet as we went by the pool, encountering a battalion of children and the accoutrements of their attempts to swim—flippers and life vests and inflatable water wings and swim rings, kickboards—and the few adults drinking spiked punch and ignoring them. We looked in all the bedrooms and bathrooms. We went to the tennis court, also ruled by an army of children, and then around the back and into the woods.

The earth changed, and I felt my sandals sinking into the deep moss and dead leaves. We walked a few feet to the gazebo nestled at the edge of the property, in the woods.

"Hey," Ramon said. He sat in the gazebo beneath a canopy of spiderwebs.

"Ramon!" I said. "We've been looking all over for you." Harriet, always the underminer, ran inside and placed her paws on Ramon's lap.

"Awww," he said as she licked his face.

"Are you crying?" I asked.

Ramon cleared his throat and leaned back.

The gazebo was musty, coupled with the yeasty scent of beer, and it was hot and moist and dark, like the inside of a tropical cave. I sat down on the bench across from him.

"What's up?" I asked. My voice was strained.

Ramon wiped his bloodshot eyes. "Nothing."

"Come on, Ramon. You're being positively misanthropic."

"Who cares?" Ramon kicked at the soft planks of wood.

"I know." I sighed.

We were silent for a moment, just sitting there, listening to far-away joy.

He shooed me away with one hand. "Go ahead." His eyes glistened.

"No," I said. "What's up?"

"You know I don't even know my father's birthday?" His words were slurred.

"Really? Is that true?"

"His parents never told him the day of his birthday. His parents were Franco supporters, did you know that? That's why he left Spain. For Italy."

"I didn't," I said. "But that's quite a trade-off."

"Seriously!" he said. "This is not an American story."

"Okay," I said.

"And now I don't know his birthday." I saw the tears streaming down his face get caught in his stubble, shining, on his dimpled chin. "Now I'll never know it either," he said.

I sat down next to him. "I'm sorry," I said. "But you never know. He might be back, like your mother says. It might be black magic. I mean, it really could be all of that."

Ramon said something, but I couldn't make it out.

"You know you shouldn't have drunk so much," I said. "You've been drinking a lot lately."

"Can you not?" Ramon sat up. "For once can you just not do that? Not berate me or criticize me or have a fucking problem? Just this once?"

I could barely understand him, but I could discern the meaning behind what he was saying. I swallowed and sat back. "Okay," I said slowly.

"Because you know what? I don't have a father and now you know what?" He stood and stumbled and then stood again. "And now I'm not going to be a father either. No more fathers!" he said, mocking the making of an important speech.

"Ramon."

"You're always talking about the mothers," he said. "But the fathers are here too."

I stood up. I put my hand on his shoulder. It was awkward for me, as I had become less inclined to show affection. "You will be a father. We will be parents. It's what you've been saying and it's true." I brushed the hair out of his face. "Okay?"

He nodded. "Maybe this is just too hard." He reached down to the floor, where a beer bottle stood. He took a long slug. "Maybe this is too hard for us."

"Stop it," I said.

Harriet had left the dank gazebo for the brighter green grass and the prospect of uneaten sausages, and I looked out to watch her approach the blankets of people, leaving mayhem and destruction in her wake.

"Jesse!" someone from within the chaos called out. "You have got to get Harriet out of here!" Children began to shriek.

I looked over at Ramon, snarling into his beer. I took his hand. "We've got to save the poor innocent children from our feral animal."

He laughed, a little bitterly.

"We can find out your dad's birthday," I said. "I mean, you can find out anything now, can't you?"

"I don't care," he said. "I guess that's the point. I can't even wake up and say, 'Today is Ramon Sr.'s birthday, how strange not to talk to him today.'"

I nodded.

"There is just nothing that makes me remember him. I don't live where I grew up. I don't have a sibling. I don't have a child. Nothing reminds me of my father."

His speech had suddenly become clear. I nodded.

"Jesse!" someone else called.

I popped my head out. "I'll be right there! Harriet, come!" I screamed, more for the people than for the dog, who I knew would not obey.

"Let's go," I said, trying to heave Ramon up.

I felt the pull in my arms, the inverse and opposite feeling of Ramon dragging me up from bed this morning. "Please," I said. "Let's grab Toto, click our heels three times, and go home."

19

———

Fall 2010

The seasons were changing; time was just going and going; there was no holding back that stream of sand in the hourglass.

We had no calls in September.

And yet, there is nothing as exquisite as that month. Though I taught at a city school, hardly a university crawling with ivy and ringed by old trees, even here, September was about promise and winning. If spring is rebirth, September is for remaking.

In September we did not hear from a birthmother, but we did get a note from Anita. I got a note, I should say. She and Paula had matched with an African-American birthmother near them, in North Carolina. *I hope it's okay that I'm telling you this,* she wrote in the e-mail. I looked over my shoulder to see if Ramon was there.

As kids we were told, There's room for everyone, don't worry. Girls, share! my sister and I were instructed. There's plenty to go around. But of course that's not true. Now there was nowhere near enough. There were fewer jobs and less food—whole countries were starving—and there were fewer babies than those who wanted the babies. So was I happy for Anita and Paula?

I was.

"Ramon!" I called out when I saw the e-mail. "Come here!" I said.

He leaned over me and I could feel his breath in my ear, and hear it stop.

I looked up at him. His face was so close. I could see his gray-flecked sideburns, and his long lashes touching down to the tender skin below his eyes and then rising up again. He rubbed his eye and cleared his throat.

"You okay?" I asked.

He cleared his throat. "Yeah," he said. "I guess I just wasn't expecting that."

"Expecting—"

"Them to be first. We started at the same time."

"They live right there," I said. "The birthmother must have wanted to be close by."

I did wonder, not for the first time, why this particular birthmother was placing her child. Was she too young? Did she already have too many children? But what does "too many children" mean?

"I just really thought we'd be first." He laughed. "I wonder when I'm going to stop thinking that."

I looked up at him again and I knew he was talking about everything.

We heard from Anita and then we heard from my mother.

I had cooked dinner—roasted salmon and lentils—and Ramon had cleaned the dining room table of his papers and computer. Ramon had just opened a bottle of sauvignon blanc when my cell rang, my mother's face lighting up the tiny screen.

"Guess what?" she screamed when, after hesitating, I picked up.

"What?" Nothing made me less excited than my mother's excitement. She will always, without qualification, ignite the teenager within me.

"Guess who's going to be here for dinner tomorrow night?"

"I don't know, Mom. Jesus? Bob Dylan?" I poured my own wine and sat down.

"No, guess again."

"Those are my only guesses." I opened up the solitaire game on my computer.

"You are no fun. Fine, fine, Lucy is coming to dinner. That's who," she said. Her grin reached me through the phone. I could tell she was ear to ear with the news itself and also with being the one to bear it.

"Really?" I said.

"Yup," she said. "Apparently your sister is on her way home tomorrow. For good, she says."

"Really," I said, more than a little put off that Lucy hadn't told me so herself.

"Can you believe it? So, can you and Ramon be here? And Harriet, of course."

"Is she coming alone?" I asked.

"I'm not sure. She called from Memphis."

"Memphis?"

"She was driving, she said. She'd been driving since Mexico." I could hear my mother moving around the kitchen, the beep of the microwave, the brief rush of the faucet. "Look, I didn't press it. Because she's coming home now. Three years. It's been three years. Are you going to come down then?"

"Sure," I said. "Of course," I said. "We'll be there."

I turned to Ramon, who was already at work on his meal. "Lucy's coming home." I pictured my sister opening up her backpack,

213

stuffed with wrinkled print skirts and tank tops. I could not even imagine those clothes now. I saw Lucy at eleven, on crutches from a fall during soccer practice; at sixteen, returning from a school ski trip. I'm not entirely sure I was excited to see Lucy now. I loved my sister, but what if I no longer liked her?

Ramon looked up from his dinner and smiled.

Lucy was coming home and once again Ramon and I were driving down to Virginia.

Perhaps Lucy was on a different leg of this same highway. What would she look like? Sound like? I thought of my mother's returns. Who will she be now? I'd wonder as we waited at the gate for her to emerge from the stream of exiting travelers. Will I recognize her? Once I'd told my father this as he stood holding Lucy's hand and mine: Maybe we won't recognize her. Maybe she's changed, I'd said.

Of course we will! my father had said, squeezing our hands tight. She is exactly the same! Just like we are.

But we were not the same, Lucy and me, and my father, too. My father had successes and failures at work. And Lucy went to Roley Poleys, and sat with Claudine as she smoked, starching and ironing my father's shirts. Presidents were shot and I kissed Andrew Tanaka on the playground and I got my period and I dissected a frog, and my mother was not there for any of these things.

Driving down our block with Ramon now, toward the house, I thought how every trip lived inside my mother, every zebra or cheetah, each marketplace where she bought bracelets for her ungrateful daughters, every field harrowed and well dug, each woman's hand held. Even if my mother was as identifiable as before she had gone, her hair the same, perhaps lighter from the sun, her glasses dusty, her all-over freckles more pronounced, she was still changed. As we were changed.

We pulled into the driveway and parked behind a red rusted Toyota Camry with a frowning tailpipe, and I ran up the stairs toward the house while Ramon let Harriet pee.

Through the window, I could see Lucy, seated on the living room couch, her face in profile, as recognizable to me as my own. Her hair was long and fine, nearly blond, and she was a soft shade of brown, not that mahogany color so many travelers to places by the sea become. Her face was a bit fuller now, which gave her the appearance of being younger than thirty-six. Her cheeks looked like they had when she was a child, not as they'd been when I saw her last; her cheekbones and chin had been defined then, her eyes deeply set.

Lucy turned toward the window, and seeing me there, she smiled. She waved and slowly rose to her feet to make her way to the door to greet me. It was when she stood that I saw it. Bisected by the picture-window panes was my sister's body, standing now, the center of her rounded. Her hands slid along her belly as she moved toward the front door.

I did not shift from the bottom of the stairs leading up to the house, and then the door was opened, and there she was, framed by the doorway. She leaned against the door now, nothing like herself and also more herself, her thighs and arms thick, her belly the shape of a small turned cauldron.

I stared. I am not sure if my jaw was slack, but I could not register the image before me. It entered me the way all the bits of necessary information I've accrued have entered me, far too slowly and without clarity.

Inside, though, the intelligence was making itself clear. And then I heard Ramon breathing next to me. For a moment, we were all silent, and then my mother peered out from the door, behind Lucy, and then Ramon charged forward, up the stairs.

"Oh my God, Lucy!" he said, taking the stairs quickly. Harriet followed him inside the door. "Look at you!"

I could see her face as she hugged my husband, whose arms seemed ever-large to me now, big enough to embrace the world, and Lucy's eyes were squeezed tight, her shoulders high.

"Hey, you!" I said, still unmoving at the foot of the stairs.

I walked up the stairs and she moved toward me and then I felt her imprint upon me, her large stomach at my stomach, her burgeoning breasts at mine as she hugged me tightly. She gripped my back, and as I went to release myself from her grasp, she continued to hug me, tighter now.

I could not explain then even one of the reasons I was crying.

"You okay?" my mother said to me inside. I smelled garlic and also cinnamon and melted butter.

"Of course!" I said.

Ramon brought our bags upstairs, and after Harriet greeted everyone, my father poured wine—"None for Lucy!" he laughed—and we all sat down.

"When did you get in?" I asked Lucy.

"Just like an hour ago." She rubbed her belly and then, when she saw me scrutinize her, she stopped. "I drove from Memphis."

"Mom said. Did you drive all by yourself?"

"Just from Santa Fe. We took buses everywhere. Greif and me, together, I mean, up the Pan-American Highway. And then we got that Toyota that's out front. He drove me to New Mexico and then headed back to California. I didn't want to fly."

"Yeah," I said.

"It's good you didn't fly, Lucy," my father said, going on his knowledge of pregnancy from 1973. That was the year Lucy arrived in a wood-paneled station wagon, a pinprick in my mother's arms. My mother held her like that for six weeks, until she went back to work.

"Did you guys know about this?" I turned to my parents.

"The traveling? No," my mother said. "I have long ago washed my hands of Lucy's choices in that regard."

"What?" Lucy said.

"I meant the baby," I said. "Jesus, Mom. Obviously the baby."

"Oh, no," my mother said, her mouth pursed. "We didn't know about this either. First we're hearing of it. You two will see. Sometimes you just have to go with it."

"Go with it?" Lucy said.

"Yes, Lucy. Just as it all falls. Plays it as it lays. Because you lose control of your children. You never stop worrying, but you lose control."

Lucy leaned her head back against the pale yellow wall, her mouth open, as if caught on a line. Then she lifted her head. "I realize I should have told you guys earlier."

I gulped at my wine and looked at Ramon. I raised my eyebrows. My father, I noted, did the same as he looked at my mother.

"Would you stop it?" Lucy said to me. "I'm sorry to let you know this way, but it is not about you. It's not about any of you, but I'm sorry I didn't warn you, I guess. I don't know, I thought you might be, like, happy or something."

"We are happy," my father said. "As long as you're happy."

I nodded. "Okay," I said. "So! When are you due?"

"We're *very* happy," my mother interjected. "A grandchild!" she said.

"End of February," Lucy said.

"And who is the father? Where is the father? Is no one asking about the father?" I asked.

There was silence.

"What color is the father?" I laughed. Perhaps this would be a family with two Hispanic children.

"That's enough," my mother said. "It's that boy she was traveling with. Lucy has already told us this."

Lucy nodded again. "Greif is the father—he's white, for whatever that's worth—but, as I said, he's in Baja, he didn't want to come back, and I did. I wanted to be with my family." She made an effort to hold back tears.

I rose and then sat next to my sister. "This is really great news." I patted her hair along her back, as if she were a pony. "It's wonderful news. It's just shocking."

"I think so," Ramon said. "I mean, that it's terrific news."

"We all do," my father said. "It's a girl," he stated. "Right, Lucy?"

Lucy smiled and nodded. "A lot could happen. I mean, she's not here yet."

"Well, I'm here to say," my father said, "that daughters are just the most wonderful thing." He got up to crack open another bottle of pinot noir. "Just the most wonderful things."

It was my mother's famous forty-garlic-clove chicken for dinner, and this time the fame I could get behind, as it was a dish I remembered having eaten repeatedly. Lucy sat across from me, my parents at the heads of the table. But for Ramon beside me, it was as if I had never left this table.

My mother spooned rice onto our plates and served the chicken out of the red Dansk casserole dish I will always associate with company, and we passed a big wooden bowl of salad, and I heard Harriet come into the room, and it was, for a moment, so pleasant to be there. Every time I looked across at Lucy, I would feel a swelling of happiness at seeing her again, and then an acute sadness whose source I would not name.

"So what is the plan, Lou?" my father asked. "We want to hear all about your travels, too, but I need to know the plan."

Lucy moved the food around on her plate. "Let me start by saying, this was planned. Well, let me back up. When I was in El Salvador, I got pregnant, uh, accidentally. That was last January, I guess, so after I lost that—"

"You lost it?" I asked.

"Yes." She looked down, touching the chicken several times with the tines of her fork.

"I'm so sorry!" I said. I remembered what that was like, the way it just slipped away, the life you'd begun to imagine and the thing itself that let you imagine it.

"Sorry, Lucy," Ramon said. "That's terrible. Especially alone."

"Greif was there! Greif has been great. Really. He started giving surf lessons to other tourists to take care of us. He was on board until I decided I wanted to leave. Leave Mexico, or any of the other beach places. Leave that whole *mode*. It didn't make sense to me if I had a child. In any case, after that I realized I was at that age when you're supposed to worry; everyone kept saying that if I wanted a baby, the time was now, how if I had the faintest desire I would regret not trying later, how in childbearing years I was already old, how my eggs were old, and then everything that had happened to Jesse"—she held her hand toward me, as if we didn't know me and my plight by now—"and so I decided I wanted to try. I wanted there to be a baby in the family."

I startled at this stinging sentiment, spoken so freely, as I did not want to be the focus of this dinner. In childbearing years I was now ancient. And so I went in for more chicken, tearing a thigh apart, first with my knife and fork, and then taking the bones up with my hands. It was succulent. Had I been wrong? Perhaps my mother had always cooked. Perhaps we had been eating out of that red Dansk casserole dish since the invention of the station wagon.

"I'm not saying that's the only reason, Jesse, but I've been away a long time and I started thinking about family, my family, families in general, I guess. We had this big family, you know? I thought of our grandmothers and great-grandmothers. All the cousins and aunts and uncles. Even Passover."

"Passover!" my mother said.

"Yes, traditions. And families in the movies, dysfunctional families, fighting, making up. I realized I wanted all of that and for some reason I was cutting myself off from it. Even its possibility."

If she said the word *family* one more time I thought I would stick my head in my mother's new oven. I looked at Ramon, who was nodding his head earnestly at my sister. My parents, both of them, were smiling.

"Family is big," my mother said. "Politics is big and the world is big, but so is family. Our family."

"Excuse me for just a minute." I got up from the table and placed my napkin, veined with grease, on my chair.

I walked slowly up to the attic—that goddamn attic where I had thought of so many things, not one of them being that I would get sick and not be able to have children. Who cared about babies? I cared about going to my friends' houses and sneaking into bars. I cared about music, so deeply I wrote the lyrics down to every song I ever loved in the neatest handwriting I would ever muster. I cared about records and talking on the phone and the movies.

I lay down on my bed. I looked at the ceiling, the same dusty track lighting from 1981, just as the blue walls, chosen because I had not wanted to be perceived as girly, had not been painted over.

"Blue?" my father had said when we were picking out the paint in the hardware store. "Won't that just depress you?"

"No, Dad," I'd said. I was already exasperated. "You know what would depress me? Pink."

"These are not the only two colors," he said. "You realize the color you've chosen is called Downpour?"

"Yes," I said. "Downpour. Let's do it."

I thought of those movies too. The ones Lucy mentioned, where people sit around tables and fight. The movies where daughters get carried on their fathers' shoulders, carried away from the dangers of growing up a girl. Kids throw their caps in the air; they hug one another good-bye. They return, back in through that front door, with their own swaddling. Any one of those frames made me sob silently. I was happy for Lucy. I was happy for us all. She was right; there should be a baby in the family. I don't know why it had to only be mine.

Briefly I wondered if our child—Ramon's and mine—whenever she came, in whatever casing he arrived in, would be loved as much as Lucy's. How could I tell? The moment was only now. Time was slowing and all we knew of the future was on a date in February, Lucy would be giving birth to a baby girl.

I heard footsteps. "Hello," I said.

"Hey," she said. "Are you okay?"

The treads were slow and heavy and I knew they would carry Lucy to the top of the stairs, where she appeared, out of breath. She made her way—she was beginning already to have the pregnancy waddle—over to my bed and sat down on the end of it. She tilted her head to the side and rubbed my leg:

The Mother.

I nodded, sitting up. "Listen, Lucy," I said. "I'm pleased for you, I am. I am relieved and happy. And I know it's not about me. But it's just a lot!"

She nodded.

"Why didn't you tell me?" I said. "It would have been a shock anyway, but to not tell me before . . . About the miscarriage, and then trying again."

"I know," she said.

"I am ashamed not to have had any idea this was even something you wanted."

Lucy swallowed. "I don't know why I just couldn't talk to you. Every time we talked I intended to. I would call with every intention of telling you. First it was about the miscarriage. And then time had passed and I felt I couldn't. And so, because I hadn't told you about that, it just grew. And then I hadn't told Mom and Dad. Because all of those things were connected. The family."

I swallowed.

"And to be honest, you never asked me. Anything. You would sort of pass judgment on me about everything, and I wanted to explain more deeply about my choices. I started to write you several times as well. But every time I did I still felt you looking down at me, like you'd be grading my letter. I thought in the end it would be better if I saw you. I knew I would be coming back soon, and I couldn't even explain that to you."

I smiled crookedly. "I understand." I likely would have been grading her letter. "I realize I didn't give you a lot of opportunity. I'm sorry. That's awful, how long you've been trying to talk to me."

We sat, silent, for a moment. I could hear the sounds of our family downstairs, Ramon's and my mother's laughter overlapping.

"Do you have a name?" I asked.

"Yes," Lucy said. "I think so. Hannah. What do you think of Hannah?"

Our grandmother's name. Life is what happens, Grandma Hannah used to say, when you're busy making other plans. "It's lovely," I said.

"I looked it up," Lucy said. "Hannah was the mother of the prophet Samuel. She was unable to have children, and so she prayed that if God gave her a son then she would give him up to be a priest."

"Are you giving her up to me?" I said brightly.

"Are you a priest trainer?"

"How did you guess? All this time hanging with Ramon's mother has turned me into a priest trainer. There's a lot I haven't told you as well," I said.

Lucy began to laugh and then stopped, her smile fading. "Anyway, the name means 'God has graced me.'"

I laughed, very softly.

"What?"

"It sounds perfect," I said. "It's a perfect, beautiful name." I took Lucy's hand in both of mine. "I can't wait to meet her."

The talking and laughing ceased when Lucy and I arrived again at the table.

"Everything okay?" my father asked cheerily.

"I see you, Dad," I said. "Feeding Harriet."

"Her Royal Highness needs some food. She's too skinny!"

"Fine," I said. "Whatever."

And then something unusual happened. My parents turned toward Lucy.

"So," my mother said. "What are you going to do?"

"I'm not sure yet."

"Do you have a job?"

"Possibly," Lucy said. "In New York. I've been talking to people at the Wildlife Conservation Society."

"Wonderful!" my parents said at the same time.

"Something along those lines anyway," she said.

"That sounds good," Ramon said. "You know who else lives in New York?"

"I know," Lucy said. "Why on earth else would I want to work for an animal conservation organization in New York City?"

"You better figure all this out, honey," my father said, slipping Harriet more chicken, totally poker-faced. "When are you due exactly?"

"February twenty-sixth," Lucy said. "To be exact."

"That was my grandmother's birthday." My father gazed away from the table dramatically.

My mother looked at my sister. "Well, you better get cracking," she said.

I leaned back, watching everyone. And for the first time in a long time, the pressure was off.

That night, after we finished dinner, and my father's famous apple pie with cheddar, the way Grandma Hannah showed him how to serve it when he first met our mother, after listening to tales of Lucy's travels, and after several glasses of wine, Ramon and Harriet and I went upstairs to bed. Harriet was reluctant to leave the living room should more food or more love be proffered, but Ramon swept her up and I watched her look out longingly as he carried her upstairs, cradled in his arms.

He set her down at the end of my bed, where she stretched out. So much so that when I climbed into the tiny bed, I could not straighten my legs. I slid her up, parallel to me. I lifted up her ear leather: *Grr,* I said, and she licked the air.

"Wow," Ramon said from the other bed, set perpendicular to mine, when we were still, in the dark.

Downpour. What a color. It made the room exceedingly dark, but for the streetlights shining through the spaces in between the slats of the blinds.

"I must say, I was very surprised," I said.

"A bit of a shock for sure." Ramon thumped his pillow.

Here we go, I thought. He's going under. "I was obviously upset, but I get upset when anyone I know is pregnant. You know? I don't think it was necessarily particular to Lucy."

"But it is your sister."

"But because of that I also feel happy about it. I'm glad that she doesn't have these struggles, you know?"

"Absolutely," Ramon said. "Look, every time someone else has a child or gets pregnant or whatever, I die a little. I do. And then I get resurrected or something. This took me a second to be happy again."

"Resurrected? How Catholic of you."

"Well."

The pillow was still beneath Ramon's head, so I continued. "But look, we have everything ready. It could be quick, the adoption. We could have kids at the same time. Lucy and us. Our kids could be almost like siblings." Of all the things I know, I know I am grateful for a sibling. I am grateful for my sister.

"Especially if she ends up in New York," Ramon said.

I imagined it for a moment, Lucy finding a place in our neighborhood, walking the streets with her and Hannah, who would resemble us almost equally. If I were to take her out alone, a neighbor might ask me how I lost the baby weight so quickly.

I was glad for Lucy's child, and for the first time in a long while, an aspect of Ramon's and my future had a face and a body and a name. Another generation peeked her head around the corner. Someone else would be there to sit at that dining room table, and listen—or decidedly not listen—and grow up there.

Ramon rose out of his bed, a ghostly shape, a darker figure than the fuzzy darkness of the room.

"Hi," I said as he crawled into bed next to me.

He moved in closer and placed his arm around me. He cupped Harriet's head. Between them, I could feel two heartbeats. "Do you think it will happen?" I asked.

He bristled. "Do I think what will happen?" he said, holding me close.

"This," I said.

He didn't pause. "I do," he said. "I know it will."

Close together in my childhood twin bed, I could feel the "we" of our bodies. My family, I thought as the two of them fell to snoring.

20

___

November 2010

The first birthmother to call was Katrina. It was just before midnight on Thanksgiving.

All that waiting, and when I saw the number coming in, I wasn't prepared.

"Ramon!" I shook him awake. "It's a birthmother!"

"Well answer it!" he said. "Before it goes to voice mail and we lose her."

"Hello?" I could not still the crazed hysteria in my voice.

"Hi," a voice said calmly. "I'm Katrina," she said. "A birthmom. I found you online."

"Wow," I said. "Thanks so much for calling." I got out of bed and went into my office/closet for my pen and notebook.

I sat down at my desk. "Hi," I said, and before I could ask her what she liked about our "Dear Birthmother" letter, as I was trained to do (was it our many travels? our diverse community?), she began speaking.

"Let me tell you about me," she said. "Because I've done this before, and I know what a gift this is for a family. I'm forty. I'm a grandmother."

"Wow," I again said. *Forty,* I wrote. *Grandmother.* "A child is a generous gift, absolutely." A generous gift? One thinks of golf clubs. A trip to Paris. What gift could be more generous? "What can I tell you about Ramon and me?" I asked. "What would you like to know about us?"

The agency told us not to ask for any information we could get from them directly, as it could be construed as pressure. This is what the agency can later tell us: what color she is, what color the father is, if she has been to the doctor, if she has taken drugs, if she is on drugs now, how old she is, if she has a job, if she has a mental illness or if anyone in her family has a mental illness, if anyone has a clubfoot or a cleft palate. How open she wants this adoption to be. Will she want to come for Thanksgiving, for instance? Like tonight. Where had she gone for Thanksgiving? Or will she only want photos? How open?

Our offering of openness was our first and last names on our profiles. I'd spent countless hours fretting over students' coming upon Ramon's and my letter and profile along my Google trail of academic articles and disgruntled Rate My Professor reviews. But what was open, really? What would it look like? And feel like?

"I want to know," Katrina said, "why you want my baby. I know," she said, "that I have what you want."

"I can tell you that we want to be parents." I doodled in my notebook. Jagged stars. "Very much." How desperate, I wondered, was it cool to appear?

I pictured this faceless woman holding her stomach. *We,* I wrote. *I.* Each of the birthmothers is a "we." There we were, our different lonely women's bodies. But the birthmother one becomes an "I," too.

"I'm not selling my baby," Katrina told me. "I'm not."

Which made me think, Is this person trying to sell me her baby?

"I've got four kids. My youngest, Connor, is three. My oldest just had a baby of his own. But let me tell you something. It's only with a daughter if you really know that baby is your grandchild. Do you know what I'm saying?"

"I think I do," I said.

"How do I really know that baby is not some other boy's?" she said. "Some shitty fuckup like the one my seventeen-year-old got knocked up with? I have five children. The last one—Davis—I gave him up two years ago. This will be number six. I see the light in that family's eyes." Katrina began to cry a little. "I see what they couldn't have without me, and I am happy that I made the decision. It was two weeks before the birth and my boyfriend left. What was I supposed to do? One minute you're preparing for a kid, and then the next? Well."

"I hear you." I pictured the CHILD PROOFING! sign at the gynecologist's office. They would have had a field day in here.

"I have a three-year-old at home, and a girl, Cassie, and even though I told my boyfriend, 'You do so much as come on my knees I'll get pregnant,' he didn't listen, and so here I am."

"Here we are," I said. "How lucky."

"But this time I want to be *there*. Last time, the decisions were made for me. I'd checked out. Emotionally I mean. But not this time. I'm talking to a lot of people. I'm going to do it right this time," she said.

"Of course," I said. "We want to be here in whatever way makes you most comfortable."

"In April," Katrina said. "I'm going to do it right."

"You're due in April?"

"The twenty-second."

"I understand," I said. "You have to be sure you get what you need. We want as open a relationship as you want to have. Whatever you need."

"I need to bond with my baby." Katrina was crying harder now. "I need to have that time in the hospital to just see him again. Last time I didn't even want to hold him."

"That must have been so hard. I'm sorry for what you've been through." I couldn't think about what that would be like. Holding a baby. After.

"I need to get the hell out of this trailer," Katrina told me.

I wasn't sure if I was supposed to answer this with reassurance of some kind. I didn't know if she was asking me for help moving and I didn't know if that was right or wrong. I had lost sight of a lot of things.

"I know I am a good woman," she said. "I know what I am on the outside. I know what people think, all the tattoos. The bad boys. But that's not necessarily me on the inside. I read a lot of books. Self-help books and books about God. I am going through a spiritual change and I know who I am now. On the inside? I have a heart as big as a cloud. And also? Jesse? I have a heartbeat that isn't just my own."

When I hung up with Katrina, I climbed back into bed next to Ramon. I lay on my back looking up at the ceiling, convex, as if the pressed tin were a bowl that held the weather.

"Do you want to know about the conversation?" I asked my husband.

"Sure, though I heard the whole thing. You were great." He patted my leg, anticipating my next question. It seemed like he might want to wait until morning to discuss this, which was an abomination as far as I was concerned. Here was progress. I thought of Carmen, the perfect birthmother who never called, and how now we were moving forward. For one split second I felt time stop. I imagined going up to Fishkill next year, holding our own baby. It was hard, I'd say, rocking her in my arms, kissing at her ear, but so worth it! I imagined Lucy and I leaning on two strollers, moving through the neighborhood we grew up in, smiling at the neighbors whose houses we once ding-dong-ditched, whose gardens we once plucked lily of the valley and lilacs from.

"She's forty and a grandmother. But it's her second adoption. I know she'll go through with it. That's what the agency said, remember?" I said to Ramon.

"Remember what?"

"The best birthmothers know how hard it is to parent." I would be lying if I said I didn't picture parenting as finally peaceful, mother and infant together on a giant bed, two spoons. But I do know—my head does, anyway—that an infant doesn't quiet from only having been wanted.

Ramon was silent. "Well," he said.

"She seems smart." I sighed. "She said she had a heart as big as a cloud." I smiled in the dark. Outside I could hear the tires of a bus singing down Smith Street. Several people were laughing out front, and then a car door slammed. Families home from dinner, far away. Families, I thought, and I did not feel like the word would make me cry. "I like that expression."

April, I thought. Already I could smell spring.

The agency was closed for Thanksgiving weekend, and Katrina called several times in the next few days. Katrina and I talked—she did mostly—for hours on end. We talked about her children, about

California, the ocean, the desert, about God. She told me she wore her heart on her sleeve, an uncomfortable place for a heart, she said, laughing, and she told me she was looking for a real connection with someone, though I was not sure then if she meant someone who would parent her child or just someone who would understand that she looked to the world like one person, but to herself she was someone different.

My phone plan had one feature: I could talk to five select people for free. That weekend, I exchanged my mother's cell (calling it amounted to listening to her trying to talk and drive, a terrifying, one-way conversation) with Katrina's, using a flower for an icon. Even though it felt like an emoticon, which I would never use, and even though my phone had a nearly unreadable cracked face, I liked that this flower represented the birthmother. It felt like Katrina was growing something beautiful.

On Saturday morning, Ramon and I looked for Katrina online. But we couldn't find her. It was strange and wondrous for someone to leave no digital footprint, as if she had wings or was merely physical flesh, only the mother of a fetus that could one day grow to be our child if we simply answered the phone late at night and listened to her body talking. Her body: a green growing place. Her body: lodging for the tiny beat of a pulse, the pin-sized black spot, the finger curled at the mouth, a curved floating form attached by corded rope, tightly tethered. Finally, the birthmother.

Katrina told me she lived in her trailer in the desert, in Joshua Tree, a place I consider magical. The first time I went, after giving a paper at a conference in Los Angeles, I got my teaching job in Manhattan. The second time, when I was visiting a friend who loved extreme sports and had rented a house there, I found out I was pregnant. Even though the latter didn't stick and the job was not tenure-track, that Katrina lived there was an intimation of magic.

The desert was extraordinary to me with its blind white heat, the flowering beaver tail and prickly pear cacti nestled between rocks, the rock daisies blossoming out of scorched earth. I was as shocked by the desert as I had been by the New York skyline, the lights switching on at twilight across the water from Brooklyn. The desert was as breathtaking as stepping onto the surface of the moon, the sudden drop to freezing, the ceaseless howl of the coyote as its night soundtrack. As Katrina talked about her children, her boyfriends, her tiny-ass trailer, her good looks and young skin, I wondered how the desert had formed her, the way the city has formed me. Surely it makes you something, I thought as I imagined Katrina leaving her trailer while we talked, looking up at the stars—the Big Dipper, Cassiopeia, the crescent moon suspended from an invisible string—her robe gathered at her throat, the silhouette of a Joshua tree at her side.

"You know we look alike," Katrina said. "I'm dark too. And like Ramon, I've got some hot Italian blood. There's a lot of me to love, but we all look alike."

All of us? I thought. She had access to our information, the many happy pictures of Ramon and me smiling broadly while cooking with his cousins in Terracina, pictures of us seated around a massive bowl of pasta in his mother's hot kitchen, us in profile looking out over the Hudson with Harriet, the changing leaves bursting into flames below.

"Can you send a photo?" I asked timidly. No pressure! the agency told us at that session. The birthmother, they told us, that most fragile bird, might fly away. We don't want them to change their minds, the agency said. We don't want to hurt them, Crystal told us. Which made us realize that the agency was there mostly to protect the birthmothers.

For our protection, Ramon and I only had each other.

"I'm on Myspace," Katrina said. Myspace. I forgot that was even still a thing. "Trina," she said. "No one ever calls me Katrina."

"Oh, *Trina*." We'd been searching under the wrong name. "Thank you so much for calling us. We will find you."

I was ready with my laptop on the coffee table when Ramon came in from his run, smelling of dried leaves and sweat. He sat next to me on the couch, breathing hard.

There she was! And she *was* pretty. Dark hair and green eyes. And there were her gorgeous children. Gorgeous children who might look like the child who could become our child.

"Why didn't we do this earlier?" I pointed to the child on the screen. "Gamble on the place where you are guaranteed to be a parent."

"I tried," Ramon began, but he stopped.

I paused and looked up at him now and saw him in Michelle's gazebo, weeping. The fathers, he had said.

Flipping through the images on Katrina's page, we came across photos we assumed were of her daughter, and the grandchild, and then some animated flowers spilling out from between animated spread legs, a lot of mermaids and fairies, and then a block of text that said: *SS. White Girls Only.*

"Whoa." Ramon touched my shoulder.

"What?" I shot three images ahead, to a photo of a kid flipping the bird at the camera.

"Go back," Ramon said.

I closed my eyes. I could feel the tears escaping from under the lids, so I closed them tighter. "No." I moved ahead, confronted now by photos of heavily tattooed men with shaved heads, one with a swastika on his bicep.

Ramon edged the laptop toward him with the tips of his tapered fingers and flipped back several images. Of course it was there again, in that special font reserved for all things Hitler: *SS. White Girls Only.*

"Who cares?" I said. I'd spent days on the phone with this woman. I haven't felt this kind of connection with anyone else I've spoken to, she'd told me. I had been silent, but it had been a while for me as well to talk to someone without interruption. With new hope. "It doesn't matter. Nurture over nature, right?"

"We have to deal with these people." Ramon stood up. "They are going to be in our lives, remember? Open adoption."

"It's always you seeing the negative! It's nurture over nature," I said. "All the research says so."

"Jesse," Ramon said. Now he bent down and held my wrists. "What is the positive here? She's forty years old. We want someone young and healthy and who isn't a fascist."

"But she chose us!" I was crying; I couldn't stop it. And forty, it was only six months from now. "That could be anything. People put stuff online without knowing what it means all the time. She might not even know what it means."

Ramon went to take a shower but our bathroom was tiny and right off the living room, so he couldn't leave the conversation.

"I'll call the agency, and they'll be able to tell us more," I said, sniffling.

Ramon turned on the shower.

"She's chosen us, Ramon," I said, louder. "She told me we are her first choice." I could hear him step into the shower. "We had a connection. I don't think we should just let this go."

On Monday, I finally talked to Crystal at the office in Raleigh. Crystal said Katrina had done an intake already and she was: Caucasian. Her boyfriend was: Caucasian with some Native American. She lived where she told me she lived, and she was the age she told me she was. Her last child, however, had been adopted through another agency. The real red flag here, Crystal said, was that she could be talking to more than one agency. And? Crystal said, we don't have a confirmation of her pregnancy.

Red flags. We learned about those in Raleigh, too, and not having a pregnancy confirmation would be a major one. Another red flag? If the birthfather does not know the birthmother's plan to give up the child. Or? If the father does know the adoption plan, because then he can hinder it. If it's early in the pregnancy, before five months, say, then the birthmother has ample time to change her mind. If the grandparents are involved, they can decide they will parent the child. And if they're not involved, that's a red flag too, because the birthmother isn't getting the support she needs.

"That's not a problem," I said. I did not mention the Third Reich imagery. "Trina told me she'd be going to the doctor on Wednesday. We're set to talk after her appointment."

"That's great!" Crystal said. "I'll let you know as soon as I get the paperwork."

Katrina did not call me after her appointment on Wednesday, nor did she call on Thursday. On Friday I left her a message, and then I tried her several days later.

"Oh hi, Jesse." She sounded very faraway. Not just alone-on-the-surface-of-the-night-desert far, but also: gone. As if I had not heard about her mother who never loved her, her daughter's drug problem, her son's anger-management issues.

"Hey there!" I was terribly cheerful. "How are you?" I thought then of something Katrina had said in one of our many hours of previous conversations: What would I have been had I the power to choose my own mother? she'd asked. I could have everything you have. I could have been a professor, like you, or a doctor or a musician. I want to choose my child's mother right.

But she was only choosing by what a mother *does*. I realized, from where she sat, trying to get herself and her children out of a trailer park I saw tilted on some desert precipice, that was important. A professor? I speak from experience: great hours, summers off, but the world is coming down around us. I thought, My mother was a good person, her job was a job that helped people. But was she a good mother? I thought of all the mothers of my youth—the ones who schlepped us across town, who cut oranges into smiles for our soccer games, who sewed patches on their kids' torn pants, the ones who were there, station wagons humming, when we got out of school. Who was a better mother? Claudine read to me before my parents came home. But does it really matter who read to me? Because I was read to. I grew up being read to every day.

"I'm in the grocery store, can I call you back?" Katrina asked.

Her tone was changed, dismissive. I wondered if she had found someone else, another person who had what she wanted, for herself or for her child; I couldn't say.

"Nope," Crystal said when I called to tell her. "We never got a verification of Katrina's pregnancy. Sometimes," she said, "the birthmothers are scared. They're so young. They change their minds."

"She's forty." The rare birthmother bird, shaking the branches of a leaf-filled tree. I pictured Carmen again, young and beautiful and hopeful, a spiral notebook at her chest as she leaned back dreamily against her locker.

"It's like dating," Crystal said now. "You get some duds before you find true love."

"She's a grandmother," I said. I still did not tell Crystal about the emblems of Nazism on Myspace, which would have precluded another date on both our parts.

"She might not have been pregnant," Crystal said. "She might have just been looking for a friend. Or she might be shopping around agencies. She might have been after money."

"Why," I asked Crystal, "am I talking to someone who has not sent in a confirmation of pregnancy?"

"Sometimes it takes a while to get that. Sometimes," she said, "we have to go on our reserves of faith. You will have a child. It might not be Katrina's and it might not be the next birthmother's, but it will totally happen for you guys!"

How many ways, I thought, my breath short, can we fail?

I called to tell Lucy about Katrina, and as the phone rang I could imagine the beat of the conversation. Did I tell you the one about the Nazi birthmother? I would ask her. She goose-stepped right out of the picture, I would say, and we would both laugh.

"Hey, Mom," I said when my mother answered.

"Hi, honey. How are you?"

"Fine!" I said cheerily. "Is Lucy around?"

"She is." She paused. "She's had a few complications," she whispered into the phone. "Nothing serious, she's going to be fine, but she's going to stay here for the birth."

"Oh!" I swallowed. "Okay."

"I'll let her tell you about it. Bye, honey." I heard my mother put the phone down and call my sister. "Lucy!" she cried. "Mommy! Your sister is on the phone."

My heart beat quickly. I pictured my sister's growing belly, stopped. Then I pictured it growing obscenely large, Hannah giving a cartoon karate chop from within, pressing out.

"Hey!" Lucy came to the phone, breathless.

"Is everything okay?" I asked.

"Just some bleeding. I didn't know what it was. I freaked. I thought it was happening again, but so late! It turned out it's going to be okay, I just need to lay low. Not run around figuring out where to live and all that."

"Okay," I said. "That makes sense."

"Any news on your front?"

"No." Nothing was funny. Nazis were never funny. "Just checking in on you is all," I said.

"That's so sweet, Jess," she said. "Thank you."

20

————

December 2010

Though we were told contact eases up over the holidays, November through January were the months of the birth-mothers. After Katrina, California Allison called to tell us there was another young person—Edwina—who might be contacting us. I heard the word clearly: *might.* She was choosing between three families. I waited for the call, but I was not surprised when Allison called to report that she had decided on a family with another child.

"She wanted siblings for her child," Allison said. "A big family, which was how she grew up."

That felt below-the-belt, as if Edwina, twenty-two and in Indiana, knew we were too old to ever do this again.

"This is such a good sign," Allison said. "So many contacts. Even if they don't work out, there's clearly a lot that's appealing about your profile."

I sniffed.

"You know what?" she whispered, and I could picture her covering the mouthpiece and looking around to make sure no one was listening.

"What?" I whispered back.

"We have this game we play here at the office. It's called: Who Would You Want to Adopt You. You know? What couples!"

"You do?" I imagined that board game, little cards of our profiles turned facedown, a tiny wheel to spin before choosing a card.

"And I chose you guys! Bethany did too. We think you guys would make such awesome parents!"

"Oh my gosh, thank you!" I said, thrilled.

It was not until I got off the phone that I wondered about this office game, these social workers, the ones who did the birthmother intakes, the ones who dealt with the prospective parents, the administrators, all of them looking at each of us, so desperate for a child that we have submitted to this wearying process. We, the prospective adoptive parents, the Christians from Mississippi, the long-distance runners from La Jolla, the Pakistani and white doctors from Indiana, all the profiles Ramon and I had looked through on the agency website to see who we were up against, all the ones we saw fall away, *Matched* stamped digitally across their photos. We were being judged not only by the birthmothers, but also by the gatekeepers to the birthmothers.

And still, I did not care. Because the gatekeepers had selected us! All I could think about as I went to call Ramon with the disappointing report of losing Edwina, was the great news that finally, we'd been chosen.

Just as I didn't speak to Carmen and Edwina, I never spoke to the following birthmother either, though looking back I think I could hear her, the steady rhythm of her breathing in the background of my conversations with the birthfather. They were a couple from Cairo who had a sick baby at Mount Sinai, on the Upper East Side. How sick, we didn't know, but they needed to go back to Egypt, where they claimed they could not get proper medical care. I wanted to visit the baby at the hospital so, as I was told by the birthfather, we could speak to the doctors directly about the child's illness.

"No way," Ramon said. "We cannot get to know these people and get caught up in their lives and then have to say no to a sick child we can't take on. They could have hundreds of thousands of dollars of bills racked up already."

"You're being negative again," I said. "We can talk to the doctors ourselves! We can talk to accounting, too." What would going to a hospital be like, I wondered, and seeing a two-week-old child hooked up to strings and needles, a marionette. I didn't know if I could bear seeing a child suffering, crying, without any sound. I had cried so often when I was alone, in the dark, and yet I could not hear myself. But this was not about that. This is to say that my mother had come every day. I could do that too, be the mother who comes each morning and leaves after dark and heals the child with her singular mother's love.

"What would be too much for care in Cairo?" Ramon asked. "Cairo is a modern place. What kind of an illness would this baby have? We are not going until the agency gets information about it. We just can't."

"Please, Ramon." I saw myself lifting a fragile child, attached by wires, a machine beeping.

All weekend I thought of raising an Egyptian child we had cured with the power of our big love and our democracy, our Americanness—well, mine; Ramon just had a green card—but the man did not put his wife on the phone. I didn't want to pressure him, as I theorized that birthfathers, while adorned with more colorful feathers, are easily frightened too, but I began to think that the mother did not want to give up her baby—a red flag, yes? I thought of her hovering next to her husband, silent, as he signed away their sick child.

A social worker I did not know called me on Monday to tell me the man had signed the release for her to talk to the doctors, but that he had also done something peculiar and disturbing. He'd asked her, she said, if there were any single women in search of children, to which she had responded, yes. He'd then asked if any of those women would be interested in marriage, because he would prefer a second wife here in the States to an open adoption.

"What?" I asked. I could not wrap my head around it and I thought of my absent father-in-law, all the way in Java with his second, unofficial wife. And then I thought that this new social worker was racist against Muslims and so was telling me something so stereotypical I considered having her fired.

"Yes," she said. "You heard me correctly. He asked for another *wife*."

"Jesus," I said.

"We're not that kind of agency," the social worker told me, as if to imply that I was that kind of adoptive parent, who, already married myself, mind you, was out to marry a married Egyptian man who would be leaving me here in the States to raise his sick child. "It was a red flag that you never spoke to the birthmother," she said.

This mistake, somehow mine, I thought, would surely make them all rescind their votes for us as parents they'd most like to adopt them. So were we back again at square one?

Square one: the place where those who haven't yet been chosen, wait.

"Jesus," Ramon said when I told him.

243

"That's exactly what I said."

"I'm just wondering, what the hell is the agency doing to help us? I mean in the beginning we were told we had such a great chance. We're straight. We are young. We're open with race."

"We aren't young." It was six months away now. The numbers were set to shift radically then.

"Compared to a lot of those couples, we're young. I speak Spanish. We translated every goddamn line of that goddamn letter into Spanish. Has one Hispanic birthmother called us? No."

"It's true," I said. "I thought all the Spanish stuff would help." So much for the Ramon Advantage.

Ramon was silent.

"I think people are scared of New York maybe," I said.

"I thought New York would make us seem cool." Ramon looked intently at his laptop.

"That's because you're from Europe."

"I thought that this was going to be easier."

My throat grew thick, as if it were stuffed with cotton. "And what are you doing, Ramon? Because I'm the one talking to these people."

"Jesse." He was still looking straight at the screen. Who knew what was on it. "It's really the woman who should field the calls. It just is."

"Hmm," I said.

"You really think I should be the first to talk to the mothers?" he asked.

"They are not the mothers!" I said. "I am the mother," I said. "Aren't I supposed to be the mother?"

22

———

January 2011

Another new year, and I started to recognize a pattern. We waited, until inactivity panicked us. Then someone made contact. It could be the agency, telling us someone would or should or might or could be calling, or the birthmother herself, like Katrina, or even the birthfather, like the nameless man from Cairo, who had found our profile online. We tried to protect ourselves. Let's be cautiously optimistic, we'd tell each other over (several) beers in front of the television (this might be our last few weeks of freedom! I mused). We thought, again, that we had been the lucky ones. And then, when the call did not come, or the call that came said we had not been chosen, when we traveled that vast terrain from almost, practically three to merely two, we grieved.

We grieved differently. Ramon railed at the agency for not vetting people, and at me for choosing this place and for screwing up with the mothers. I wept. And then, as he railed, I wept again, for being married to someone who railed instead of being supportive in times of grief. I thought of the men I knew and felt sure they would not behave this way. I thought of Anita, and her care and feeding of all those gorgeous animals.

"This hurts me too," Ramon said, many times. "It is not just you who wants this."

And now I see that I knew this was true but I did not care. The loss of these birthmothers was unbearable to me. They were the loss of everything.

But inevitably, after a day of chaos and misery, I got up and went to teach my classes. I met friends for drinks or coffee or dinner. I attended a colleague's book party, a lecture. I went to a movie or to hear live music. In this way, I moved on.

Until we were fortunate enough to be contacted. And then, well, as my grandmother used to say, it was déjà vu all over again.

It had been several weeks since the Cairo Incident, as we had come to call it, when Ramon and I went to meet several of his cousins who were in New York on business. (Business? I'd asked, and was brushed off.) On the train uptown, I removed Katrina's flower icon from my phone. As I heard the swishing sound of the deletion, I thought of Katrina's heart, as big as a cloud, and it seemed to me the bigger the cloud, the more bad weather it could hold.

We were out to dinner at their hotel, an Italian place—why must Italians always eat Italian cuisine when not in Italy? So they can say how terrible it is by comparison? Will they die without a plate of pasta?—when another call came in to the 800 number.

"Hello?" I was breathless, crazy, as I always am when I know it might be a birthmother calling.

Just from that first ring our percentages of becoming parents went from zero to a hundred.

"Hi," the young woman said. "I'm Heather."

I went out to the lobby, opening my purse and struggling to get my pen and a pocket-sized Moleskine as I walked. "Hi!" I said.

"I saw you and Ramon online. I'm having twins." She said all this at once, a torrent of rain. "Are you open to twins?" Heather asked.

Am I open to twins? Not really. We live in a fourth-floor walk-up, for one. But twins, we know, is our only chance for siblings. I had, after all, checked the box for twins on our client profile form.

"Of course we're open." I sat down on a bench against the wall of the hotel before a window facing the street. I thought of Carolyn and her forthcoming twins and I imagined us blocking all the non-mothers (suckers!) with our double strollers on our neighborhood sidewalks. "We love twins."

"Oh," she breathed out, relieved. "Great."

I wrote that down. *Twins,* I wrote. *Great.* "Thank you for reading our profile. What was it you liked about our letter?" I asked Heather.

"Your education," she said. "And the way you and your husband spoke about each other. You have a beautiful relationship."

I snorted, but silently, as I wrote down: *Jan. 18, 2011. Heather likes our education and our relationship.*

"Thank you, Heather," I said. "We are fortunate. Can I ask your last name?" Several couples walked in and out of the shining lobby, the women's heels *click-click*ing along the floor.

"Sure," she said, and she told me. I wrote it down. We love to cook! I told her when she asked what we do together. Big meals for our friends and—I coughed—*family.* And go to museums! And the movies! Also, lest she think we spent our lives inside, I told her, We really love to hike!

"I'm in Westchester with my parents," she told me. "Well, we're in Westchester," she giggled.

This is all so good! Suburban, young, with prenatal care. "I hope they're being supportive," I said. And, in imbuing all things with magical thinking, I thought that by excising Katrina's flower, I had lighted a path for Heather to get to us. For Grace.

"Absolutely. They've been awesome. We were on a cruise to Mexico over the holidays. I realized after the cruise, actually, because I thought it was being on the boat that was making me so sick."

"Right!" I said. "Of course!" The only red flag here was the grandparents, who were edging in like the shadows of circling birds. "And how are you feeling now?"

"Tired," she said. "But done with the morning sickness. Thank God. It would wake me up in the middle of the night. Not sure why they call it morning sickness."

I laughed. Lucy had told me the same.

"I'm due on June eighteenth."

My heart flipped, that goldfish slippery in a hand. Here was a date, five months from then, and three days from my own birthday. Hannah would be four months old; it would be like having triplets in the family. I pictured my digital calendar with the June 18 date embroidered in pink: *Baby.* No. *Babies.* I thought of all the showers I'd been through in the past five years, women's faces pitched into bowls, biting at nipples, sipping on strawberry sparklers. No matter what happened, I had resolved not to have a baby shower. Now I instantly revised this: I will not have a shower until I'm holding a child in my arms.

I looked out at the street. They were calling for a storm but now snow was just beginning to fall, ever so lightly. Fairy dust. I watched people look up at the sky, their faces smiling, catching snowflakes, arms outstretched to the weather. Twins.

"Look," I said. Already I was having memories and making

memories, simultaneously. My father, my sister, and me building a snowman. Big black buttons for eyes set in the packed snow. Ramon and two blank-faced children padded up in purple snowsuits. "Look," I said again. To Heather. "It's starting to snow."

Heather's story was this: She was taking a year off between high school and college. Her boyfriend (part Caucasian and part Hispanic, she offered) had broken up with her before the cruise, and though she had tried to get in touch with him since discovering she was pregnant, she'd had no response. She'd heard from friends he was overseas. Perhaps, she said ominously, fighting in Iraq.

When she told me that she'd considered keeping the child, but with two there was no possible way, I thought of her leaning over the rail and looking out at the Pacific on the deck of a massive ship strung with fairy lights.

I love the ocean at night, how it meets up with another darkness at a horizon point I cannot recognize. I thought of Heather, before she knew her youth would be cut short. She looked out and dreamed of this boy who had stopped calling. Perhaps she was sad about those promises not kept as she gazed out at the sea, heard it breaking against the boat, heard the tinkling sound of people eating and drinking, caught the sound of her future.

Twins. We will have to move but no matter. I was fed up with this apartment, with its pocket-sized bathroom, its gapped floorboards, the scratch of mice in the bedroom walls. Besides, I'd heard from a colleague there would be an opening, tenure-track, at a small liberal arts school upstate; I could apply for that job in the fall. I'd heard a friend from graduate school would be on the search committee. By the summer, the five of us could be in the country.

I thought of a house with open sunlit rooms, copper pots hanging over a gleaming steel stove, pies bubbling in the oven, a pair of toddlers with their too-big mittens attached to the sleeves of down-stuffed little parkas, giggling as they lie back, moving their arms and legs, angels in heaps of snow.

I called the agency the following afternoon.

"I just talked to a Heather from Westchester who's having twins. Did you do the intake with her?"

Crystal said she was the one who talked to Heather when she called in, but that Heather from Westchester was Heather from the Bronx; she lived with her boyfriend, who was half African-American, half Hispanic. She was attending college online, studying to be an accountant. She might have smoked pot once before she knew she was pregnant. But remember, Crystal said, this is a self-report.

"That must be a different Heather," I stated after I had written the information down.

Crystal was quiet. "It isn't, I'm afraid. Sometimes the birthmothers say what you want to hear. Just like prospective adoptive parents."

"That's bullshit." I stopped myself. If we are the sorts of parents who curse, who will give us a child? Panicked, I continued. "We have never lied about anything." Had we? I wondered. "Why would she lie? I don't care if she's from Westchester or the Bronx. What a terrible way to begin a relationship." My heart drummed so hard in my chest it was in my ears, but I was not hearing that there was anything necessarily *wrong* with Heather. Perhaps she was trying to impress us, which sounded positive.

"Birthmothers often feel that the adoptive parents, the women in particular, look down on them. Everyone wants to feel loved and approved of," Crystal said.

Really, I thought. "That's just awful. I'm sorry to hear they might feel that way."

I was sorry Heather felt she had to lie about her situation. That she told the agency the truth, however, showed authenticity and ambition.

This is what I informed Ramon of when we were out to dinner in our neighborhood, at a place that puts popovers sprinkled with salt and glazed with honey on the table as soon as you sit down.

"Ambition?" He was incredulous.

I could see he was letting go of Heather, heading to the rage part of what had become an unbreakable cycle, but I was still in our cautiously optimistic stage.

"Yes, she wants a good family for the child. Wouldn't you call that ambitious?" I bit into a popover: eggy, light, sweet, delicious.

"No," Ramon said. "I would call it untrustworthy."

"Don't." I looked hard at my husband. "It's maybe a little weird, yes, but her boyfriend is part Hispanic. See? The Spanish stuff is working!"

Ramon looked back at me. Big almond eyes; that dimple; wavy black hair that was nearly gray. When did he get so gray? He shook his head. "You know, Jesse, we're not desperate. We're not."

I felt my face grow hot and I imagined being plunged like a vegetable into a pool of cold water to stop my cooking and retain my vibrant color. "Speak for yourself, Ramon," I said, waving the waitress down to order.

Walking back to our apartment, Ramon disappeared, and then reappeared in the fluorescent-lit threshold of a deli on Smith Street holding a clutch of wilting little daisies.

"A flower for my flower," he said, and I hugged him, taking the sad bouquet.

When we got back to our apartment, I put the flowers in one of the vases on the mantel, beneath a print of *Guernica* Ramon had insisted on hanging.

We sat on the couch beneath my daisies, and Picasso's depiction of war, searching the web for Heather. We found a young blond woman guzzling beer on Facebook, but that was Manhattan Heather, and apparently we needed Bronx Heather. Soon we came upon a young woman in a local paper. At eighteen, she'd been arrested for prostitution, a year ago almost to the day. There was a mug shot of this Heather and a friend of this Heather, young girls whose faces were ravaged. Their hair was stringy; their skin was thick and their eyes were dark, set deep in their sockets.

Before Ramon could say anything, I said, "I don't care."

"You don't care," he said. "That's just brilliant."

"No," I said. "I don't. As long as she's not doing drugs while she's pregnant."

"Look at her!"

I closed the screen.

"If she wasn't doing drugs, why else would she be a prostitute and a liar?"

"That was a year ago!" I said. "She could be a totally different person now."

I thought of myself a year ago, which hardly reinforced my point. I was unbearably the same: filled, as ever, with want. "She could be seriously reformed. Which is why she didn't have an abortion. Maybe she went to Narcotics Anonymous and found her higher power and now she's religious, Christian religious, and so she doesn't believe in abortion anymore."

Ramon sat back and closed his eyes. He took off his wool cap. We hadn't even removed our coats, and the snow—the big wet flakes we stomped off our boots in clumps before walking in—was melting. The wool of our coats and hats and mittens smelled like honey and rosemary and hot wax.

"Wait," he said in that way that means he's going to say something disingenuous. "So are you thinking that the father is her boyfriend or are you thinking that—and please tell me you're at least entertaining this idea—it is some horrible guy who paid her to have sex with him sometime after being arrested for soliciting undercover detectives at a Best Western in Queens? And you remember, this was the girl who told you she got knocked up at her prom in Westchester."

"She did not say it was her prom, okay? There is never going to be an ideal here." I closed my eyes. "There just isn't." I won't lie. Once we had thought the girl on her way to Princeton who got knocked up at the prom was a likely scenario.

"She's lying to us," Ramon said.

"To me, you mean," I said. "She's lying to me. Because I'm the one who has been talking to her."

"Yes. She is lying."

"Don't be so negative," I said. "Please?"

"Seriously?" Ramon turned toward me. "You think I'm being negative? This is a child. You'd be more cautious about buying a used car."

"Used?" I got up and paced the living room. "Used."

"A car," he said. "Jesse, just a car."

If I pressed this I knew we could lose Bronx (prostitute) Heather. "Why isn't the agency helping more? What are we paying them for?" I was gesturing wildly, as I often do while lecturing in the classroom. "I don't understand. We're getting all these calls. So many people aren't even getting calls. They don't even get seen." Again I wondered which was worse.

"To vet the prostitutes and the Nazis," Ramon said.

"Stop it. And anyway, they're not even doing that," I said.

"Remember when Nickie asked us if we would be comfortable adopting a child of rape?"

How could I forget. How could I—would I—ever forget any of this.

I crossed my arms. "Having sex for money is not rape."

"Prostitutes and Nazis," he stated again. "What did people do before the Internet?"

I headed into the bedroom. "I can't do this," I said, trying to slam the door, but it was a cheap, hollow, piece-of-shit door that wouldn't slam.

I flopped onto the bed. Here we go, I thought. Here is the cycle again, but how do I break it? Then I heard the scrape of a chair moving out from the table, the padding of my husband coming to the door.

"Jesse." Ramon knocked, quiet as a mouse. "Okay in there?"

I rolled over onto my stomach but didn't say anything.

"We are going to get a child," he said. "We are. You have to believe."

I felt my stomach flat against the mattress, the pillow at my turned cheek. What I thought was: When oh when will this story end? I could not bear the smooth rounded belly of one more friend, not one more curly-haired cherub of a child reaching out with the teensiest hand, not one more person saying the wrong thing to me. Let it end like this, I thought then: We will get those twins and I'll get that job upstate. I saw a meadow spotted with wildflowers, and two children seated there, facing the sun, holding buttercups beneath each other's chins, just like Lucy and I had done behind the stables, the smell of horse and hay and sweat surrounding us.

What I thought was this: What if the cancer comes back? Maybe the cancer will come back, and if it does, all of this will be over. I will not be able to adopt a child. What a relief that would be, I thought, turning on my back.

"Do you hear me?" Ramon was still outside the bedroom door. "We are going to be parents. I promise. Please," he said. "Let me in."

The next morning, our neighborhood was blanketed in white. Harriet stood on her hind legs at the window, a child waiting to get to play in the snow, when Heather called.

"Hi, Heather!" I said. "How are you feeling?" I didn't know how to broach the subject of what I had come to think of as conflicting stories.

"Hey," she said. "I talked to the agency and I've chosen you guys."

"Really?" I said. "Heather, that's amazing!" I pushed away that she hadn't talked to Ramon yet, a red flag, though likely not more so than the lying and the prostitute issue.

"Yeah," she said. "You guys are totally great."

"Thank you! We really look forward to getting to know you better. I just want to let you know," I said, "that whatever you want to tell us is okay. We understand this is a hard time for you."

"Thanks!" There was a sunny barrier of false happiness in Heather's voice. No longer could I picture her, a heartsick teenager beneath a splash of stars leaning out onto the water, listening for her future on the waves. No longer were Heather and I versions of each other; I could not see myself in her, or her in me. "So I'm going to the doctor in two weeks. And I'll send in the pregnancy confirmation then. But for now I have the ultrasound photos. Do you want me to e-mail them?"

"Sure," I said. But I did not want them.

"Awesome!" she said. "I've got to run, Jesse, but I'll talk to you soon!"

Please don't send those photos, I thought.

When I heard the ping of my computer, I clicked on. The ultrasound. *Nice Talking To You.* The text said, *enjoy :)* And there it was: two fetuses, stacked little birds, one in silhouette, one looking straight on. Even my body has been inwardly imaged, that snapshot marked along the top with my name and the date, on all those mornings when hope was an entirely different animal. I had seen Lucy's ultrasound too, the profile of her daughter already forming, a curled fist at her mouth, the stamp of my sister's name above the developing head. Heather's blurred photo was framed by no such information. The information that did arrive did so the way memory does, as knowledge I have always held: These babies were not real. None of the babies had been real. There will be no snow pants and mittens in the coming winters, fields of light come spring, and if I apply for that job upstate and out of the five hundred applicants, I actually get that job, I will likely be going there alone. Ramon might not leave New York. If Ramon is at ease in European cities, and less so in New York City, in the country he is a tourist. He wears street shoes on our hikes. In the woods his elegance reads as small, as if he could too easily get lost there.

The birthmothers have only been women.

The door was closed.

"You just don't know," Ramon said when I told him. He looked up from his computer. "Maybe she had a really messed-up scanner."

"Maybe," I provisionally agreed. But by his impulse to mollify I realized: he knew too.

He turned back to his work. "Why do they all keep telling us the babies will be here for spring? What," Ramon asked, "is it with springtime?"

The next morning a call came in from the agency.

"Hi," Crystal said. "So I'm not sure if Heather told you yet, but she lost her babies in the night. She left a message on the office machine. I'm just calling to let you know. Sad."

I laughed. I put down my pen.

"I'm sorry," she said. "This is hard. For many prospective adoptive parents, matching takes a while."

God forbid she said adoptive *mothers*. If she used the word *mother* on us, what would we women do? Start a riot so big and angry that no amount of tear gas, Tasers, or armored vehicles could hold it back? "You know she didn't, like, lose two babies in the middle of the night, right?"

"Not likely, no." Crystal sighed.

"So it was a scam then, right?"

"Yes, it appears to have been. Though a scam tends to mean you gave her money, which you didn't, thankfully. But I am flagging her profile."

The red flagging of the red flag. "I can't help but wonder if all of these aren't scams. We haven't talked to one viable birthmother."

"It's usually one in, say, thirty that's not real. But with the economy as it is, we have seen a rise in them."

"Hmm," I said. "Very interesting," I said. "Okay, thanks for letting me know, Crystal."

Then she assured me that despite these few bad dates there would ultimately be a match, and that while we were having all these unusually crazy experiences, when we did get our match, when we found the right birthmother, it would all make sense. And this, Crystal had said, would all disappear, not unlike childbirth.

Childbirth?

The pain of childbirth, Crystal had told me.

I walked the five steps into the dining room, where Ramon was working or playing his hedgehog mouse game or playing billiards or poker or whatever the hell Ramon had been doing. "It was a scam," I said.

He was silent.

"That was Crystal. Well, we knew it probably was." I thought to touch his shoulder but did not. "We knew."

There was a long sigh. "Seriously?" Ramon looked up, his fingers still poised over the keyboard. "When is the part that is mutually beneficial? The altruism part. The goddamn *adoption* part. Because this is ridiculous. Who does that? It's like preying on the elderly."

"Thanks." I thought, If I get a child right this minute, when that child is my age, if I am still alive, I will be just about eighty. Just about.

"You know what I meant."

I went to check my e-mail, trying to get far away from this moment, a trick that I can only say I have learned from growing up a girl.

Among my accumulation of morning e-mails there was one from that friend who consistently sent out mass messages about dogs.

I clicked on the link and, as always, there was a dog in need. This one, a beautiful gray pit bull with a creamy white chest, maybe eight months old, had been found chained to the Williamsburg Bridge during the snowstorm the night Heather called. Who would do that? Who would leave a beautiful, helpless animal that way? I tried not to think about Harriet's ever leaving us. I started sobbing for the dog, abandoned and freezing, all alone on the bridge. What did the world look like to him now? I thought.

Who would do such a thing?

After several hours, I left my office/closet and went to the kitchen to make a sandwich. Ramon and Harriet were on a walk, and while they were out, I noticed that the daisies Ramon had gotten me on the way home from the restaurant two nights previously, delicate as wildflowers, had drunk up much of the vase's water and perked up. I was about to trim their stems and add more water when my phone rang. Katrina. I had removed her icon but I had not expelled her from my phone book altogether, and now I made out her name through the fractured face and leaking ink. It had been well over a month since we'd spoken, and I didn't know if she was pregnant, or if she was ever pregnant. I didn't know if she was looking for a friend or for money, and I didn't know if she was a Nazi, and still? I was excited.

Because, I thought, Katrina from Joshua Tree might be our birth-mother. Because she might hold what we want like a cloud holds the rain. Because perhaps she had her pregnancy confirmation and had talked to other prospective adoptive parents, from many agen-cies, but she had still decided we were perfect, and, because she lives across the country, we will send photos and letters as our child grows and we will not have to deal with the host of Aryan Nation boyfriends she courts.

"Hello?" I answered in that breathless way I will never be able to control. I grabbed a pen and turned a bank envelope blank side up.

No one said anything but I could hear movement in the background.

"Hello?" I said. "Trina? Are you there?"

Still there was no answer, but I could hear her speaking. Oh, that looks cute, she said. There was murmuring, and then the sharp knifelike sound of a hanger moving along a rack, the ruffle of clothing, the smack of plastic hangers hitting other plastic hangers. Let me see, I heard Katrina say. Turn around, she said.

I sat down on the couch, where I could see that on the fire escape, the snow was still piled high.

Cassie, that tank top is so cute! I like the way it hits you just here at the waist. Right here, she said, and there was again the sound of movement. I knew Katrina was touching her daughter at the hip. Come on, let me see. We should get that one.

I lay back on the couch and looked up at the bowed ceiling. I held my breath. I couldn't hang up.

Oh, do you see those boots there? Do you want to try them on?

Something was said that I could not catch, and then I heard Trina's voice again. Oh, that is nice. Go try that on, honey.

Then there was a voice from a distance. Mom? It was farther away than Trina's voice but I could hear it clearly; I could hear its youth. Do you think this is too small?, the voice, the voice of a teenager, said. Mom?

I stood up, cradled the phone between my neck and shoulder, and pulled a daisy, dripping with water, from the vase on the mantel. I watched my thumb snap the bloom from the stem. I pulled another and flicked it off. And then another.

There was a short silence, and I pictured Katrina's daughter spinning around for her mother. Also there is my own mother turning me by the shoulders in front of the full-length mirror in

Garfinckel's, where I was almost born, in the coat department. There was a spot there that marked that moment. Then the spot was gone. That department store is gone now too, but my mother's chin hooks over my shoulder, and she's smiling. Look at you, my mother says, all grown up.

I flicked the head off another daisy and watched it—the face of the sun—fall to the couch, join the small accumulation of the heads of all the little daisies.

What do you think? the girl's voice said now. Mom, she said. Do you think I look pretty?

Part 4

FLYING

23

February 2011

Still it waged on, the saga of the birthmothers. I knew they were not all bad people; I knew that the ones who were pregnant, who truly were birthmothers, were just doing what they could. And yet, I could not help but think, as we hurtled toward Hannah's due date, toward spring, about all the babies that might have been: soon time would move through their arrivals as they passed into the arms of other mothers.

It defies storytelling, waiting. We think if there is a beginning, surely there is an end. That is the way a story works. The end of this story can only be the end of waiting. And yet we were still waiting for the birthmothers, for our birthmother; she was as invisible to us as the future.

At the end of January Anita had e-mailed that their baby had arrived. It had been hard, she wrote, as there had been a moment when they thought it would not happen. The birthmother disappeared. We had a room filled with baby things. A changing table.

A Diaper Genie. A hanging mobile. Paula took leave from work, Anita wrote, but we could not find the birthmother. It turned out she had given birth and the birth grandmother stepped in and took the child. And then a month after she was born, they got a call . . . The point is, Anita wrote, we thought it was over and it was so awful, I couldn't even write to you. And now? Now. It really is just all behind us now. I hardly remember a bit of it.

Attached was a photo, the three of them in front of a picture window. I couldn't help myself, still I looked at real estate—the elegant view of their vast backyard.

"Ramon!" I called into the dining room. "Look!"

I heard him sigh. For a moment there was no movement, and then there was the sound of his chair against the floor, his feet walking.

"What?" He stood at my office/closet door.

I pointed to the photo of the child on an unmade bed swaddled in a muslin cloth printed with swinging monkeys. A puppy sniffed at her ear.

Babies and puppies. What's not to love?

He laughed.

"This is good," I said to Ramon, but I still wondered just whom it was good for.

He nodded. "I know." His chin was hooked over my shoulder. "Not everything has to end in tears, does it?"

I laughed. Because of course, I was crying, but not all tears are sad ones.

Not long after, a young woman named Jordi began to e-mail our account. Like me, she was a student of history, she wrote. Still in college, she had big dreams of academia (which I did not put her off of), and her boyfriend, an artist, like Ramon seemed to be, had big dreams too. Too big, Jordi wrote, to have a baby now. You two, she said, are a perfect match, LOL.

When I first received the e-mail—again the *beat beat* of my heart, indication now of the conflation of excitement and fear—I remembered that couple on the film, the young and beautiful couple who had chosen the parents for their child based on the prospective father's interest in music. And so every time I wrote Jordi about what I'd cooked that day, about my students, my own studies, what I was reading, I tried to decipher her own sets of likes and dislikes, as if I were cracking code.

Jordi wrote back that she would like to be more brave with food. *I'd like to be braver in general,* she wrote, and she had me. *You are brave!* I responded, *and very generous, too,* and she replied with a smiley face and updates on the papers she was writing and how she wished she could cook. I sent recipes.

Eventually Jordi told me her own story of being adopted, and I in turn explained how Ramon and I were a little gun-shy, as we'd had several people lie to us in our most raw and tender moments. My exchange with Jordi grew over the weeks to a daily correspondence, nearly fifty e-mails. We made several distinct plans to speak on the phone, but when I would call at the designated time, I would get her cheery voice mail. I ignored this issue, understanding Jordi to be shy, bookish even, someone who preferred writing, which I understood, believing in our forged link.

Then one day, Jordi decided she wanted to meet. I called Crystal, who told me that she did not yet have Jordi's paperwork, but if we wanted to take the risk we should go ahead.

There are a few other families I am choosing from, and I want to be sure, Jordi wrote, and so Ramon and I felt compelled. That day Ramon and I drove to meet Jordi in the Garden State Plaza in

New Jersey. We were stopped in traffic at the George Washington Bridge. I thought of what Jordi would look like. *My pale skin is so burned today!,* she wrote in an e-mail, which only now made me realize both that she was white and that she felt it important to let me know this.

Eventually traffic abated, and while we thought we might have trouble finding this mall, we didn't, because it was nearly as big as the island of Capri, and instead we couldn't find the restaurant Jordi and I were set to meet in. Soon, we parked in a lot bigger than an airport, and Ramon, who had spent about as much time in malls as I had spent on the shores of Italy before meeting him, staggered into the massive building to kill time.

It was three thirty or so and I was the sole person in the restaurant. I sat in a booth and watched the teenagers pass by, impossibly young girls, their thin arms and legs tan and exposed, wrists wrapped in bracelets. There was a distinct smell of something foul covered over as I waited, staring at the menu and rubbing my thumbnail along the polyester tablecloth.

An hour after we were set to meet she entered the restaurant, and I knew it was her because her eyes searched for me. She was white. She didn't look particularly pregnant, but she was heavy enough that it was difficult to discern. She sat down across from me and I tried to ease the awkwardness by giving her some Italian face creams and telling her how wonderful it was to meet her.

"I'm starving," she said.

"Order something," I said. "Please."

She ordered a burger, very well done, and I ordered chicken soup. When the food arrived I picked a fry off her plate without thinking; perhaps I was trying to show her how comfortable I was with her, and with this fraught situation.

"Tell me everything." I chewed on her fry.

Her iPhone rang (How can she afford an iPhone? I thought, looking at my banged-up, cracked phone) and she took the call. Then she hung up and, after several failed tries to many different pizzerias, she ordered a large pie for her mother, who was apparently at home.

"Sorry." Again she picked up her burger.

"How open do you want your relationship with the adoptive parents to be?" I asked.

Jordi shrugged. "I'll figure that out later," she said. "I'm talking to two other families. One keeps drunk-texting me that they want a girl. They want a white baby, which this is."

I expected her to look at her stomach but she didn't. I had been where those families were sitting—I sat there now, in fact, in a not-so-comfortable chair—and I didn't believe anyone would text a birthmother, drunk or not, to demand a girl baby. "When are you due?" I asked, realizing that one of the few details Jordi did not know about us was the many boxes we'd checked.

"Sometime in June," said Jordi.

"Can I ask what made you decide, so unselfishly, on open adoption?" As I posed this question, only then did it arrive, again, knowledge, the sort I already held: She can't have made a decision. If she is actually pregnant, she is not yet pregnant enough to feel what this will mean.

She shrugged again. "I'm adopted too? Like I told you, my boyfriend and I have big dreams. A baby doesn't fit into them?"

I nodded. "I understand," I said. "I hope we can continue talking."

She nodded back, looking away.

After I paid the bill and Jordi wandered away and into JCPenney, I called Ramon and he pulled the car around.

"You've been in the car?" I got in and slammed the door shut.

"It's more comfortable here," he said. "That place is horrible."

Following a long silence, he asked, "Are you going to tell me about it?"

"I'm not sure what just happened. She didn't sound like the person writing all those e-mails. But I'm wondering if that's not my issue. I mean, maybe she is."

We drove onto Route 17, and then there was more traffic at the bridge.

"I just don't know," I said.

I conjured Jordi leaving the mall and heading to her doctor's, faxing the paperwork immediately, so moved was she by me and my creams and my comfort in sharing. I thought of riding my bike with my about-to-be husband onto the George Washington Bridge, the brilliant skyline before us, the thrilling feeling of having ridden so far uptown. I didn't know yet that my vertigo would not allow me to make it across.

A few days passed and then Crystal told me the paperwork had still not been sent in, and so I wrote Jordi that we'd need her paperwork to go forward. Her e-mails ceased.

After a week or so of silence between us, a time where I parsed each past e-mail, searching for clues, analyzing emoticons, I got a text from Jordi that she'd been to the doctor. *It was so good!,* the text said. *We know what it is!* I thought of Heather, those blurry birds peering out from the unfocused ultrasound, and I felt I was being played. I tried to imagine myself in Jordi's situation. Would I not just tell me the sex of the child? Would I not write me a more feeling e-mail? If Jordi was like me then she most certainly would.

But she was not like me and so she did not write me a more feeling e-mail. And I did not write her. She texted me again this time with the question, *Do you want to know what your baby is?* Again I did not respond. Another text came in several hours later. *Don't you want to know the sex?* When I did not respond to this, Jordi texted me: *It's a girl!* She offered this at least ten times a day for a week: *It's a girl!* Again and again: *It's a girl! A girl! A girl!*

"This is just torture," Ramon said. "Can't we silence your phone?"

"We can," I said. "But it's all still there."

This, Crystal told me, when I'd reported in, was an emotional scam.

"Emotional?" I said.

"It doesn't seem like she wanted anything but to talk to you and keep your attention."

"That she got," I said. "Why did she keep telling us it was a girl?"

Crystal paused. "Everyone wants a little girl."

Do they? I thought. Because little girls do, one day, turn into women. And women want so much. "How do I make this stop then?"

I thought about what we wrote in our home study form for Lydia about open adoption: *We are sensitive to birthparents' desires and needs, and compassionate toward birthparents, who we know are making an altruistic decision to give someone else the opportunity to parent when they cannot.*

"Eventually," Crystal said, "the texts will stop if you don't respond. I'm so sorry. I realize this has all been just crazy."

She was right; Jordi's texts did stop. And I had learned to shut myself off more from these experiences; each one, as it revealed itself, felt less violent. The mark of that experience, though, lived brutally inside me, as I had trusted someone who had found out who Ramon and I were, and had exploited that.

"There is nothing more evil than someone who scams couples in the desperate state of trying to have a child," Crystal said.

There. She'd said it. It was getting to—no, it was very far beyond being in the middle of—a desperate state. "I just want to know for sure what happened. I want to understand it," I said.

"You cannot understand insane. It's just insane." Crystal's voice sounded deeper now, as if she'd aged considerably or taken up smoking. Had she become jaded in the year and a half since we'd met? I wondered if, exposed now to the harsher elements of life, she had lost her No More Tangles smell. "It's happened to many prospective adoptive parents, I'm afraid.

"You can't let this inform your next potential birthmother relationship. It will happen and all of this will be behind you. What you and Ramon have been through is just so unusual. I wonder," Crystal asked, "if you could write any of this down. You're a scholar, after all. Perhaps you could keep a journal."

I laughed. *Keep a journal,* I wrote. My red leather notebook was almost filled. "I have thought about it," I said.

"Good!"

"Listen, Crystal." I put down my pen. "Can I ask you something?"

"Sure," she said. "Shoot."

"Can you please stop calling us prospective adoptive parents? I mean, just on the phone? I am not in denial or anything about my role or our position here, but just on the phone. When we're talking, just us."

Crystal laughed. She laughed! Her laugh was ragged and scratchy. She had most certainly taken up smoking. "Absolutely," she said. "I absolutely can."

24

School had begun again and I gave myself over to the daily focus of my long-neglected work. I attended departmental meetings I had once avoided; I met with students; I planned new assignments; I graded and returned papers promptly; I worked on improving my handwriting. I took long walks through the neighborhood with Harriet, and I concentrated on Lucy, making plans for Ramon and me to be there when Hannah arrived, red and screaming, into our lonely family.

Sometimes we are moving when we think we are standing still. That is what I have learned about waiting.

It was Valentine's Day when Crystal called. I remember looking out my office window at the ridiculous red construction-paper hearts and pink cupids pasted, ironically perhaps, along the hallway. It gave the impression that we had retreated backward, to elementary school, that there was no future to be had at all, that there was only the past to carry us through these brief sunny corridors.

"Remember Carmen?" Crystal said.

Two colleagues in our shared office looked up from their work at the sound of my sobbing.

"Ramon!" I collected my scattered books and folders and papers. I gathered up everything. "It's happening."

He was silent.

"Carmen," I said. "The first one. The very first one."

Zero to one hundred. That evening we were on a plane, and we were flying. We soared over New York City and our city glittered below us, glowing, jeweled, an answer to so many of our questions, and we were heading to light, to desert, to perpetual spring.

To Carmen, the first one to break our hearts, but she had changed her mind and she had chosen us, and she was to be induced the next day, and we were flying.

Shakily, I held Ramon's hand. "Let's rent a convertible," I said. We could be in California for several weeks waiting for the paperwork to be finalized. I imagined us high in the hills, the desert extremes; Joshua Tree would be in full bloom now. I imagined our hair flying behind us, the sun to our cold, chapped faces.

What would Carmen look like—beautiful or plain, fat or thin, dark or light? I had spoken to her only for a moment. Hello, she had said softly into the phone. Is this Jesse?, she had said, and I had answered, Yes, it's me.

"We can't carry a newborn around in a convertible," Ramon said. "Are you nuts? We will have a *baby*. What we need is a car seat and diapers."

Startled, I looked over at Ramon. "Oh my God," I said. "This is happening. Is this happening?" There was, after all, the chance that Carmen would keep the child, or that her parents would. There was a chance that we would be coming back alone. Still, there was the possibility for anything.

"I believe that this is," Ramon said, turning to the window. "I believe it," he said.

When we'd spoken, I had thanked Carmen for her altruistic act, and I had thanked her for choosing us, however she had come to choose, in whatever way she had come to that decision. We'll take good care of your daughter, I'd said, and I saw Ramon then, bent over a little girl who was growing clearer, a photograph in a dark-room, coming to light. I saw Lucy and me running through the sprinkler in our suburban backyard. Claudine was at the screen door, her hands on her hips, and the wet grass was between my toes.

Let her be real, I thought.

The lights of the city—our city—receded as we ascended until pinpricks of fuzzy light embroidered the sky.

We were headed there, closer and closer. Outside our window, the sky was pitch-black. She is real, I thought.

We have found her.

Acknowledgments

THANK YOU TO THE MacDowell Colony, for the time and space to begin making my way to this project. Thank you to Meg Wolitzer, for her unwavering support. Thanks as well to Nina Revoyr and Jen Loja, always faithful early readers; to Allison Devers, who lent me Asbury Park; to Mitchell Kaplan, who encouraged me to use my real voice; and to Elissa Schappell, who demands bravery. I am indebted as well to Suzanne Nichols and Mia Diamond Padwa for their unremitting work off the page. And deep gratitude to the mothers: Judy, Voula, and Kate. Thank you to all the great people of Scribner, including Kelsey Smith for her terrific input and Kate Lloyd for her publicity prowess. Thanks to Clay Ezell of ICM for his constant work on my behalf. And big love and appreciation to my tireless advocate Jenn Joel, for her support, and to my editor, Alexis Gargagliano, whom I've been lucky enough to have with me for every book, and who gave this one its happy ending.

About the Author

Jennifer Gilmore is the author of *Golden Country,* a 2006 *New York Times* Notable Book and a finalist for the Los Angeles Times Book Prize and the National Jewish Book Award, and *Something Red,* a *New York Times* Notable Book of 2010. Her work has appeared in magazines and journals, including *Allure,* the *Los Angeles Times, The New York Times, The New York Times Book Review, Tin House, Salon, Vogue,* and *The Washington Post.* She has been a MacDowell Colony fellow and has taught writing and literature at Cornell University, Barnard College, Eugene Lang College at the New School, New York University, and Princeton. She lives in Brooklyn.